# Something to
# BELIEVE

TORONTO PUBLIC LIBRARY
Sale of this book
supports literacy programs

# Robbi McCoy

Bella BOOKS
2010

Bella Books, Inc.
P.O. Box 10543
Tallahassee, FL 32302

Printed in the United States of America on acid-free paper
First Edition

Editor: Katherine V. Forrest
Cover Designer: Linda Callaghan

ISBN 13:978-1-59493-214-4

**Also by Robbi McCoy**

Not Every River
Songs Without Words
Waltzing At Midnight

*To Pollyanna*

## Acknowledgments

My deepest appreciation and affection go to my life partner, Dot, for her patience, understanding and indulgence during all of the trials I put her through during the painful writing of this book. Your wisdom and unfaltering devotion, darling, have made this story what it is, a testament to enduring love. You are my rock.

Many thanks also to my editor Katherine V. Forrest, an expert guide in our fictional landscape. Yet again, she's the bomb!

## About the Author

Robbi McCoy is a native Californian who lives with her partner and two cats in the Central Valley between the mountains and the sea. She is an avid hiker with a particular fondness for the deserts of the American Southwest. She also enjoys gardening, culinary adventures and the theater. She works full-time as a software specialist and web designer for a major West Coast distribution company.

# PART ONE
Yangtze River, China, before the dam

# CHAPTER ONE

"The water's going to rise a hundred meters in some locations when the dam is in full operation." The slight, gray-haired engineer, whose name Lauren had already forgotten, raised his hand level with his forehead, as if to illustrate a hundred meters. "Two million people will have to be moved, which means rebuilding cities from the ground up. Whole cities, *big* cities, brick by brick."

"A massive undertaking," Faith said, her attention completely caught up in the conversation.

She had that rapt look on her face, the one that encouraged people to go on talking indefinitely. As soon as Faith had heard this guy was an engineer with more than a casual knowledge of the dam, she'd parked herself at the top of the staircase and engaged him in conversation. She now stood leaning against the brass railing, one hand in the front pocket of her jeans, her sunglasses on top of her head where she'd perched them after moving from the afternoon sunshine into the interior of the ship. Her straight, thin nose was pointed directly at the engineer, who stood no more than two inches above her five-five height, and her forehead was knit into her serious business-like expression, the one Lauren thought of as "the scientist."

Lauren stood self-consciously near the doorway, her attention drawn to the artwork on the walls and the richly patterned carpet, the gleaming stair banisters and the chandelier above them. It wasn't that the Three Gorges Dam project didn't interest her. It was just that they had boarded the ship only moments before and she was anxious to see everything, especially their cabin. Besides, she had read about all of these statistics already while researching the trip. Lauren smiled to herself as she recognized one of the essential differences between them, that Faith preferred to get her information from people and Lauren preferred to get it from books, or from the written word, at least, in whatever form it came to her these days.

"In the United States," continued the engineer, "such a thing just wouldn't be possible. Can you imagine the outcry, all the lawsuits, everybody asserting their rights? I'm not knocking America. I'm just saying it's different here in China. They'll all cooperate and lend a hand. Whoever doesn't like it will keep their mouth shut and plenty of people will get screwed."

"It's a different mindset," Faith agreed. "Do you think they'll make the schedule?"

"Fully operational by 2009? I think they might, yes, with the exception of the ship lifts. Those suckers probably won't be up until 2014, but the dam will be producing electricity in just a few years. No doubt about it." He shook his head, awed at the prospect. "This kind of job would take twice, maybe three times as long somewhere else. At this level of technology, I mean. They're going to tear down these towns and rebuild them with manual labor! I've seen crews of workers everywhere breaking up concrete with hammers and chisels."

"One thing they have in China is people power," observed Faith.

He nodded. "Amazing what people can do when you've got enough of them. Look at the pyramids, for instance, and they didn't have a single truck. At least here they've got a few machines."

Her cheeks flushed, Faith said, "Speaking of the pyramids, all things being equal, do you think there's any modern engineering feat to rival them? I mean, given all our technology, have we achieved anything as impressive as that?"

"God, no! We'd have to build a stairway to the moon to claim something equivalent."

Faith laughed her deep, carefree laugh.

"I'm going to go find our cabin," Lauren said, excusing herself.

"Okay," said Faith, glancing around at her. "I'll be right there."

Lauren turned into the narrow hallway, which was flanked on both sides by identical doors, reading numbers as she walked the length of the hall to locate their room. When she arrived at their cabin, she realized with frustration that Faith had both key cards. She could go back, but decided to wait. She stood her suitcase against the wall, then sat on it facing the door to their cabin.

Another passenger came along, a tall, athletic-looking blonde wrestling a large suitcase. She stopped to look at the room numbers, then came up to Lauren and said, "I think ours is just past you."

"Oh, sorry," Lauren said, standing flat against the wall to let the woman pass by. She was in her mid-twenties, Lauren guessed, cute, dressed for warm weather in a short-sleeved shirt and twill cargo pants. Her straight hair was in a ponytail under a white baseball cap. She stopped at the cabin next door, verifying the room number.

"Thanks," she said, parking her suitcase and shoving her hands in the pockets of her pants one by one until she produced the card that would open her door. Her suitcase, Lauren noticed, had a rectangular rainbow sticker on it. Lauren looked her over again, more interested, as she stuck the card in the slot and pushed the door open, then shoved the suitcase in the doorway to hold it ajar.

"Cassie!" she hollered, waving her arm and looking back down the hallway. "Right here!"

Lauren turned to look at the woman heading toward them pulling another suitcase. She was older, about Lauren's age, mid-thirties, had thin, brown, shoulder-length hair parted in the middle and swept behind her ears. She wore a plain yellow T-shirt and blue jeans. Her glasses reflected the overhead lights, obscuring her eyes. She was nice looking, Lauren thought, in a casual, comfortable sort of way. There was no doubt now. Their neighbors were lesbians. American lesbians. Strange coincidence, she thought, as Cassie caught her eye and smiled warmly. She too wedged past.

"Looks like we're neighbors," Lauren said.

"Yes." Her eyes were clearly visible now. They were deep brown, lit by enthusiasm and amusement. "I'm Cassie Burkett."

Lauren took hold of her offered hand briefly, noting the dimples which appeared as she smiled again.

"Lauren Keegan."

The cute blonde took Cassie's suitcase and carried it inside. Cassie turned back to Lauren and said, "That's Jennifer."

Lauren recognized the awkward moment of not knowing how to introduce the lesbian lover—*partner, girlfriend*? No matter how comfortable you were with yourself, this scene played out over and over with strangers. Is this a moment to make a stand? Take a chance, knowing nothing about this other person? Or just let the moment go down easy for everyone?

"My partner Faith is just around the corner," Lauren said, offering a crucial piece of information.

"Ah," said Cassie, looking enlightened and surprised. This wasn't an Olivia cruise, after all. No reason to expect more than one gay couple on board a boat with a mere sixty passengers. Not to mention having one next door. "Nice to meet you, Lauren. We'll see you at dinner, then."

Cassie disappeared into her room just as Faith rounded the corner, key card in hand. She looked bright-eyed and invigorated, her cheeks still rosy.

"Sorry, honey," she said as she arrived at their door.

"That's okay. It's been more interesting waiting here than you might think."

Faith opened the door and led the way inside the small cabin, their home for a four-day cruise on the Yangtze River. There were two twin beds separated by a small table. Sliding glass doors opened onto a private balcony with two plastic chairs. The shower was tiny, but functional. All very cozy and smart.

Once they were inside with the door shut, Faith slipped her hands around Lauren's waist and kissed her. "Welcome to your stateroom, Madam," she said.

Lauren ran her fingers through Faith's short, platinum hair, noting the childlike glee in her eyes. Faith pulled her closer and kissed her more passionately. She felt a familiar need rise in her. Later, she promised herself, pulling reluctantly away.

After the long flight from Portland to Beijing, then the flight from Beijing to Wuhan, they had slept in their hotel for a solid ten hours last night. Now it felt like they had finally arrived, refreshed and ready for this first leg of their vacation.

"Let's get unpacked," Faith said. "Only twenty minutes to dinner. By the way, what was so interesting about waiting in the hallway?"

Lauren heaved her suitcase onto one of the beds. "I met our neighbors."

"Stuffy old retired postal workers from Florida?" She pulled a stack of shirts from her suitcase and placed them in a dresser drawer.

"Couldn't be further from it. They're lesbians."

Faith tilted her head and eyed Lauren with curiosity. "No shit? Are you sure?"

"Positive. Their names are Jennifer and Cassie."

"Oh, you know their names and everything."

"Well, not everything. Actually, that's all I know."

Faith stood and looked at the wall separating them from their lesbian neighbors. "You don't suppose somebody did that on purpose, do you?"

"Put the lesbians next door to one another?" Lauren laughed. "No, I don't think so. There are dozens of widows and divorcees on this boat, all sorts of women rooming together. I'm sure it's just a coincidence. I mean, I don't know about you, but I don't recall checking any box that said 'lesbian.' Or even any euphemistic, badly-translated Chinese version of that, such as 'women of the Sapphic persuasion.'"

Faith brightened, recognizing a challenge. "Or women *sans bon hommes*."

"Or even women *sans mal hommes*."

Faith struck a whimsical pose. "Women who go gaily amid perverse delights."

Lauren laughed, then shook her head. "You win. But, seriously, I think it's just a coincidence."

"Yes, you're probably right, but you know what your Aunt Rachel always says."

"There's no such thing as a coincidence. Yes, I know, but Aunt Rachel also believes in leprechauns and dragons."

Faith grinned. "Don't you?"

Lauren smiled at the irony of the question. Faith believed in nothing that wasn't a scientific fact. She was a refreshing and unlikely combination, a cynical optimist. The things she took pleasure in—myth, magic, science fiction—they all occupied the realm of fantasy for her. She saw a sharply delineated line between the real world and the imagined one. Though she lived exclusively on the harsher side of that line, life in general delighted and rewarded her. She expected the best things to come her way and she was not often disappointed.

Living with this paragon of positive thinking, Lauren struggled with her natural tendency toward pessimism and managed, most of the time, to land somewhere in the middle.

"No," Lauren said with finality. "Merely a coincidence, I'm sure. But it might make the cruise a little more interesting."

"It's hard to imagine it being more interesting. We're about to travel back through two thousand years. No rift in the space-time continuum necessary."

Lauren huffed at Faith's sci-fi reference. "Based on that hotel we stayed in last night, I'd say we already traveled back a few hundred. This is much nicer."

"Oh, much nicer, yes." Faith put her hands on her hips and frowned at the beds. "Let's move that table out of there and push these beds together."

"Are you expecting to get lucky tonight?"

"You never know. Gotta be prepared."

6

Faith's eyes twinkled mischievously. At forty-four, she was a dynamo of energy and Lauren had trouble keeping up with her, despite being seven years younger. Faith just seemed more alive than most people. More lively, anyway. She got up in the morning ready to attack the day and went to bed at night generally satisfied with how well she'd done. Lauren, on the other hand, had never been able to muster that kind of *joie de vivre*, especially in the early morning. They were just different types of people. And that was okay. Fifteen happy years together had shown this to be a compatible pairing with little strife and no regrets.

"I wouldn't be a bit surprised," Lauren said, pulling the table out from between the beds, "if we *both* get lucky tonight."

# CHAPTER TWO

The dining room was arranged eight to a table with a complement of eight tables, precisely accommodating the sixty-four passengers. Faith felt an involuntary smile come to her as she made this observation. That was typical of the Chinese. They wouldn't have considered a scattering of two or four-person tables, allowing some flexibility for the passengers, even though the room could have fit more tables. That would not have been the most efficient design. The Chinese were masters of efficiency.

Cassie and Jennifer and four other women were already seated at their assigned table. Was this part of the plan, too, Faith wondered, that the straight married couples would be seated together and the apparently single women would be grouped at women-only tables? The table was round. The dishes were placed on a lazy Susan in the center so the diners could spin them around and help themselves. Faith recalled their earlier trip to China. This was the arrangement for all lunches and dinners. Breakfast was different, usually an American-style buffet with a few Chinese items, like rice and stir-fried vegetables, thrown in.

The first offering tonight, a whole fish, milky eye looking up, was laid down as Faith and Lauren arrived. This was Faith's first look at the other lesbian couple. She picked them out easily by their ages—as the only women at their table under sixty—remembering that Lauren had described Cassie as close to her own age and Jennifer as younger. Cassie looked up with recognition as Lauren approached. She had a comfortable smile and an animated face. Her glasses made her look intelligent and down to earth. Jennifer was stunning, a beautiful young woman, dressed in a smart two-piece outfit, tan knit slacks and a short matching jacket.

Among the older women, one of them might have been as old as eighty. Her hair was dyed bright red and she was serenely attractive in the way of certain women who have led untroubled lives, making her age indeterminate.

As introductions were made, Faith learned that three of the four older women were widows and the fourth was a divorcee, all of them long divested of husbands. Cassie and Jennifer were from Albuquerque where Jennifer was an EMT and Cassie was a high school English teacher. Faith noticed they didn't mention to the group they lived together.

Lauren's eyes lit up when she heard the phrase "English teacher."  She'd been an English major in college too before she changed to soil science. Maybe they'll hit it off, Faith thought, scooping a chunk of flaky white fish from the platter in front of her. Lauren was shy and awkward with strangers, but Cassie, it was obvious after just ten minutes, was outgoing and unselfconscious, and would easily take charge of any social situation. If the odd coincidence that had thrown them together as shipboard neighbors should extend to friendship, even only four days worth, so much the better.

When it was her turn, she said, "I'm Faith. I teach at Portland State. Anthropology."

"Oh," said Nancy, one of the widows, "that's wonderful."

"Lauren here is my life partner," Faith continued, laying a hand on her shoulder. "Fifteen years of unwedded bliss."

Faith smiled at Lauren, hoping she wasn't embarrassed. She colored a little, but smiled back.

"And I'm Lauren," she said. "I'm a soil conservationist with the USDA in Portland."

"Oh, well," said Cassie gleefully, "if we're coming out, Jen and I are lesbians too!"

Jennifer's mouth fell open and she stared at Cassie, who grimaced in mock horror at her indiscretion. Lauren giggled discreetly. Faith glanced around at the other women. None of them seemed particularly alarmed. They were all probably seasoned travelers. They weren't the sort to be disturbed by a few lesbians. Or if they were, they weren't the sort to show it.

These women exhibited varying degrees of competence with their chopsticks, with most of them managing well enough, but Jennifer didn't even attempt it, asking immediately for a fork and saying, "I've given up on those things."

"Since you're an anthropologist," said Pamela, the redhead, "maybe you can tell me if this is true. Someone once told me there are cultures where a widow is forbidden to ever remarry after her husband dies."

"That's true," Faith confirmed. "Not so much in the modern world, although there are still some enforced mourning rules. Even in our own culture, it's considered at least a little crass for a widow to remarry too soon after her husband's funeral."

"Yes, but it isn't a law."

"No." Faith took another bite of her fish. "The Chickasaw required three years of mourning. That's one of the longer ones. Among several other Native American tribes, the rule was that the widow had to sit by her husband's tomb for a year. Her family members brought her food, but until a year had passed, she was forbidden to leave the spot."

"Oh, Lord!" exclaimed Pamela. "Two days after my Richard's funeral, I was on a plane to Tangiers. And I haven't stopped traveling since. That was thirteen years ago. I'm having the time of my life. He was a good man, Lord love him. He worked hard and made a lot of money."

Faith smiled at her. The huge diamond on her hand hinted at how much money her Richard had made.

"So under practically anyone's rules," said her roommate Nancy, "you're now free to remarry."

Pamela scowled. "Why would I do that?"

Cassie laughed.

"Mourning is an interesting subject," Faith said. "It was originally instituted in many societies as a way of isolating family members of the dead from the rest of the community."

"Why?" Cassie asked.

"If you look at it as a practical measure, it may have been to prevent the spread of communicable diseases. Along with isolation, sometimes people burned all the possessions of the dead person to destroy any evil spirits hanging out with the dead guy. But, really, what they thought of as evil spirits may in fact have been bacteria or viruses."

Cassie nodded thoughtfully. "Yes, that makes a lot of sense."

"So what is the appropriate period of mourning today?" Nancy asked.

"Some modern sociologists say one month for every year married can be expected. I think a formula like that is useless. Mourning is a highly individual process. Some people never recover from the death of a spouse. Others bounce right back." Faith gave a nod toward Pamela, who grinned. "Fortunately, we don't have to abide by anyone else's rules."

By now the fish had made its way around the table and was back in front of Faith.

"What kind of fish is this?" Pamela asked, flaking it with her chopstick.

"Whatever it is, it's good," Faith said. "When you're traveling in foreign countries, I've always found it a good rule not to ask questions like that. Eat everything and just enjoy it."

"Have you two done a lot of traveling?" Jennifer asked Faith as two plates of vegetables were set on their table.

"Luckily, yes. We've been all over the world. Every continent except Antarctica. This is our second trip to China. We managed to hit most of the usual tourist stops on our first trip. The Great

Wall, Xi'an, The Forbidden Palace, that sort of thing."

"That's what we're doing," Cassie said. "Two weeks, and this cruise is the last thing. So far, it's been fabulous."

The others started comparing notes about their travels. All three widows had impressive lists, even from Faith's point of reference. Their main form of amusement, it seemed, was traveling.

"What major European city would you most want to live in?" Pamela asked the group.

After hearing London, Paris, Barcelona and Prague, she turned to Faith and said, "What about you, Faith? You've been to all of these cities, right?"

"Actually, we've been all over the world, but my research takes me to some unlikely places and we haven't had the chance yet to see very many of the usual ones."

"Right," Lauren said. "We've been to Ghana, Madagascar and Syria, but we've never been to Paris. Or London, other than the airport."

"We *have* been to Rome," Faith pointed out.

"Yes. The catacombs." Lauren laughed shortly.

Faith turned to face her, recognizing her sarcastic laugh. Turning back to the group, she said, "All those places, all the beautiful cities of Europe, are on our list. Including Tuscany, Lauren's heart's desire. But Paris and London and Tuscany will wait for us. The Yangtze River will not."

For the first time Faith noticed the musical soundtrack playing in the background. Betty Hutton was singing "Things Like That There." A funny old song, she mused.

"That's Shanghai chard," Lauren offered to Sharon, the divorcee, who was staring with curiosity at the greens on the lazy Susan. "It's like bok choy. And this is a type of small round eggplant. Looks like they've done it Schezwan style, so it will be spicy. Nothing scary, though."

"How do you know all that?" Sharon asked, spooning some into her plate.

"Just a hobby of mine. Food. I like to cook. I like to try different things. In Portland, we're lucky to have some really good farmer's markets. There are actually a lot of Asian vegetables there."

"Lauren's a remarkable cook," Faith said. "Living with her is like going to a restaurant every night. Actually, better than most restaurants."

Lauren smiled thankfully.

"So, Jennifer," Faith said, "you're an EMT. That must be an exciting job."

"For sure. Some nights you wouldn't believe." Jennifer eyed the Shanghai chard suspiciously before spooning some onto her plate. "It can be pretty hairy sometimes. Probably not something to talk about at dinner."

Cassie, her mouth full, nodded emphatically. Because Lauren had identified the vegetables, the group now looked to her to name and describe each new dish as it was placed on the table. It was the perfect subject, Faith thought, to draw her out. Lauren, however self-deprecating, was an extremely knowledgeable expert on food. Between her job and her personal interest, she had both the science and the art well covered.

"I'm curious," Cassie said, addressing Faith. "Why'd you come back to China? Just loved it so much the first time?"

"We did love it, but we're here because of the dam. To see the area before it's flooded."

"We've heard some alarming statistics," Cassie said. "Nearly two million people will have to be moved to higher ground. Whole towns."

"Some really big cities, actually," Lauren said, "Fengdu, which is one of our stops, has a population around seven hundred thousand. The city is being rebuilt across the river from its current location."

"They've put markers along our route here," Faith said, "so you can see where the water level will be after the dam is in full operation. The result will be electricity for millions, but you can't help looking at this beautiful scenery and think about what's about to be lost. But it's like that with dams all over the world. Hetch Hetchy in Yosemite. Glen Canyon in Utah. Lots of archaeological sites were lost there too. There was a huge push before that dam was built to recover as many cultural resources as possible, just like there is here. That's really why we're here." Faith served herself some eggplant. "As much as I love beautiful scenery, the real purpose of this trip is to see the hanging coffins."

Jennifer dropped her fork, which clattered across the floor under the table. "Hanging coffins?"

"You haven't heard of those?"

"Oh!" said Pamela, "I've heard of them. Can't remember what they are, though."

"They're ancient, hand-carved wooden coffins suspended on the sides of the cliffs above the river. A people called the Bo are responsible. Some of the caskets have survived for two thousand years."

"What?" Jennifer gaped. "There are dead bodies hanging on the cliffs in this river?"

"They're skeletons now, of course. But, yes, there are. Most of them have long since fallen into the river. And many of those still in place will be submerged when the dam is built. They'll be underwater. Well, the sites will be underwater. The coffins themselves will be removed before that."

"We're going to hike up to one of the sites day after tomorrow," Lauren said, "in the Shen Nong gorge. You can't see much from water level, even with binoculars, so we wanted to get a close-up look."

"Wow!" Cassie said, her dark eyes widening at the thought. "That sounds fun."

Jennifer turned to Cassie, startled. "Fun?"

"Would you like to go?" Faith asked. "We'd have to get permission, but if you're interested, we can ask. We'd enjoy the company. Isn't that right, Lauren?"

She nodded enthusiastically, confirming that she was warming up to their new acquaintances.

"But we're going on the tour to the temple day after tomorrow," Jennifer said when Cassie looked at her for her buy-in.

"Oh, come on, Jen. We've seen a dozen temples already. This is something unique."

"It is," Lauren agreed. "A once in a lifetime opportunity to see the hanging coffins of Bo."

Cassie's eyes lit up with interest. She looked at Jennifer again with a hopeful expression.

Jennifer sighed. "Okay," she relented. "It's not going to be dangerous, is it?"

"No," Faith replied. "But it might be muddy. It's been raining. So wear hiking boots if you've got them. Anybody else?"

Faith looked at the others, who all declined a muddy hike, which didn't surprise her. "I'll make a call first thing in the morning to make sure there's no problem having you join us."

A waiter came by with a replacement fork for Jennifer and a platter of small red crustaceans. Faith couldn't suppress a delighted squeal and immediately grabbed one, though she had to reach across Nancy to do so.

"What is that?" Jennifer asked, wrinkling up her nose.

"Spiny lobster," Faith said, tearing open the claw. "I love lobster."

"They don't look like lobsters." Jennifer looked dubious.

"Not the kind you're used to, but they taste wonderful. So delicate and sweet. They're like crawdads. Try one."

At the mention of crawdads, Jennifer's mouth fell open and she just stared.

"Never eaten a crawdad?" Faith asked.

Jennifer shook her head as Cassie took one of the lobsters.

"Lobster may be my all-time favorite food," Faith said. "I don't think I could ever get too much of this stuff."

Conversation lagged as the number of dishes placed before them mounted. Faith was just breaking into her second lobster when Jennifer suddenly leapt to her feet. Her chair went flying back, toppling over. Everyone stopped eating, watching her streak across the room to one of the other tables where an elderly woman started screaming and an elderly man appeared to be choking in a manner that sounded serious. Apparently Jennifer had heard this, somehow, before any of the rest of them, over the din of conversation, dishes and the music, which was now onto Frank Sinatra singing "Come Fly With Me."

Jennifer grabbed the old man, kicking his chair away, and yanked him to his feet, his back to her. He was easily twice her size, but she managed to manipulate him into position with her arms around his chest. His wife had now stopped screaming, but as the rest of the room began to realize what was happening, there was a general round of gasps. Several people were on their feet, including Faith and Lauren, as Jennifer performed the Heimlich maneuver repeatedly. Everyone waited in tense silence as Jennifer made three attempts before a chunk of food shot out onto the table.

Faith had been holding her breath. She let it out and took another deep breath as Jennifer let the man back down to his chair. He gulped air and swallowed several times and gradually grew calm.

"Is it all out?" Jennifer asked, kneeling beside him.

He nodded.

"Okay, then," she said with authority, rising to her feet and giving him a pat on the shoulder. "You'll be fine."

"You saved his life!" said the old woman, gaping at her husband, her eyes still wide with fright.

Jennifer shrugged. "No biggie."

"On the contrary. You should have a reward." She reached for her purse.

"No, really. I do this all the time. But I wouldn't turn down a beer if you want to spring for that."

When Jennifer returned to the table, she was grinning, looking deservedly pleased with herself. Cassie put an arm around her and hugged her. "Good job!" she said. "You responded so fast."

"Didn't even think about it," Jennifer said, taking her chair.

"Very impressive," Faith said. "Good training, right?"

"Right. Becomes instinctive."

Faith nodded and sat down, knowing that although the response to distress might be instinctive, the Heimlich maneuver was not. That was learned.

"What did he choke on?" Cassie asked.

"Who knows?" Jennifer shrugged. "Probably one of those spiny crawdads."

A few minutes later a waiter brought her a Tsingtao beer in a green bottle. She raised it toward the old man's table in a silent salute. His tablemates were still talking excitedly about the near tragedy. The old man gave Jennifer a grateful smile.

# CHAPTER THREE

On a ship this small, when official entertainment was offered, there was one choice and only one choice. If you didn't take it, there wasn't much else to do, so why not take it? That was the reasoning that led almost all the passengers to this evening's organized activity: Chinese fan making.

After the instructor displayed several beautiful examples of folded paper fans decorated with lotus blossoms, fish, birds, dragons and other traditional motifs, he let them loose with wooden sticks, glue, sheets of paper and watercolor paints. They were four to a table, so Cassie and Jennifer joined Lauren and Faith for the craft session. Lauren was glad to see them there because she already felt closer to the two of them than anyone else on board.

"I feel like I'm in kindergarten," Cassie said with a gleeful snicker.

"I'm hopeless at this sort of thing," Faith announced, staring at her blank piece of paper. "Lauren, what are you going to paint on yours?"

Lauren briefly studied the sample fans at the front of the room. "Goldfish maybe. I like goldfish."

Cassie nodded, dipping her paintbrush in a bottle of blue ink. "Good choice."

Jennifer was already painting intently, her face close to the table, the tip of her tongue protruding from her mouth.

"Can we talk while we do this?" asked Faith, addressing herself mainly to Jennifer.

Jennifer looked up. "Sure. No problem."

"In that case, how about coming out stories?"

Cassie peered over the top of her glasses at Faith, her lips curling into a one-sided smile. Faith apparently interpreted that as concurrence.

"You go first, Lauren," she instructed.

Lauren suspended her brush over a small round blob of orange paint. "Been gay all my life," she said. "By the time I was sixteen, I was exclusively into girls. Lost my virginity to a girl named Stormy my senior year in high school."

"Stormy!" Cassie yelped. "How romantic."

"It wasn't her real name. But that's what everybody called her. It was intense, but more about sex than love. After that, nothing serious until I met Faith at twenty-two, the first real love of my life." Lauren briefly held Faith's hand. "My first and last, my one true love."

Jennifer glanced up from her work to smile at Lauren's sentiment.

"You next, Faith," Cassie urged.

Faith set down the paintbrush that hadn't yet touched paint. "I had no clue I was gay. I thought you had to be a jock to be a lesbian and I was so far from being a jock I knew I couldn't be one, despite the erotic fantasies I had about my Physics teacher. Still, I only dated boys in high school and married my steady boyfriend after graduation."

"Skippy," Lauren interjected.

"Yes, good old Skippy. He dated my older sister Charity

briefly before he cast his eye my way. I don't think she ever forgave me for that." Faith laughed.

"Charity?" Cassie looked thoughtful, then quoted, "'And now abideth faith, hope, charity; but the greatest of these is charity.'"

Faith nodded. "Believe me, my sister Charity used to quote that passage frequently, with her nose in the air."

"Your parents were very religious?" Cassie asked, painting thin black lines on her paper.

"Yes," said Faith. "I had a younger sister named Hope, so you've guessed the source of our names. I've always thought my family was cursed by irony."

Cassie pushed her hair back behind her ear. "How so?"

"Well, Faith ended up with no faith. In the case of Hope, things were always hopeless. She had a terminal illness from birth and died when she was ten. And Charity has turned into the most uncharitable of women. At least toward me. I decided a long time ago that if I ever have a daughter, I'll defy the God of Irony and name her Cruella Ugly."

Cassie cackled and turned to Jennifer, who smiled uncertainly.

"If she's my daughter, too," Lauren said, "I think I'd prefer Lisa or Christine."

Cassie nodded at Lauren, looking amused, then turned back to Faith. "So what happened to Skippy?"

"We were married just over a year." Faith glanced around the group and lowered her voice suggestively. "And then I met a woman."

Everyone nodded knowingly. Faith ended her story there, stopping short of talking about the "woman." The girl, really—Faith's college romance. Janie was a shadowy figure to Lauren. She had seen photos, but Faith hardly ever spoke of her. It was so long in the past and not long-lived—two years at most. There was probably not a lot to say. Faith's equivalent to her Stormy, she'd always assumed.

Lauren glanced at Faith's paper, which remained completely blank. Faith shrugged at her and lifted her paintbrush in an encouraging first step.

"Jen," Cassie directed, "tell your coming out story."

19

Jennifer swished her paintbrush in a glass of water. "Not much to tell. I never had a boyfriend. I always knew I liked girls. Had my first girlfriend when I was fourteen. Been through bunches of them since." She grinned tauntingly at Cassie, who shoved her playfully.

Jennifer returned to her painting, which was turning into an intricate floral design.

"Cassie?" Faith prompted.

"Yes, all right." Cassie glanced at Lauren with a comfortable smile. "I struggled with my sexuality as a teenager. I thought I was a lesbian, but wasn't sure and didn't really want to be. I liked boys okay, as friends, and at that age, it was hard to tell the difference, so I ended up getting married after high school, like Faith. We had a son, Eric, who's being raised by his father. He's fifteen now."

"Your ex-husband has custody, you mean?" Faith asked.

"Right. With Lucas, Eric's had a stable home." For the first time since they'd met, Lauren saw Cassie grow solemn. "When we got divorced, my life was a mess, so it was the best thing for everyone."

"Do you see him?" Lauren asked, pausing her brush to give her full attention to Cassie.

"Yes. He comes for visits. A very nice boy. Not into sports. Studious type. Lucas and Judy have done a great job with him."

"He *is* very nice," Jennifer said. "They live in San Francisco, so we don't see him much. We had him for two weeks this summer. He's interested in cooking, so we let him take over the kitchen while he was there, which was fine with me." Jennifer and Cassie smiled knowingly at one another. "It was fun. We never knew what we were going to see on our plates."

"Maybe spiny lobster," suggested Faith.

Cassie laughed. "Could have been if he'd have seen any around."

Noticing that Faith had still put nothing on her fan, Lauren pointed threateningly at the paper in front of her.

"Okay," Faith relented, dipping her brush in a random bottle of paint.

Cassie was drawing birds, white and black birds with long

legs, most likely storks or cranes. Jennifer's design was becoming something unexpectedly attractive. She had gnarled branches of red and pink blossoms nearly covering the space, looking remarkably adept. A few spiky leaves appeared here and there. At the moment she was drawing convincing Chinese characters in a section of open space above her branches. Obviously, Jennifer wasn't new to watercolors.

Impressive, Lauren thought, then caught Cassie watching her. Indicating Jennifer's painting with her eyes, Cassie gave a nod of agreement and a close-lipped smile before returning to her own painting.

Cassie's face was very expressive, hardly ever at rest and often amused. She smiled a lot with her eyes, her lips pressed tightly together like now, but when she laughed, it was a wide-open laugh that showed all her upper teeth.

I like her! Lauren thought, surprising herself.

She painted some green shapes amid her orange shapes, trying for lily pads. She put some black dots on her fish for eyes and decided she was done. Besides, the instructor was now calling for the group to fold their fans and glue them to the sticks.

"How did you two meet?" Cassie asked, applying a thin line of glue to her paper folds.

Faith, who had now managed to paint a single, solid yellow circle on her paper, glanced at Lauren. "Do you want to tell it, honey?"

"Okay." Lauren tore her gaze from Faith's stark painting. "I was working for the USDA as a soil conservation technician, an entry-level job. It was my first real job out of college. So, you know, young, no clout. I met Faith when I was called out to an experimental lawn seed farm."

"Lawn seed?" Cassie asked, wrinkling her nose.

"Like you plant in your yard. Fescue, ryegrass. That sort of thing. It's a big business in Oregon. Rains all the time, so grass grows like, well, like weeds. The farm itself was powered completely by solar energy. Very progressive at the time. So they were partly funded by a government grant. Anyway, they were just getting started, plowing the land, and they turned up some bones."

# CHAPTER FOUR

Traveling upstream on the Yangtze from Wuhan, the ship entered the Three Gorges area on the first full day of cruising. Most of the time was spent gawking from the top deck of the ship at the deep, dramatic V plunge of the mountains on either side of the river. The color of the water in the Xiling Gorge was reddish brown like mud and the sky was gray and thick, overhung with low, wet clouds. Dark green vegetation was interspersed with buff-colored rock on either shore.

Everybody was crowding the stern, taking pictures. Occasionally, a burst of narration came from the loudspeakers with facts about life on the river, the history of the area and the changes that were expected once the dam was in place. The story of the Yangtze was now meshed inextricably with the progress of the dam.

Lauren hugged her jacket over her sweatshirt as they passed a wall pockmarked by small caves and topped with intricately-shaped pinnacles.

"The cliffs on either side of the gorge," boomed the heavily-accented voice on the loudspeaker, "are composed of limestone, easily soluble by groundwater. In a landscape like this, which is called karst topography, caves are common features. We are now passing the Three Travelers Cave, named for three famous poets from the Tang Dynasty. Inside the cave are numerous inscriptions from visitors throughout the ages. The interior of the cave serves as an impromptu museum of the development of the Chinese alphabet over the centuries."

Lauren looked around for Faith and located her on the port side of the ship, bundled up with a knit cap and muffler. She hurried across the deck as the narrator continued.

"The Three Travelers arrived at different times in history, discovering the cave by chance. They stayed briefly and left their poems on its walls. They never met one another, but their words live here together for all time."

Lauren sidled up to Faith, observing her red nose. "I'm going inside for a while. I'll be back when we get to Wu Gorge."

"Okay. I'm going to stay up here a little longer."

Lauren nodded, then made a dash for the stairs, skipping down to the main deck and the galley. Inside, she saw Cassie sitting alone over a steaming mug at one of the tables. She had on a cable-knit sweater and jeans. Her jacket hung on the back of her chair. A camera sat on the table beside her mug.

"Hey," Lauren said, "what are you drinking?"

"Hot chocolate."

"That sounds perfect." She went to the beverage machine and served herself a mug, then returned to Cassie's table. From where she sat, she could see the legs of people on the deck above through the window.

"I didn't expect it to be so cold," Cassie said. "I didn't even bring gloves. You know how you can't conceive of cold weather when you're home packing in the summertime."

"I know. But I've been caught so many times without the right gear that I pack it all now."

Lauren removed her gloves and wrapped her hands around the mug to warm them.

"Actually," Cassie said, "I don't even own a pair of gloves. Even in winter, Albuquerque is usually very mild."

Lauren gulped down some of the hot chocolate. "Is that where you're from, originally?"

"No. I was born in Montana. We moved to Nevada when I was in high school, mainly to get out of the cold. That's where I met Lucas and got married. Then, after the divorce, I moved to Albuquerque because that's where my girlfriend's family was. Been there ever since."

"And Lucas moved to California?"

"Right."

"Siblings?" Lauren asked.

"I'm an only child like my son Eric. What about you? What's your family story?"

"Born in Washington, just across the river from Portland. Never moved around much. My parents divorced when I was six and then my mother remarried a couple years later. I've got three brothers, but the only one I'm close to is Jim. He's the youngest."

"No sisters?" Cassie pushed her empty cup aside.

"No. I always wanted one. I begged my parents for a sister. And then they had another boy. I thought they were extremely unreasonable."

Cassie smiled, displaying her dimples. "Are your parents living?"

"My mother is. She and Riley, my stepfather, still live in the house I was born in. But we don't see each other. They aren't happy about the direction of my life."

Cassie nodded knowingly. "They've got something against the Department of Agriculture, huh?"

Lauren let out a sputtering laugh.

Cassie put her hand on Lauren's, saying, "Sorry. I couldn't resist that. And I'm sorry your family is unsympathetic. That's always tough."

Lauren glanced at Cassie's hand covering hers and it was immediately withdrawn.

"That hot chocolate really hit the spot," Cassie said. "Feeling much warmer now."

Lauren took another drink. "I meant to tell you Faith got permission for you and Jennifer to come on our hike tomorrow."

"Oh, that's great news! What time do we leave?"

"As soon as we dock. I think it's around nine." Lauren noticed the serious-looking camera on the table between them. "That's a nice camera."

"Thanks." Cassie put a hand on her camera. "I've been really happy with it."

"Are you a photographer?"

"Oh, no! I just dabble, but I enjoy it. It's a hobby. With the mist and the drizzle we've got today, I'm getting some fantastic shots."

"Neither of us is much of a photographer," admitted Lauren. "Faith is forever cutting the tops off people's heads. So much so I don't ever trust her to take a picture anymore. I'm not a lot better, but with the no-muss, no-fuss camera we've got, you can't go too far wrong. I generally take the pictures when we're on one of these research trips."

"I'd be happy to do that tomorrow," Cassie offered, patting her camera. "Maybe that'd be a way of saying thank you for the adventure."

"That's a good idea. Thanks."

The song playing on the ship's omnipresent soundtrack, an instrumental version of "Fascination" broke into Lauren's consciousness. "Do you know this song?"

Cassie narrowed her eyes and tuned in. "Oh, sure. I love it. An old favorite."

"Me too."

Cassie hummed along with the song, then smiled warmly at Lauren. "My grandmother had a seventy-eight with that song on it. I think I still know all the words."

"Was it the Nat King Cole version?"

"No. A woman." Cassie looked thoughtful. "I think it was Jane Morgan."

"I don't know her."

27

"She was a big sensation during World War II, but people don't remember her. We used to listen to those records all the time, me and Grandma. She never did get rid of them. Dinah Shore, Doris Day and Nat King Cole too. I still have some of her seventy-eights, though I have nothing to play them on. Just one of those things that's hard to get rid of. Such happy memories."

"It'd be fun to play those again, wouldn't it?" Lauren suggested.

"Yeah, it would. It's funny they play this sort of music here, don't you think?"

"They're trying not to offend anybody, I'm guessing. Personally, I wouldn't mind some traditional Chinese music. Same thing in a Chinese restaurant. Give me Chinese music, not Tony Bennett. Or Greek music in a Greek restaurant. I never understand why that isn't just standard practice. You don't go to a restaurant just for the food. You go for the atmosphere."

"I totally agree with you," Cassie declared. "We were at this Japanese restaurant a few weeks ago and I thought the same thing. Here I am sitting beside a huge Buddha statue in a red throne, amid watercolor murals of blossoming cherry trees and girls in colorful kimonos, eating this soba noodle soup and drinking sake accompanied by 'Do Ya Think I'm Sexy?' Now, I'm a big Rod Stewart fan, but that just wasn't right, you know?"

Lauren nodded as several pairs of legs walked past the window. "Looks like the sun's coming out."

Cassie turned around to look. "Good. Maybe I'll wander back up on deck."

"See you in a while, then."

As Cassie left, Lauren watched her denim-covered legs climb up the stairs outside the galley and onto the top deck. She finished her cocoa slowly, noticing that the song now playing was "I'd Like to Get You on a Slow Boat to China."

# CHAPTER FIVE

The ship's lounge was dimly lit, crowded with square tables, chairs and loveseats, with a small stage at one end. A piano player provided a background of instrumental versions of familiar pop songs which could be easily tuned out. The four women sat at one of the tables, no one else near, with drinks in front of them. It had been Lauren's suggestion to meet Cassie and Jennifer in the lounge after dinner. Faith was glad because there was no entertainment scheduled tonight.

"I hope the weather's better tomorrow," Lauren said, leaning drowsily against Faith. "By better I mean warmer. I thought my nose was going to fall off today up on deck"

"As long as it's not raining," Faith said. "Rain would be the worst."

Cassie reached for her glass. Like Lauren, she was drinking

scotch. Faith had never liked scotch. To her, it tasted like burnt wood. But she wasn't much for any type of hard liquor. She preferred wine or fruity mixed drinks like the margarita she'd ordered tonight.

"Will we cancel if it rains?" Jennifer asked.

"No," said Faith. "You can decide tomorrow morning if it's worth it to you, once we see the weather forecast. We're going, regardless. This entire trip was planned for the hanging coffins."

As the waiter passed near them, Jennifer waved him over and ordered another glass of wine. "I'll buy this round," she offered.

"In that case, I'll have another," Cassie said. "Lauren? Faith?"

Lauren nodded. Faith waved the offer off, as her first glass was still half full.

When the waiter withdrew, Cassie asked, "Is this research for a book, or what?"

"An article," Faith said. "Eventually maybe a book."

"Second book," Lauren said. "Faith's already published one."

"Oh, really." Cassie looked intrigued and trained her gaze on Faith. "What's it about?"

"Burial customs," Faith answered. "The rituals and beliefs surrounding death and life after death. Like mummification. That sort of thing."

"That's morbid," Jennifer said, looking like she'd eaten something nasty.

"You must encounter some grisly scenes in your line of work too," Faith pointed out, "with considerably more blood and gore than my old bones."

"Yes, but most of those people are still alive. They're just people. They aren't skeletons or mummies or something creepy like that."

The waiter returned with their second round of drinks, disrupting conversation as he cleared the empty glasses.

Cassie leaned toward Faith and said, "Give an example of some strange burial practice from your book."

"Here we go," Lauren warned with a short laugh. "You're in for a lecture now." She picked up her glass and tucked her legs into the love seat, getting comfortable.

"For Jennifer's sake," Faith promised, "I'll stay away from tales of disembowelment and cannibalism."

"Oh, Christ!" Jennifer winced.

"How about this one? The ancient Syrians put the bodies of their dead in huge pots of honey as a way of preserving them. Honey kills bacteria, so the body never spoils."

"Interesting," Cassie said. "Similar to the Egyptians with the embalming. But why, exactly? I've never thought much about that. Why did they care if the body decayed?"

"Good question. In the case of the Syrians, they thought that if the body decayed, the spirit would die. They thought there was still a connection between the spirit and the body after death. It's an interesting idea. Not unique in the world, but rather foreign to us. In our culture, and I mean the Judeo-Christian tradition, the spirit completely detaches from the body at death."

"In Buddhism too," Cassie said. "We just heard that on a tour in Beijing."

"Yes, quite a few cultures believe that. But there are so many variations. In some South American tribes, they believed the spirit was free to come and go while a person was alive, and while the spirit was away from the body, the person was asleep. If the spirit left the body and didn't return at all, the person died."

"Are you talking about the soul?" Jennifer asked, pulling her knees up and wrapping her arms around them.

"If you wish," said Faith. "The thing that's interesting to me about the idea of a permanent link between the body and the spirit is that it has ramifications while the person is still alive. In a belief system like that they don't think of the body so much as a vessel, as a disposable container. The body, like the spirit, is also considered sacred. Our culture has traditionally viewed the body as unimportant and transient. That has consequences."

"I never even thought of that before," Cassie reflected. "Very interesting. What's another one?"

Faith was thrilled with Cassie's interest. She glanced at Lauren, who gave her an encouraging smile.

"This is one of my favorite stories," Faith said. "It's not in my book because I haven't been able to visit the site yet, but maybe it will be in the next one. There's an island in the Pacific, one of

31

the Solomon Islands, used for generations as a burial ground. The island was never inhabited. It's small, the top of an old volcano. The people who used this place, which they called Sky Mountain, lived on a larger island several miles away. From their island, the top of Sky Mountain was frequently in the clouds, seeming to touch the sky. It was the tallest point around and, in their view, closest to the next world where the spirits of the dead went for rebirth."

"You mean Heaven?" Jennifer asked impatiently.

"That's a Christian concept," Faith said in her patient teacher voice. "These people weren't Christians. In their belief system, there were four phases of being. We're occupying the third. The fourth and last was ascension to the sky spirit world which they believed was literally in the sky. When someone died, they carved a dug-out canoe for the deceased and tied it to their boat, then rowed over to Sky Mountain. They carried the canoe up to the top of the mountain, where they left it."

"They didn't bury it?" Cassie asked.

"No. They left it open so the spirit would have no trouble rising into the sky. The carrion birds took care of the rest."

"Oh, my God!" Jennifer said, closing her eyes. "This is horrible."

"It's fascinating," Cassie said, wrinkling her face playfully at Jennifer.

"The practice was abandoned in the seventeen hundreds," Faith explained, "but the story of Sky Island persisted in the people's lore, which is how it was rediscovered in the twentieth century."

"Where is this island again?" Cassie asked.

"Solomon Islands. Off the coast of Papua New Guinea."

Cassie reached for her glass. "Why do you like that story so much?"

"It's a very clean and simple representation of several universal archetypes. It makes a good illustration. But, mainly, I think the idea of the mountain in the clouds is beautiful and romantic. It's such a pure example of how people transition to the afterlife. It's not muddied up with any notions of penance or sin or even evil spirits. There's no purification ritual involved.

Everyone who died automatically got taken to the mountaintop and ascended into the sky."

"Faith is a scientist," Lauren said, "but she's not immune to beauty and romance."

Faith put her hand over Lauren's. "When the island was discovered by researchers in the nineteen forties, it contained hundreds and hundreds of these coffin canoes. The mountainside was littered with the bones of all of the bodies that had been left there. It was quite a find."

"I can't imagine seeing a real live human skeleton without freaking out," Jennifer said.

Lauren snorted loudly and Jennifer looked confused.

"You said '*live* skeleton'" Cassie pointed out, her amusement tinged with affection.

Jennifer frowned. "You know what I mean."

"You get used to it," Lauren said. "I have. There's even a human skull in our house."

"Are you serious?" Cassie asked, her eyes wide.

Lauren nodded. "We call him Yorick."

Cassie laughed. "Of course you do!"

Jennifer looked frustrated now. Cassie put an arm around her shoulders and said, "It's from Hamlet. He picks up a skull and says, 'Alas, poor Yorick, I knew him well.' Famous line."

Jennifer nodded uncertainly. Faith began to wonder what these two had in common.

"So they did that just so the dead people were closer to their spirit world?" Cassie asked. "To give them a boost into the sky?"

"That and to remove them from their own island. Primitive people had some interesting ways of dealing with the problem of soil and groundwater contamination. I've always been interested in the way people build their mythology around real, practical concerns. Myth isn't arbitrary, usually. It's based on some fact or serves some useful purpose."

Cassie looked thoughtful, leaned back, and said, "So you've never been to Sky Island?"

"No," Faith said. "I hope to go, eventually. It's a place I've wanted to visit since I first heard of it."

"It's not quite so high on my list of vacation spots, though,"

Lauren said. "I mean, a rock covered with old bones? Not quite Tahiti."

Cassie laughed. "By the way, Faith, what's the title of your book?"

"*Paradise Lost.*"

Cassie looked intrigued. "Like Milton?"

Faith nodded.

"Do you talk about original sin?"

"In a way, yes. It's about how human societies face their mortality. In many cultures, including Christian ones, there's the idea that humans lost their immortal status at some point and are struggling to regain it. In most belief systems, that can only happen after death, as if human life is some sort of digression, even punishment, rather than the truly important thing."

Faith realized she was dominating the conversation, but Cassie seemed genuinely interested and Lauren, she knew, was happy just observing and listening.

"Isn't all of this death stuff depressing?" Jennifer asked.

"Not to me. Death customs are really all about life, aren't they? Life after death for both the deceased and the loved ones left behind. The afterlife, in any of its many forms, is the main source of hope for billions of humans since we first became human. There's almost no society without a tradition of an afterlife in some form or another. With the rare exception, like the Maasai of Kenya, every culture we know of believes in something beyond this life."

"So, really," Cassie concluded, "your specialty is life after death?"

"You could say that. I don't happen to believe in it myself, but I think it's an endlessly fascinating concept. As soon as humans became conscious of their mortality, at least as far back as Neanderthalensis, and maybe even further, they started to create realities beyond this one."

Cassie looked skeptical. "How can we know that?"

"Because of burial practices. Because, if there was nothing after death, there would be no reason to prepare for the afterlife. The earliest known burial sites show evidence that the dead person would be going on to something else."

Cassie sat back, her glass in hand, looking satisfied.

"I believe in it," Jennifer said firmly. "I believe in Heaven."

They all turned to look at her. She looked mildly defiant, leveling her gaze at Faith, as if she were preparing for an argument. But Faith merely smiled and raised her glass to Jennifer. She suddenly felt neither superior nor disdainful, but, just for that moment, she felt envious. That was an admirable accomplishment in its way, the ability to believe something for which there was absolutely no tangible proof. The vast majority of humans were apparently capable of it, but Faith never had been, not since she was a small child. Like other children, as she grew older, her myths left her one by one: the Easter bunny, Santa Claus, the tooth fairy. And God.

When her younger sister Hope died at the age of ten, she had tried hard to believe in Heaven. Everybody told her that's where Hope was. She had desperately wanted to believe that Hope was still somewhere, anywhere. She had been a sickly child since birth and Faith had always felt protective of her. She had loved Hope in a way she never loved her older sister Charity. She managed to convince herself briefly that Hope was a happy, healthy girl living in Heaven, but with no reinforcement, she eventually lapsed into non-belief. She didn't know why she didn't believe. Charity, older by only a year, had grown up in the same Christian family, had attended the same church and been taught the same things, and she had emerged as steadfast a believer as her parents.

Faith, ironically, couldn't comprehend blind faith. She'd been researching it for decades, but it remained a deep mystery to her. She was no more capable of believing in the God of her parents than she was of believing the moon was made of cheese or that everything happens for a reason, as people were fond of saying at times of incomprehensible tragedy.

Last year, at her mother's funeral, relatives thought they were offering comfort with statements like, "Now your mother will be with her little Hope again." That thought was comfort for her father and Charity, she supposed, but it held no meaning for her.

"What do *you* think happens after you die?" asked Cassie pointedly.

"Nothing," Faith replied. "End of story."

"That's so sad," Jennifer remarked, looking genuinely gloomy.

Cassie slipped an arm around her shoulders and gave her a heartening squeeze.

"Not really," Faith said, "depending on what you do with that idea. It definitely makes me appreciate life. This is my one shot and I try to make the best of it. Live every day with determination to make it a good one. I'm grateful to be alive, every day."

"It's true," Lauren said. "She lives like that, like today is always the most important day there is. Not to be wasted."

Cassie raised her glass and said, "To today!"

The four of them touched glasses.

Faith drained the last of her margarita. "I'm afraid today is over, girls," she said. "At least for me. But I think we did a damn fine job of using it up."

# CHAPTER SIX

It seemed Jennifer was nervous, even fearful, as the four of them left the cruise ship and boarded a motor-driven sampan to take them deeper into Shen Nong gorge. She had said something earlier about going off on their own, as if it were reckless. Lauren couldn't blame her, really. They were far from home in a tremendously foreign place and had left the security of their structured tour. Lauren had spent some of the early years with Faith being similarly uneasy. Faith never seemed to be concerned about all the ways in which an adventure like this could go wrong. Lauren had learned, in time, to worry less, though she had never become so carefree as Faith. She decided to tell a story as the four of them sped between high rock walls on the Shen Nong River.

"We once missed the sailing of a cruise ship," she said to

Jennifer. "In Alaska. We were on an Inland Passage cruise and we decided to rent a car in Skagway because there was a Tlingit site Faith wanted to visit. None of the tour buses stopped there."

"What's a Tlingit?" Jennifer asked, her face peering through the circular opening of her tightly-cinched hood.

"Native of Alaska. One of the tribes. There's only one rental car place in Skagway. We got our car from a cranky old woman there named Birdie. The day turned out beautiful and we made it to the site with no problem. We had plenty of time and no worries as we drove leisurely back to town."

"But then?" Cassie asked.

"But then a moose appeared right in the middle of the road. Faith was driving. She swerved to avoid it and ran us into a ditch."

Jennifer gasped.

"Nobody was hurt," Lauren said.

"Not even the moose," Faith added.

"We'd been seeing buses all day from the various cruise lines, driving up and down the road. But by then the tour buses had already headed back to the dock. The road was deserted. It's hard to get how isolated that place is until you're standing on the side of a highway for an hour and not a single vehicle comes by."

"Lauren thought we were going to freeze to death out there," Faith confided.

"And we could have! It was getting late and really cold. Finally a guy in a tow truck came along. He said Birdie had sent him out to find us because we hadn't come back. Well, I took back all the nasty things I'd said about Birdie at that point. The guy pulled our car out and we rode back to town. But the ship had sailed."

"Oh, no!" Cassie said. "What did you do?"

"We asked Birdie if we could keep the car for another day," Faith said. "We figured we could drive south and catch our ship at the next port, which was Juneau. Not that far, right, I asked Birdie. Nope, not that far, she said. About ninety miles as the eagle flies. So, we're thinking, fantastic. We'll be there in no time, have a nice dinner, just wait for the ship to arrive."

Faith looked at Lauren, wordlessly handing the story over.

"No, said Birdie, you can't do that. There's no road to Juneau."

Cassie's mouth fell open. "What? Juneau is the capital of Alaska."

"Right," Lauren confirmed. "But no road to Juneau. Not even by a roundabout way. So Birdie hooked us up with a bush pilot for the next day. We stayed in Skagway that night and flew to Juneau in the morning."

"I loved it!" Faith said. "I'd been wanting to fly with a bush pilot every day since we arrived in Alaska. Seems so adventurous, you know. "

"It was fun," Lauren said. "We were actually glad we missed our ship. The pilot gave us a fascinating tour on our way to Juneau."

"You were lucky you weren't eaten by a grizzly bear," Jennifer said. "Are there any bears here?"

Faith laughed loudly.

"Things do sometimes go wrong," Lauren said, "despite Faith's unflinching optimism. But usually not irrevocably. And sometimes something unexpected turns out to be the best thing of all."

"Still," Cassie said, "I'd just as soon not miss our embarkation time today."

"Plenty of time for our little excursion before that," Faith assured her. "As long as we don't run into a moose."

The multi-hued cliff walls narrowed as they went further upstream. The color of this river was a deep green, not the muddy brown of the Yangtze. It was a gorgeous place, Lauren thought, craning her neck to look high above them to the open sky, blue and cloud-free. No chance of rain today.

"Look!" Faith said, pointing high up on the left river bank. "You can see them!"

They all followed her finger up the sheer cliff two-thirds of the way to a spot where three hunks of wood protruded from the rock wall.

"Those are just tree trunks," Jennifer said after looking through the binoculars.

"Right," said Faith. "They are. That's what they made the

coffins out of. But as you can see, there are no trees growing on these steep cliffs, especially no trees of that size. Those things were carried up there somehow."

"Why here?" Cassie asked. "These cliffs are practically vertical. Why choose a place so hard to reach?"

"You have to assume that was the idea. We don't really know. To keep something away from the bodies."

"Something?" asked Jennifer, grimacing.

Faith grinned, but didn't offer an explanation. Their guide cut the boat's engine and pulled over to the river bank, gliding gently to shore. Now that the boat was stationary, they could feel the warmth of the sun. It was a fine day for a hike.

"Leave your coats," Lauren suggested. "It's going to warm up once you start walking. You'll probably just want a vest, if anything, over your shirts."

They peeled off their outer layers, down to short-sleeves, except for Jennifer, who wore a sleeveless top. Lauren admired her muscular arms momentarily before unzipping the legs of her convertible nylon pants. Both Cassie and Jennifer pulled on ball caps, Jennifer threading her ponytail through the opening in the back of hers. Faith put on her Tilley hat and Lauren tied it for her under her chin. Once they were dressed the part, they piled out of the boat to begin their hike.

The guide was a small man, shorter and thinner than all four of the women. He was gaunt, but quick and agile, moving rapidly along the rough terrain in open sandals. He never said his real name, but they were instructed to call him Joe. They followed Joe in single file, Lauren first, then Cassie, then Jennifer, with Faith bringing up the rear.

The path alongside the river started out flat and easy, but soon began to climb, getting steeper and sometimes slippery. Most of the time it was wide enough to give them a sense of safety, but in a few places, the trail became a narrow ledge on the cliff face. They slowed down considerably at those spots and picked their way carefully, aware of the peril of plummeting to their deaths. Faith and Lauren were used to this sort of hike, but it was clearly an unaccustomed adventure for Cassie and Jennifer. From what Lauren had gathered, Jennifer's finely-toned body was the result of daily trips to the gym rather than sports. The going was much slower with the two of them along, but Lauren decided it was nice to have them anyway. Cassie at least, because she seemed to be so delighted with the day.

They took frequent rest stops, during which they could survey the steep green mountains surrounding them, shrouded in mist, and watch the river below. The landscape was breathtakingly beautiful and Cassie snapped photos regularly on the way up.

At one of the stops, Cassie removed her vest, leaving just a T-shirt layer. Sweat glistened on her forehead. She stuffed the vest in her backpack, then turned to look at Lauren and smiled broadly. "This is fantastic! Thanks for letting us come along."

Cassie patted Lauren's shoulder, then, to signify she was ready to continue. Lauren cast a glance over at the others. Jennifer was staring at the ground. Faith was grinning with the sheer joy of being here.

"What a place to be put to rest!" Faith exclaimed, sounding a little winded.

"Ready," Lauren said to Joe, who sprang off ahead. They didn't really need a guide, since the trail was easy to follow, but it was a political requirement. The Chinese government liked to keep track of its tourists. They were visiting a cultural heritage site, so this was a sensitive situation. Faith had had to obtain permission, a process that had taken months. She'd had to submit her reasons and her credentials to government scrutiny. If she were not a qualified scientist, she wouldn't be allowed to make this trip. Ordinary tourists were only able to view the coffins from water level.

Periodically, Lauren stopped to observe an interesting plant—interesting to her, at least. If they weren't bursting with showy flowers, they didn't have any appeal to the others, so she kept these stops brief. Once she squatted next to a small fern surrounded by tender grass, its leaves just beginning to unfurl. She slipped her index finger into the curl of one of the fronds, letting it hold her finger like people do with newborn babies.

"What is it?" Cassie asked as the troop came to a halt.

"A fern. Not one I'm familiar with. I've always liked ferns. In some ways, they're very simple plants. They have no seeds and

41

no flowers. Yet they've survived so many millennia with their basic structure unchanged." Lauren slid her finger gently from the grasp of the plant and stood.

"That's the law of the jungle, right?" Cassie said. "If it ain't broke, don't fix it."

Lauren nodded. "I like the idea of something staying the same for so long that you can almost call it forever."

"But nothing lasts forever," Faith announced cheerfully.

Lauren smiled to herself. She knew Faith didn't consider that a negative idea. They were living in the same world, but somehow they seemed to see such different things. Faith was unquestionably a glass half-full sort of person. Lauren could tell that Cassie was one of those too. Although she wasn't one herself, she did admire the point of view.

As they plodded up a steep, muddy incline, she heard a sudden cry from behind and turned around to see Jennifer being held securely in Faith's arms. Faith laughed as Jennifer got her feet under her and stood.

"She slipped," Faith explained.

"Thanks," Jennifer said, hitching up her shorts. "If you hadn't caught me, I'd have been sitting in the mud."

"My pleasure," Faith said, a hint of the flirt in her voice. Lauren narrowed her eyes at Faith and she winked her response. She was in very high spirits today.

After an hour, they had climbed two-thirds up the height of the cliff to reach the site. There were three hollowed-out tree trunks set in natural recesses in the limestone, resting on wooden poles wedged into the rock face to form supports. Silently, the four women removed their packs.

"Don't touch them," Joe warned.

"I'd like to look inside," Faith said. "I won't touch anything."

Cassie slipped an arm around Jennifer's waist and asked, "You want to look inside?"

Jennifer shook her head and shivered.

"Well, I do," she said.

The coffin Faith approached was carved out of a single tree trunk and rested in a shallow, natural depression in the cliff.

"This is Song Dynasty," Joe said. "Eight hundred years old. The oldest ones are twelve hundred years old, Tang Dynasty. They used to have lids covering them and artifacts inside. Textiles and pottery. Weapons too. Knives and spears, that kind of thing."

Faith turned from the coffin to face them and Cassie took her photo.

"The artifacts have been removed," Joe added.

"By whom?" Faith asked.

"Researchers. Sometimes vandals. These coffins will be moved before the water rises. You can go to the museum to see the artifacts that have been found. There were hundreds of these here once."

"Don't miss the inscription on the rock here," Faith said, coming away from the coffin. "It's very faint, but there are some marks done in cinnabar."

When it was Lauren's turn, she stood on tiptoe and peered into the coffin. A layer of sand several inches deep filled the bottom, but didn't completely cover the skeleton within. The rib cage was partially visible, as was the skull. She had seen more than her share of skeletons during her fifteen years with Faith, but they never failed to move her, even so. Her mind always managed to put skin and muscle on them, as well as an imagined life complete with emotions, loves, losses, triumphs and defeats. Although there were many things you couldn't know about a human life, any human life, one thing that no one ever disputed was that each one was special and unique. One of the things Lauren loved about Faith was that even though she approached her subject matter with a cool, scientific expediency, she never lost sight of the human component. She retained respect for the people she studied, keeping in mind that they once had been people with dreams and imaginations as rich as her own.

Cassie took her turn after Lauren, snapping several photos of the interior of the coffin. When she came away, she grinned and said, "This is so cool." She was obviously thrilled.

"Come on, Jen," Faith said. "Take a look. You'll regret it if you don't. Always do everything."

To Cassie, Lauren said, "She always says that. Do everything.

Take both. You know, when somebody says, do you want the cheesecake or the tiramisu, she says, 'both.'"

Cassie laughed, showing all her teeth. "I like that!"

Faith's philosophy of life was always to grab whatever gusto life offered. She wasn't one to sit on the sidelines of anything. It was one of the great advantages of being her partner. Lauren knew that her own life wouldn't have been nearly as exciting if not for Faith. She had a tendency to hang back, approach life tentatively. She recognized her younger self in Jennifer.

Faith took hold of Jennifer's hand and walked her up to the coffin. She continued to hold her hand as Jennifer peered over the edge. As the tallest woman present, Jennifer was the only one who didn't have to stand on her toes to see inside.

"Oh, shit!" Jennifer whispered.

Cassie and Lauren sat on a mossy boulder to take in the view. The river far below was silent from this height. There was a lone hawk gliding on air currents at eye level. Like the mountain they were perched on, all the mountains as far as they could see were round-tipped triangles pointing into gray mists. The moist mountains were covered with verdant green vegetation except in this channel where the river had cut down through the soft limestone, creating sheer borders of bare rock, interspersed with an occasional small tree. The cliffs of this gorge were too steep and unstable to support much plant life.

Cassie, who had been sitting silently observing the scenery, turned and smiled at Lauren, a tranquil, undemanding smile. In that moment, Lauren was struck with the feeling they had known one another for a long time. Cassie was one of those rare people who felt familiar almost immediately, like you had known her in another lifetime and were picking up again in this life where you'd left off some centuries ago.

"Better than a Buddhist temple?" Lauren asked.

"Yes. Much better, although we've seen some really great temples. Everything is so ancient here. It's hard to get your mind around it. The Terra Cotta Warriors, the Great Wall, the Forbidden City. All the things we've seen are hundreds or thousands of years old. This culture has been here for so long. It's mind boggling."

"I've felt that way so often on our travels. In awe, you know, of what people have accomplished."

"You've been all over the world," Cassie observed.

"Still a lot of places to go, though. One thing about Faith's research is that she'll never exhaust her subject matter."

"Everybody dies."

Lauren nodded. "Everybody does die. And most of them don't do it without making a little fuss. Or a lot of fuss."

"Like this." Cassie pointed to the three coffins. "So nobody knows why they did this?"

"No. Nobody knows how they did it either. Some of these things are suspended on completely sheer vertical walls with no place for anyone to walk or stand. And those coffins are heavy. I imagine when Faith writes this up, she'll back one of the theories, but they're all just educated guesses. The Bo people had no written language. Not much is known about them at all. Their culture was wiped out during the Ming Dynasty. These coffins are the main thing they left behind."

"You know, before I met you two, I never thought much about how important the burial customs of a people are. It's like the key to everything, isn't it? Their philosophy, their mythology, their identity as a culture. How they died tells you a lot about how they lived."

Lauren nodded and smiled at Cassie, thinking she was a very likable woman. She was curious and intelligent, good-natured and kind. She was probably a good teacher.

Faith and Jennifer were no longer looking at the coffin. They were standing near the edge of the cliff and Faith was gesturing in a way that took in the mountains around them. She's explaining about terrace farm irrigation or some such thing, Lauren guessed.

"Do you usually do that?" Cassie asked. "Learn all about the stuff Faith is working on?"

"I like to know what we're looking at, yeah. I enjoy it. I'm kind of a research nut. Sometimes when we go to a place like this, she'll be asking *me* questions about it. Details, you know, that she doesn't remember."

"You two make a good team. You seem like a strong couple."

45

Lauren glanced at Faith, who was still talking animatedly to Jennifer. "We are."

"What about your own work? Does it absorb you?"

"Over the years it's become very routine, like most jobs. It has its moments, but nothing like this. This isn't routine for her either. We usually manage two trips a year. The rest of the time, she's a teacher, like you."

Since they had been motionless for a while, it had gotten cold again. Lauren took her windbreaker out of her backpack and pulled it on. Cassie helped her find the sleeve, then gave her a friendly pat on the back.

Faith and Jennifer walked over to where they sat.

"Are you glad you looked?" Cassie asked Jennifer.

"Yeah. It wasn't that bad."

"Time to head back," Faith said. She took one more deliberate look around at the mist-filled gorge and the three coffins. Then she turned to Lauren with a look she knew well. Faith was happy beyond expression, like a child at Christmas.

Lauren couldn't help but feel some of her joy.

# CHAPTER SEVEN

Lauren's hips rose up each time Faith's hand thrust down, driving her fingers deep inside. Lauren locked her arms around Faith's back, her grip desperate, her moans muffled by sheer determination, as per their agreement. We can leave the balcony door open to the cool night air, Faith had agreed, if you don't frighten the farmers and livestock on shore. So Lauren was attempting to comply, suppressing her usual vocal enthusiasm.

Faith felt Lauren's body tense into the last stage of frenzy. There was one cry of ecstasy that escaped into the night, but it was brief and probably would not bring the Chinese authorities out to the ship to investigate. Faith smiled to herself in the dark as Lauren's body fell back on the bed, spent and satisfied.

It wasn't really the farmers and their livestock she was concerned about, nor even the people who might be still on deck above. It was the neighbors. Although they were becoming friends with Cassie and Jennifer, they didn't need to share everything. They had retired to their cabins at the same time, so Faith knew they were just on the other side of the wall.

She kissed Lauren, savoring her lower lip, which smelled and tasted of sex.

"That was a good one," Lauren said, breathless.

"Despite no Uncle Dick?" Faith joked.

"I was just asking if you'd brought it. Obviously, we don't *need* it."

"I almost did bring it," Faith said, turning on her side and inviting Lauren to spoon. "Maybe if it wasn't purple I would have, but the thought of some juvenile baggage handler flashing that thing around put me off the idea. Carrying it in the carry-on would have been even worse, if my bag got searched going through security. Uh, what's this, ma'am?" she mimicked.

"How would you have answered that?" Lauren asked.

"I don't know. Uncle Dick? The only part of him worth bringing along, anyway."

Lauren snickered, her hand sliding along the curve of Faith's hip. She moved closer, wrapping herself around her back. "What a day!"

"Fabulous. It was a bitch to arrange, but absolutely worth it."

"I think Cassie and Jennifer enjoyed it too."

"Cassie, at least." Faith gripped Lauren's hand to her stomach. "Jennifer too, I guess, to some extent. I hope so."

"I like her," Lauren said. "Cassie, I mean."

"Yes, I can tell. You usually take longer to relax around new people."

"I feel like I've known her a lot longer than two days."

That was apparent, Faith thought, remembering how lively Lauren's conversation with Cassie was earlier in the evening. Lauren had been positively vivacious, talking and listening enthusiastically to Cassie's views on the importance of maintaining the literary tradition in modern English-speaking cultures to include people who were totally unreadable nowadays like Henry James. Then they had compared books they'd read and authors they admired, and finally Faith had left them there by themselves, absorbed in their conversation, while she went to the room to read. Lauren wasn't normally so unguarded. It was nice to see her like that.

"She was very funny at dinner tonight," Lauren said. "Talking about the absurdity of golf. A bunch of guys in loud pants hitting a tiny dimpled ball around a cow pasture, looking for gopher holes. Didn't you think that was funny? I couldn't stop laughing. It was the way she told it that was so funny."

"Um," Faith mumbled, feeling suddenly very drowsy.

After a moment of silence, Lauren whispered, "I love you."

"Love you too."

Faith lay facing the open balcony door, relishing the warmth of Lauren's body tucked close up against her back. The only light in the cabin was a faint glow rising up from the ship's halo of light on the water below. The sound of the river splashing against the ship came in through the open door. A tender breeze wafted over them intermittently.

Faith was almost asleep, or maybe she had been asleep and wakened again, when she gradually became aware of the sound of voices. They were indistinct, but clearly querulous. As she focused on them, she realized they were coming from the next cabin, from Jennifer and Cassie, a few feet beyond her head. They were arguing. Bits of their conversation came on the air currents. Their balcony door must also be open. What she was hearing, she realized, was Jennifer as she moved close and then further away from the open door. All she heard from Cassie was a muted voice through the wall, barely audible.

The phrases she could understand—"embarrass you," and "you always do that," and "am I supposed to ask your permission?"—were like one of those exercises where you're given a photo with several pieces cut out and your brain fills in all the missing bits. A few phrases were all you needed to reconstruct the entire argument.

After dinner, the four of them had gone again to the lounge for drinks. It had been comfortable and friendly. But there was that awkward moment when Jennifer had called the waiter over to ask for another glass of wine and Cassie had looked

49

concerned. It was instantly apparent that she didn't want Jen to have another, but how could she say that in this group of new friends? So she said nothing. At the time, anyway. And Jennifer had gotten noticeably loud after that drink. Not obnoxious. Just slightly more rowdy than before. It had been nothing to Faith and Lauren. Maybe it had seemed worse to Cassie. Later, if she said something to Jen, something like, "I wish you wouldn't have had that last drink," that might have been enough to cause a fight, depending on what buttons it pushed.

Of course, Faith realized she was imagining all of this. They might have been fighting over something completely different.

Lauren slipped out of bed, leaving a cool vacuum behind, and Faith watched her walk to the balcony door. The faint light in the room was no brighter than a single birthday cake candle might produce, but it was enough to create a silhouette of Lauren's body, a classic female shape.

Lauren slid the patio door shut almost silently, then returned to bed. Faith could hear nothing now but the faint sound of women's voices next door, far too quiet to understand words or to keep her awake.

Seeing Lauren's outline at the patio door reminded her of Janie because of the way she used to stand naked in the doorway of their darkened bedroom, backlit by the bright nightlight she always insisted on in the hallway. Like a child, she was afraid of the dark. Janie had been someone completely unsuited to her, as often happens during the sexual rampages of youth. But Faith had loved her anyway, deeply and painfully. Painful because they were constantly finding fault with one another, were disapproving and disappointed even while craving one another. It had been an immature romance, which wasn't surprising considering how young they were. Even now, thinking of Janie, Faith felt wistful. There are some people you never really get over, even after twenty years.

It would probably hurt Lauren to know that another woman still owned a piece of her heart, so Faith was careful to never say such a thing. The closest she had come was one day early in their relationship when, answering Lauren's questions, she had described her love for Janie as "different." Lauren had wanted to know how it was different. Was it better? Worse? Less intense? Faith had decided it was wiser not to try to explain that and had stuck to "just different," an explanation that clearly hadn't satisfied Lauren. What she wanted to hear, Faith concluded, was that any previous love Faith had felt was of no consequence in comparison to what she had with Lauren. Faith didn't see any point in making such comparisons. It didn't make any sense to her. Every relationship was its own reality.

Lauren was idealistic and, in some ways, innocent. Not unlike Faith had been when she met Janie. She had been only twenty-one and had thrown herself into that love affair without reservation. She had nearly drowned trying to keep them both afloat. It had been a constant struggle. Though she had eventually escaped and survived, she had lost something there, had left something behind. She assumed most people did leave something behind when they left their first real love, some slice of joyful innocence that was unrecoverable.

Lauren had never had that experience. She was so young when they met that she had very little baggage. Faith knew she was Lauren's first real love. Lauren had never had to leave that shattered piece of innocence behind. Faith hoped she never would have to. Lauren would be one of the lucky ones, Faith thought. Her heart would never be broken.

As soon as Lauren was tucked up against her again, Faith fell asleep.

# CHAPTER EIGHT

The evening's entertainment was a production featuring traditional Chinese folklore and folk dance. The costumes were brilliant and beautiful. The music was exotic. The dance was slow, a cross between ballet and a martial art. A narrator, wearing a turquoise robe decorated with gold piping and gold dragons, told the story like a Greek chorus as the actors went through their steps without speaking.

Lauren sat between Faith and Cassie, clasping Faith's hand discreetly between them.

"This is the story of how the four great rivers of China came to be," said the demure narrator, her hands pressed together in front of her. Then she bowed her head slightly and moved to the side of the stage.

The lights went down as four people walked out dressed in

drab peasant clothes. They knelt and appeared to be praying. The narrator, who was now in shadow, spoke again. "The people of the world suffered a great drought. Their crops died. They had nothing to eat. They prayed for rain."

Four dragons leapt onto the stage, a pair of actor's legs visible under each of the costumes. Each dragon was a different color—red, yellow, white and black. They danced, undulating and dipping between one another like huge paper streamers. Lauren turned to catch Faith's glance and they smiled at one another. Faith squeezed her hand.

The narrator, heard but not seen, seemed to be a disembodied voice. "The four dragons who lived in the Eastern Sea, the Long, Black, Yellow and Pearl dragons, were flying in the sky, playing with one another like children, when they heard the people's lament. They stopped their game to listen."

The dragons immediately stood still, huge heads cocked at a listening angle.

"The dragons felt sorry for the people who had no rice to eat, so they decided to ask the Jade Emperor to send rain. They flew up to the Heavenly Palace to make their request. They found the Jade Emperor relaxing, being entertained by singing fairies."

Lauren turned to catch Cassie's eye as the peasants withdrew and a large, regally outfitted man on a huge throne was pushed onto the stage. Four nymph-like girls attended him, costumed in filmy robes. The dragons approached the Jade Emperor.

"The Jade Emperor agreed to send rain," said the narrator. "He promised to send it the next day, so the dragons, satisfied with their accomplishment, left and returned to their game. But the promise was false. The Jade Emperor was annoyed with the dragons for interrupting his leisure. He agreed to their request to get them to leave. After ten more days and no rain, the people of earth were near death and the dragons realized the Jade Emperor had lied to them."

The emperor's throne was pushed off stage and the peasants returned to their imploring positions. The four dragons danced around them.

"The dragons decided to take matters into their own hands and save the people. They scooped up great mouthfuls of the

East Sea and sprayed the water into the sky so it would rain down on the people's crops. They did this many times, creating a downpour which saved the people."

As the dragons ran across the stage, the peasants leapt up and down in celebration, now holding bowls full of rice.

"The dragons knew that what they were doing was risky. When the Jade Emperor found out about it, he was enraged that they had defied him."

The throne returned and the peasants withdrew.

"The Jade Emperor ordered the four dragons to be seized. He then called upon the Mountain God to move four mountains to imprison the dragons forever, one dragon under each."

Everyone left the stage except the dragons, who each went to a corner of the stage to lie down.

"Even though they were imprisoned, the dragons were determined to help the people so they would never starve again. They turned themselves into rivers and crossed through the mountains and valleys, flowing to the sea, providing water to the people forever."

The narrator returned to the center of the stage. "That is how China's four great rivers came to be—the Black River, the Yellow River, the Pearl River and the Long River, which you know as the Yangtze." She pointed to each dragon in turn as she named the rivers. "The four rivers continue to flow across the land to this day, giving life to the people."

The lights came up and the actors came out for bows.

"What a charming story," Cassie said, clapping.

When the ovation subsided and the actors dispersed, Faith said, "All of their plays are so beautiful, so colorful. I think it's interesting, too, to compare the two traditions of the dragon, the East and West. Here, the dragon is a playful, friendly creature, dedicated to helping mankind. In the West, the dragon is a monster."

"The personification of evil," Cassie added. "The dragon is a stand-in, in fact, for the devil in so many stories."

"That's very interesting," Lauren said, "how two such opposite views of the same mythological beast could evolve. Sounds like a subject for a master's thesis."

Cassie laughed. "Yes, and it's probably been done already."

"Hasn't everything?" Lauren remarked.

As they stood, Cassie slipped an arm around Jennifer's waist and smiled fondly at her.

"Do you want to go to the lounge for a while?" asked Lauren.

Jennifer gave Cassie a suggestive smile, at which Cassie turned to Lauren and said, "Not tonight, I think. We'll see you in the morning."

After Cassie and Jennifer had left the room, Faith said, "Looks like those two are happy with one another again."

Lauren nodded, wondering at her odd, uneasy feeling as she imagined them going back to their cabin to make love.

# CHAPTER NINE

"Follow the blue flag," instructed Meilin, raising a sky blue pennant high above her head in front of the group of thirty. "Be careful. Big market. You stay close."

The after-lunch tour, and one that Lauren was tremendously excited about, was a trip through the public market in Wanxian. This was where the locals shopped for their food. There were no provisions for or expectations of tourists here. Normally, the cruise patrons didn't even see this, but a rain-induced flood had closed the trail to the waterfall they were supposed to have visited. The waterfall was reputed to be very tall, very beautiful, filling a misty gorge, but Lauren considered this change of plans a lucky break.

Meilin led them up the wide, concrete steps from the dock to the city, rows of multi-storied white buildings under a dark gray sky, and the obedient group followed. Rain was still a possibility, so they carried umbrellas. All of them were by now used to following a flag in this way. All of the tours in China were led by guides with colored flags. It was a good idea, a system that worked. Lauren was unable to see Meilin up ahead. At five feet tall, she was obscured by the other tourists, but her flag bobbed up the stairs, clearly visible. Five hundred feet to the west, also moving *en masse* up the stairs, was another group from another ship, following an orange pennant.

"This is going to be so much fun," Lauren said as they reached the city and plunged into a busy street. "To see how the people live day to day. So much of the time tourists are kept isolated from real life here."

"Right," said Faith. "Last trip Lauren and I snuck out of our hotel in Beijing early one morning and took an impromptu tour of a little residential neighborhood. The people there were very surprised to see us. They all stood still, stopped what they were doing, and stared."

"And what did you see?" Cassie asked.

"Similar to what you've seen from the buses. The people were getting their breakfast, sitting in front of their houses with bowls of rice. One old woman was making something that looked like pancakes over a fire in a drum. It was peaceful. Old men sitting in open rooms playing board games. Small children sitting on the ground, some of them unclothed. Bicycles going by. It was hard for us to say if these people were poor or not. From our perspective, they looked very poor, but maybe they were average city dwellers."

"I'm so glad we went for that walk," Lauren said, remembering the day fondly.

Meilin led them down a narrow side street with bicycle traffic and almost no cars, then turned again into what looked like an alley lined with tiny shops. They passed some young men walking with poles across their shoulders, two heaping baskets of apples hanging from either end. One of the men turned to smile at them with a look of friendly amusement. A woman stood in a doorway of a shop holding a baby on her hip, watching them pass, her expression impassive. Jennifer waved at the baby. An old man pulling a two-wheeled cart loaded with bananas walked

57

rapidly along with his load, his face shaded by a straw paddy hat. Three young men sat on the curb smoking cigarettes. One of them was reading a newspaper. All three of them wore black pants, work shirts and sandals.

Lauren felt conspicuously American.

They passed a cart loaded with flowers—daylilies, carnations—and the floral aroma wafted into their path.

"Is this the market?" Cassie asked.

"No," Lauren said. "It's inside a building. That's what I heard from one of the guys on board when we were talking about raingear."

"That's good." Jennifer sounded relieved.

Even though Lauren didn't know what to expect herself, she was sure that whatever Jennifer was envisioning was going to end up being a huge misconception. She would not have been surprised if Jennifer was imagining a Chinese version of Safeway.

At last they filed under a bright green awning into a wide passageway to enter an open building choked with stalls, tables, people, a profusion of sights, sounds and smells, too much to immediately process. As Lauren became oriented, she thought the interior of the building resembled an underground parking garage, an open space with concrete pillars at regular intervals and banks of fluorescent tube lights hanging below a network of water pipes and electrical wires.

They had entered at one end. The building stretched out in the other direction with so much activity in between that they couldn't see the other side. The group crowded together, following the blue flag through an aisle between wooden counters bursting with wares. Lauren was suddenly overcome by the smell of fish and noticed she was walking beside a table covered with open plastic tubs and bowls, all of them filled with water and shellfish. She took a closer look in the tubs, recognizing clams, oysters, mussels, shrimp and a writhing coil of foot-long eels.

Jennifer peered into the tubs and then jumped back. "They're alive!" she shrieked.

Faith nudged Lauren and whispered. "It's alive, Igor. It's alive."

Lauren giggled, then turned to Jennifer and said, "No question about freshness."

A young woman sat behind the table, her black hair pulled

back into a stubby ponytail, shucking oysters over a stained towel across her lap. She smiled at Lauren, who smiled back. She didn't seem disturbed by this troupe of tourists gawking at her merchandise. Lauren turned away from the eels, as that was enough to make her queasy.

The tubs of water continued, containing endless varieties of thrashing fish, octopi, squid, scallops and multi-colored seaweed. Faith stood near a large tub of lobster, pointing at it with a salacious grin while Lauren snapped a picture, careful to include one of the ubiquitous hanging red paper lanterns. As they moved away from the seafood aisles and into the produce, the group of tourists seemed to calm down, as if the agitated fish had been infecting them with anxiety.

Rows and rows of colorful fruit were lined up along both sides of the walkway. Scales stood at each station to weigh the fruits and vegetables. Most of the vendors, Lauren noticed, were women. Some of them smiled at the tourists. Some of them frowned and some of them seemed indifferent. They passed by tomatoes, pears, onions, peppers and wide tables of leafy greens. There were trays of rice, potatoes, bamboo stalks, cucumbers, melons, ginkgo nuts, dried leaves, pods and roots, many of which Lauren didn't recognize.

"This is incredible," she said to Faith as they passed a table covered in mushrooms, most types unfamiliar to her.

Then they came to a booth containing mountains of citrus fruit. Lauren stopped and handed the camera to Faith. "Take a picture of me here with the Buddha hands...and don't cut my head off this time."

Jennifer and Cassie stopped too as Faith snapped the picture.

"Buddha hands?" Cassie asked.

Lauren pointed at the pale yellow fruit with fingerlike projections.

"Is it good?" Cassie asked.

"Not really. It's good for using like lemon rind. Mostly rind. Not much to eat there. But I'll tell you what is good. These little mandarin oranges here. We had some of these when we were here before. They're wonderful. They're called the honey citrus of Wenzhou. They're seedless and very sweet."

"Should I get a couple?" Cassie asked.

Lauren nodded. "I'll get some too."

"You're not supposed to eat the local produce," Jennifer cautioned. "Not raw."

"This is safe," Faith said. "You'll peel it. The fruit's protected inside."

"I don't think we should," Jennifer persisted.

"I'd like to try them," Cassie said, picking one up. Then she took another one and waved them toward the woman behind the table, a toothless gray-haired ancient.

"One dollar," was the familiar response they heard so often all over China.

Cassie turned and smiled knowingly at Lauren, then reached into her pocket.

"She's ripping you off," Jennifer said, pointing to a sign with a number five on it. "They're probably selling for five yuan a pound. Even at five yuan apiece, that's only about a quarter for both."

Cassie deftly removed a single dollar bill from her pocket stash and handed it to the old woman, who grinned and bowed slightly. Then she turned to Jennifer, who was frowning, and said, "It doesn't matter. I don't mind."

Lauren bought four of the mandarins, giving the old woman two dollars.

The four of them moved off toward the blue flag. Their tablemates grabbed Lauren to identify several unfamiliar vegetables, but soon let her be when they realized even she was out of her comfort zone amid all of this exotic produce.

The next area they ventured into was the meat section. That's when Jennifer really started freaking out. Slabs of beef and pork lay on tables. Cow livers and pig's heads hung in the stalls from hooks and live chickens and ducks sat cramped in cages. Feathers and flies were everywhere. Tongues and kidneys and chicken feet lay out on tables with no covering. All of this was fascinating to Lauren. She openly gawked.

"This is disgusting!" Jennifer declared, obviously disturbed. "It's so unsanitary. What are these people thinking?" Then she turned to Lauren and said, "Don't you think somebody should do something about this? Food safety, isn't that your job?"

Lauren, taken aback, said, "Uh, well, in a way, although I'm not an inspector. And even if I was, this isn't our jurisdiction. They have their own regulations."

"Jen," said Cassie gently, "can't you try to be a little more open-minded?"

She turned a contentious look toward Cassie. "Open minded? Are you kidding? Look at this! These are the people spreading swine flu and bird flu all over the world. After seeing this, I'm not surprised."

"I think you're overreacting. You should try to be more tolerant of cultural differences."

"Cultural differences? This isn't like a weird hairdo or something." Jennifer stared, then scowled, rapidly losing her temper. "Am I embarrassing you in front of your new friends, Cass? Is that your problem? I'm sick and tired of you complaining about my behavior. I'm just being myself. If that's not good enough for you, then fuck you!"

Lauren stiffened, then saw Pamela and Sharon swing around to stare. Cassie looked stricken.

"I'm going back to the ship," Jennifer announced. She turned and walked rapidly back the way they'd come.

Cassie ran after her and grabbed her by the arm. "You can't do that. You have to stay with the group."

Jennifer shook her arm free. "Leave me alone! I'm going back."

Cassie stood where she was, watching Jennifer weaving her way through the market. Lauren came up behind her and touched her shoulder. Cassie turned, looked at her solemnly, then attempted a smile.

"Sorry," she said. "I don't know why she's acting like this."

"Don't worry about it," Lauren said, taking her arm. "People get tense on vacation. Happens to everyone. Come on. We've fallen behind."

The blue flag was marching off in the distance, so the three of them hurried to catch up.

"She shouldn't have gone off like that," Faith said. "I'm going to tell Meilin."

Lauren nodded. "Good idea. She's going to find out

61

somebody's missing anyway when she does her next count."

Faith went ahead to talk to the guide. The group was now heading outside, emerging from the market into the dampened light of a cloudy afternoon. They gathered together outside the exit, a loose group, atwitter with the excitement of the wonderful sights they had just seen.

Faith returned. "She's really agitated now."

Sure enough, Meilin started barking orders at them as if they were a unit of army recruits. Her diminutive stature did not make her any less menacing. They were to stay close and follow the blue flag. They were not to wander off. But before that, they were to line up to be counted. They obeyed without hesitation, as if trying to make up for their renegade member with military-style precision. When the count was over, one person short, Meilin shot a disapproving glance at Faith. It must be her fault that Jennifer was missing, she seemed to imply, since she was the one who had reported it.

Nancy nudged up close to Pamela, who was standing to Lauren's right and asked, "What happened?"

"Lovers' quarrel," Pamela whispered.

Nancy nodded knowingly, glancing at Cassie.

Meilin made a phone call, then summoned them to attention and marched them back through the streets to the ship with no stops. Lauren walked beside Cassie, who was understandably subdued. It would be extremely embarrassing, she thought, to have your partner say "fuck you" in public like that. It would be bad enough in private. Lauren herself was still stunned by it. She couldn't imagine Faith ever saying such a thing to her.

As they walked down the concrete steps toward the river bank, Cassie said, "I hope she made it back."

Unfortunately, that wasn't the case. When they boarded, they found out Jennifer had not come back. Meilin's call to the ship had put the crew on alert, so they'd been waiting. There had been no sign of her.

When Cassie heard this, she started to panic. "I'll go back. I'll go find her."

As she headed for the gangway, a male crew member stepped in front of her, blocking her way.

"Cassie," Faith said, "they won't let you go. And they're right. You don't know your way around. You don't speak the language."

"But—"

"They're sending out a couple of ship hands."

"We're going to sail in an hour," Cassie said, glancing toward shore.

"They'll find her," Faith said firmly. "Let's go have dinner. By the time we're done, she'll be back on board."

Cassie pulled aside. "I'm going to wait here until they get back. You two go ahead. I'll see you later."

"I'll wait here with you," Lauren offered.

"No." Cassie turned to look into Lauren's eyes, revealing how troubled she was. "There's no point, Lauren. You go to dinner. I'd rather you did."

Lauren nodded, then followed Faith to the dining room where everyone was now aware that Jennifer was missing. Faith explained in abbreviated details that Jennifer had not felt well and had, rather unwisely, decided to return to the ship on her own. Those who had been there and had heard the exchange between Jen and Cassie didn't contradict her account, not openly anyway.

"White slavery," said one of the older men. "They nabbed her for the white slave trade. Cute young girl like that. That's the way they do it. Take them right off the street, throw a burlap sack over their heads and you never see them again."

"Oh, God!" Faith said under her breath to Lauren, "I'm so glad Cassie isn't here to hear that idiot."

Their table of six was more than usually quiet, since Cassie was absent and Faith was not in the mood for conversation. When the omnipresent watermelon arrived at the table, Lauren set aside some sesame chicken, stir-fried Chinese broccoli and three wedges of watermelon on Cassie's empty plate. She took it up on deck, finding Cassie where she'd left her, standing at the railing looking out over the town.

"Brought you something to eat," she said.

Cassie glanced at the plate, smiling appreciatively. "How do you know my favorite things?"

"Food is something I pay attention to. You said how much you liked the sesame chicken the first day and I saw you take three helpings of broccoli at lunch yesterday. And everyone knows your favorite part of the meal is always the watermelon. No great powers of deduction required."

"That was very thoughtful." Cassie sat on a bench and ate a piece of chicken. Lauren sat beside her.

"If they don't find her before we leave," Lauren said, "you know they'll just bring her to Fengdu by car."

Cassie looked up and cocked her head. "Is there a road to Fengdu?"

Lauren laughed lightly, thankful for Cassie's sense of humor. "I don't actually know. Never bothered to check that out, since we were coming by boat."

Cassie ate most of her food, including all of the watermelon, then put the plate down on the bench. "Jen is usually more easy-going than she's been the last couple of days. I think she's a little intimidated by you and Faith. She's not really into these topics we've been talking about. Literature, history, science. Not her thing."

Not interested in the things you're most passionate about? Lauren thought, then asked, "What is her thing?"

"Sports, for one. She loves to watch all kinds of sports. We go to see the Lobos play all the time. Baseball, football, basketball."

"Lobos?"

"That's our university team."

"I'm not much for sports myself, but Faith is. She's a fanatic over baseball. Maybe those two can find some common ground there. I'll mention it to her as a conversation topic. For tomorrow."

Cassie glanced at her watch. "If she makes it." She stood up to watch at the railing again and Lauren did the same. They both caught sight of Jennifer simultaneously at the entrance to the dock, standing with a tall Chinese boy, gesturing emphatically as if in an argument.

"Jen!" Cassie hollered, waving, then she ran over to the gangway where she was again prevented from leaving the ship.

Lauren followed, watching Jennifer as she handed the boy

64

some money, then turned to run up the gangway. The man at the top of the ramp opened the gate for her, then shut it with a bang behind her.

Jennifer flew into Cassie's arms and they hugged each other enthusiastically.

"I'm so sorry I did that," Jennifer said. "So stupid! I'm such a jerk."

"I'm just glad you made it back," Cassie said, then kissed her. "I was so worried. What happened?"

Cassie held Jennifer's face in her hands, having forgotten all about Lauren, who took a couple steps back, planning an unobtrusive exit.

"I got turned around," Jennifer explained. "Went out the wrong door or something. That damn market was huge. It took me a while to realize I was lost. Then it took a while to find a guy who spoke English. He led me back to the dock. Then he wanted a hundred dollars! Do you believe that? Asshole! I gave him twenty."

Lauren went downstairs and reported that Jennifer was on board and the search could be called off. Fifteen minutes later the search party was also aboard and they were pulling away from the dock and on the way to Fengdu.

# CHAPTER TEN

The following morning, Faith and Lauren got up early to sit on their balcony to watch the shore drift past. Faith ran down to the dining room to bring back two mugs of coffee that sat on the little table between them, along with two of the mandarin oranges.

Every so often, something of interest would draw their attention, such as a thin waterfall cascading down the cliff wall. They passed a grotto with a small temple built into it, then some Chinese letters carved deeply into a smooth slab of rock. They couldn't read these inscriptions, nor did they know how old they were, but as they passed the markers showing the expected new water level, it was clear that all of these things would be underwater in a few years.

Lauren had her journal open, and occasionally jotted a note.

"Fengdu should be a fascinating place," Faith said. "I'm really looking forward to it."

"Me too. We should be able to see both the old city on this side and new one on the other. That should give an interesting perspective of the impact of the flooding."

"Fortunately, a lot of the ghost city on Ming Mountain will be above the water level, so it will be saved."

Lauren leaned back with her coffee and perched her feet on the balcony railing. "Do you remember why they call it that, the ghost city?"

"Some old folk tale that said the king of the underworld resides there. Supposed to be a place full of devils. Or a place where the spirits of the dead come to be reborn. Either way, not inhabited by living humans."

"So it's a ghost town in more than one sense."

Faith nodded, then took a drink of her coffee. "There are more than seventy temples in the ancient city, which is supposed to be the gateway to the underworld. Basically, it's a recreation of Chinese hell through statues and inscriptions. Should be a lot of fun."

Lauren laughed, then took one of the tangerines and easily slipped off the peel. She broke the fruit in two and handed half to Faith. As Faith bit into it, juice ran down her chin. Lauren reached over with a napkin and wiped it off.

"Thanks," said Faith. "These things are heavenly."

Watching the river, Lauren saw a group of women in the water up to their knees. "What's this?" She stood and leaned against the railing to get a better look. More of the women came into view.

Faith stood beside her. "They're washing clothes," she observed.

The women were bent over, scrubbing clothes on wash boards. Higher up along the river bank were earthen-colored houses, all small, all plain, surrounded by bare ground. These houses were different from most they'd seen, the familiar multi-storied apartments that appeared in every city and town. These were single-family homes of a simpler sort, occupied by farmers. There were no cars, no garages.

"It's wash day!" Lauren announced.

Faith waved at the women and a couple of them waved back.

"Do you think those houses will be flooded when the dam's built?" Lauren asked.

"There's no doubt they will."

Lauren sat back in her chair and wrote in her journal for a couple minutes, then set it down on the table. "I'm going to get another cup of coffee," she said. "You want one?"

"Yeah, sure. Thanks."

Lauren left with the mugs and Faith sat back in her balcony chair watching the hills float by. What a wonderful morning, she thought. So peaceful and cozy. Faith read what was written on the open page of Lauren's journal. She recognized some of the sights they'd seen so far this morning.

*Old walls of cobblestones, glued together with earth and moss, remnants of some long-vanished settlement, stand crumbling on shore. Jutting white spires of rock, capped by a woolly mantle of forest greenery, form a vertical palette for some ancient calligrapher. Thin, curling fingers of smoke-like clouds slither down to touch the churning current, smelling like they look—wet and gray. Barges laden with heaps of coal push upstream. Horizontal stripes of bright yellow-green crops line up on narrow terraces cut into the steep hillside, rising up on its flank and into the clouds. The sky sits heavily on the tops of mountains as if it has sagged down to rest there under too much weight. Washerwomen stand in the mud-colored river up to their knees, scrubbing clothes, their baskets on shore, chattering with one another in high-pitched choruses of communal contentment. Behind them, several small junks tug at their moorings and somewhere in the mountains, someone is blowing out a call on a horn. Not a musical instrument, but something organic—the horn of an animal.*

It struck Faith, reading these details, that everyone's memories of this place would be significantly colored by what he or she took away—in photos or notes or actual memories, with the memories being the most transient and faulty. Those who took only photos would forget the smells and sounds. But more than that, they would forget their impressions at the time. Lauren was capturing the total sensual experience. She was exceptional at capturing that. Sixty-four identical photos of

Wu Gorge might find their way into photo albums when their companions returned home, but these memories of Lauren's were hers alone.

If she's willing to share, though, Faith thought, smiling to herself, a few of these details might also find themselves into my article on the hanging coffins of the Bo.

A few minutes passed before a small village came into view. A dozen sampans with their distinctive curved sails bobbed in the water. Faith took the camera and snapped several photos, hoping Lauren would return in time to see this. She heard the door open behind her. "Lauren, come here!"

Lauren hurried over and set the coffee on the table, then leaned over the railing to watch the boats. Faith watched Lauren, her beaming face, her hair blowing back from her forehead, and felt a wave of affection that prompted her to pull her close and kiss her cheek. Lauren turned to look at her, her expression serene, then they both sat down to wait for the next bit of excitement.

The warmth of the coffee mug was welcome between Faith's palms. The morning was chilly, especially out here on the balcony, but not cold enough to drive them inside.

"I saw Jen and Cassie in the dining room," Lauren said. "They both seem very happy this morning. No lingering negative impact from yesterday, not that I could see anyway."

"Good. I get the feeling they're used to fighting and making up."

Lauren sipped her coffee tentatively, steam rising past her nose. "What do you suppose they have in common? I can't really see that they have much. I mean, Cassie seems to have a lot more in common with me, for instance, than with Jennifer."

"Well, they love each other."

"I know, but that's my question. *Why* do they love each other?"

"Have you seen that Jennifer?" Faith laughed lightly.

Lauren scowled. "Seriously."

"It's hard to say what draws two people together. I mean, look at us. I'm beautiful and you're homely. I'm brilliant and you're a simpleton. I'm insightful and compassionate and—"

"Oh, stop!" Lauren slapped playfully at Faith. "You're arrogant is what you are!"

Faith grinned as Lauren settled back in her chair. "Why two people love one another is one of the unanswerable mysteries of the universe. It's so mysterious, in fact, that traditionally people relegate it to a function of the soul. Your elusive, inexplicable soul is the part of you that falls in love."

"But you don't believe in a soul," Lauren noted.

"No, not in the sense of a supernatural entity that never dies. But I do believe there's something in each of us that's unique and more than the sum of our physical parts, something that holds the key to our personal identity. In the perpetual search for self, it's the thing we're searching for. And it's that part of us that falls in love." Faith turned to look pointedly at Lauren. "And I do believe in love."

"I'm glad to hear you believe in *something*."

"Everyone has to believe in something. I believe in the mystery and majesty of the human mind."

"Not the heart?"

"The heart is just an organ that pumps blood. But the mind is where everything interesting takes place, including love."

"Of course I know that. The heart is merely a metaphor for love." Lauren picked up another mandarin and tore off its peel. "Where did that idea originate, do you think, that love was the business of the heart?"

"I don't know." Faith sipped her coffee, then said, "That reminds me of the Egyptian feather test. Did I ever tell you that one?"

Lauren shook her head and handed half the mandarin to Faith.

"In Egyptian mythology, when someone died, their heart, which was considered the location of the soul, was placed on a scale to be weighed against a feather from Maat, the goddess of truth. If the heart and feather were in balance, the person was allowed into the Field of Reeds, their paradise."

"And if their heart was heavy?"

"Then a monster ate it and they ceased to exist."

Lauren looked thoughtful. "Is that the origin of the expression, to have a heart as light as a feather?"

"I wouldn't be surprised."

"That's a good story," Lauren observed. "I think you would pass that test."

Faith smiled. "Do you?"

"Yes, without a doubt. You're lighthearted. No problem for you to get through to the Field of Reeds."

"If I am lighthearted, it's because I'm in love." Faith cast a sideways glance at Lauren as she ate a section of the orange.

Lauren smiled, taking hold of her hand. "Me too."

"Love is one of those intangible universals," Faith said. "It's something that's highly valued in every human society. Even God isn't as universal as love. The Nootka, for instance, don't worship a god. They believe in magic and animal spirits and such, but no divine personage, no creator or ruler."

"Really? That's interesting. I guess I thought God was universal."

"Nope. Neither God nor the Devil is universal. But they're pretty damn prolific."

"Speaking of devils," Lauren said, leaping out of her chair. "Look at this!"

Faith joined her at the railing as they came toward a gradually rising hill, at the top of which was a gigantic human head carved out of white stone. The headdress on it was flat and squared off, giving the entire head a rectangular shape. The eyes were closed and the mouth was framed with a sharp-angled mustache. The huge sculpture embedded in the hillside included two hands folded under the head, holding some sort of tablet. Both of them stared in amazement as they came closer and the statue grew larger.

The ship was turning now, heading toward shore where two other cruise ships already lay anchored.

"The Ghost King," Faith said quietly. "Are you ready to meet the king of the underworld?"

Lauren nodded emphatically. "Bring him on, Baby!"

# CHAPTER ELEVEN

The ship's lounge, with its dark paneling and sofas and mismatched tables, had become the regular evening hangout for the four new friends. The cabins were so small they weren't suited to socializing, especially at night when it was too cold and dark to sit on the balcony. On this, their last night of the cruise, Faith sat in one of the stiff-backed chairs at a square table, writing out postcards to friends and family members. Lauren and Cassie sat on one of the soft couches, side by side, drinking scotch and talking. Faith had not been aware of their conversation for the most part, but at the moment she was idle, trying to think of something to say to her sister Charity. That was tricky because Charity was so contrary on all possible subjects that Faith imagined even the idea of China would grate on her, would trigger some religious, political or cultural controversy in her mind. On all of these subjects, Faith and Charity were total opposites. There were almost no safe topics between them. Not that they tried to have a conversation all that often anymore. It was helpful that Charity lived in Colorado. She was much easier to take at a distance.

She had chosen a postcard with a lovely mountain scene showcasing the velvety green hills surrounding the Three Gorges area. Surely that wouldn't give Charity any cause for objection. Faith studied the photo, reassuring herself there were no possible ideological arguments leaping out from the idyllic landscape.

Her attention moved to her right hand, to their grandmother's diamond and sapphire ring, the source of a big blow-up between them after Grandma died. Unfortunately, Grandma hadn't specified anything in her will about the ring. But because of Faith's open admiration of it, Grandma had told her more than once it would be hers. Faith turned the ring to catch the light. Charity hadn't believed her and they had had a horrible fight, one of those emotional monsters that drags into play every unresolved bit of pain about every slight from a lifetime of troubled sisterhood. Predictably, when Faith tried to give the ring to Charity to placate her, she refused to take it. It had taken years of angry silence to move past that, six or seven years ago now. Although they were speaking again, their relationship remained touchy. Every word and every gesture on Faith's part was carefully considered, designed to avoid conflict.

She removed her reading glasses and rubbed her eyes. Lauren and Cassie sat facing one another on the sofa, both of them looking relaxed and contented.

"It's a pipedream, I suppose," Lauren was saying. "But I've wanted to try it for a while. I've made a few small attempts. Articles in our local paper, you know. Little travel pieces."

Cassie took another sip of scotch. "The articles, the ones you've gotten published, what were they about?"

"Kind of funny things, really. Like cranberries. One was about cranberries."

"Not the Celtic music Cranberries?"

Lauren laughed. "No! The fruit. They grow them in Oregon."

"I didn't know that. I thought cranberries only grew on the East Coast."

"No. Both Oregon and Washington."

"I should read your article," Cassie decided brightly. "Then I'd know all about it, right?"

"Right." Lauren looked excited and flushed. "Then I did this one about where to go to sample and buy the largest variety of apples."

"So you write about food!"

Lauren nodded. "I didn't really plan it that way, but it seems I gravitate toward that subject. In general, I'd like to be a travel writer. I like to travel and I like to write."

"Sounds like a wonderful dream." Cassie patted Lauren's arm. "Perfectly possible, too."

"Except for the need to make a living," Lauren observed.

"Yeah, except for that." Cassie laughed.

The waiter came by to bring them fresh drinks. They were on their third round. Jennifer had declined to sit in the lounge this evening and was in the ship's tiny exercise room on the lone treadmill. Faith was certain both Cassie and Lauren were glad of that, glad of the chance for this one-on-one visit before the end of the cruise.

Faith finally wrote an innocuous and cheerful greeting to her sister which could easily have been translated as, "Having a wonderful time. Wish you were here." At least she'll know I'm thinking about her, Faith thought, and thank God she won't know *what* I'm thinking about her. She smiled and took up another postcard. Looking at the tiny address book she traveled with, she came next to Emma McKinley. She hesitated.

"What about you?" Lauren asked Cassie. "What are your dreams for yourself?"

"I do have one, actually. For a long time I've wanted to be a lawyer. Oh, I know, lawyers are the scum of the earth."

Lauren shook her head. "No, that's just a stereotype. There are plenty of exceptions. Lawyers can do a lot of good if they want to. They can empower people."

"Yes, that's exactly it." Cassie nodded enthusiastically. "I want to be in a position to do that."

"What's holding you back?"

Cassie shrugged. "Law school. Seems intimidating. I don't

know if I could do it. And it wouldn't be easy, financially, since I can't see how I could do that and teach full time. I'd hate to change direction and put all my resources into that and then find out I wasn't up to it."

"Why wouldn't you be? You're an intelligent woman. You obviously know how to deal with school. I've heard English majors make very successful law students."

"I don't know. Maybe I'll do it someday."

She didn't sound convincing, Faith thought, then returned to her postcard problem. Should she send Emma a postcard or not? Why are postcards so difficult all of the sudden? Faith wondered. Emma, her graduate student, would be ecstatic to get a postcard from her. Emma had taken all of her classes during the past few years, starting with cultural anthropology. But Faith had grown wary of her lately. Over time, their relationship had gradually changed from student and teacher to something more personal. They had met for lunch twice off campus. Emma often came by Faith's office late in the afternoon and they sat in conversation for an hour, easily, some days, so that when Emma left, Faith had to call home and tell Lauren she was running late. It was beginning to feel too much like deception. If Emma had been a girl of twenty like the other girls with crushes on their teacher, this would have been completely harmless. But she was a woman of thirty-four, a reentry student. As such, they had found more common ground than Faith did with most students. But like those fawning young girls, Emma was beginning to reveal deeper feelings. She was more self-controlled than the others, but Faith had seen it in her eyes and in gestures like small gifts and the way she turned up on campus so often where Faith happened to be, much too often to attribute to chance.

Faith was now her thesis advisor. As a result, they were working more closely than ever. Every move had to be carefully orchestrated now. No more off-campus meetings, for one thing. Faith had been setting up rules for herself in her mind like an alcoholic sets up rules to regulate her drinking. She hadn't worked out all the rules yet. She didn't know what the rule was about postcards.

The card she was considering for Emma was an image of the

Terra Cotta Warriors from one of the most elaborate tombs in the world, that of the first emperor of China. Faith suspended her pen over the card and listened again to the conversation nearby while she mentally composed her message.

"God," Cassie said, "that place we saw today was weird, wasn't it? The Ghost City."

"Weird and wonderful," Lauren agreed. "Like a bizarre funhouse. Some of those faces reminded me of the witch doctor masks in Faith's collection. Too outlandish to be scary, though."

"Oh, right. It wasn't scary, although it might be if you went there alone on a moonless night and stood on the Bridge of Helplessness over the River of Blood and heard some ghostly cry of agony."

"What a fantastic place for a Halloween party!" suggested Lauren.

The two of them laughed gleefully at this notion. Faith had to admit it was an interesting thought. She considered telling them festivals not unlike Halloween parties were actually held there, but decided to stay out of their conversation. They didn't need her breaking into their fun.

"I love that hat," Lauren said. "It's so cute on you."

Cassie touched her knit cap, tugging down slightly on the bill. "Thanks. After all that drizzle today, my hair was hopelessly flat, so I decided to just hide it tonight."

"It makes you look like a little street urchin or something. One of those adorable orphan children with gigantic pleading eyes. You know what I mean. I can't think of the artist."

"Yes, I know what you mean."

Cassie took off her cap and pulled it carefully onto Lauren's head, then sat back admiring the look. Her hair was definitely flat tonight, Faith noted.

"Well, you look adorable too!" Cassie exclaimed. "It looks better on you, even."

Lauren tilted her head with an air of conceit, then laughed self-consciously. Faith had rarely seen her enjoying herself so much. It was a curious thing to watch. Maybe it was the scotch. Alcohol did tend to loosen her up quite a bit.

"Why China?" Lauren asked Cassie, still wearing the cap. "What made you choose this as your vacation?"

"Oh, it was sort of a mess, really. Started last year. Jen latched onto this idea of adopting a baby. These friends of ours did it. They came over here and got a newborn. Cute little girl. Well, you know, it would never be a boy here, would it? I wasn't surprised when Jen fell in love with the little sweetheart. She decided she wanted us to do the same thing, adopt a Chinese baby."

"Did you want another child?"

"Let's put it this way, I wasn't dead set against it. And I want Jen to be happy. I had a child, but she didn't. Why shouldn't she have one if she really wanted one? So we started planning how to go about it. Made inquiries and set aside a chunk of time to travel to China. The closer the time came, the more Jen started having second thoughts. She kept changing her mind. About three months ago, she finally decided for certain she wasn't ready. We put a stop to the baby plans. But we kept the trip to China."

"Were you glad she decided against it?"

"Frankly, yes. I wasn't sure I was up to that kind of commitment. I mean, I really blew it my first time around." A sad smile appeared on Cassie's lips. "I was envisioning Jen as the main mother figure in this case, although if I was supposed to teach the tyke how to play softball or fix a car, I wasn't really going to be of much use there either. I guess, ultimately, I'd have made as lousy a father as I did a mother."

Although Cassie tossed the remark off with a laugh, Faith detected some serious misgivings beneath it. No doubt Lauren sensed the same thing because she looked sympathetic and put a comforting hand on Cassie's forearm.

"Do you think of yourself as a lousy mother?" she asked.

"Oh, maybe 'lousy' isn't an accurate description. Absent is more like it. I really do think it was the right thing to do, though, to let Lucas raise him. I'm sorry I haven't had a larger role in his life. But at least we've kept up our visits. Two or three times a year. And I have to wonder if my son would have been such a good reader if he'd been raised by his English teacher mother. So many of my colleagues end up having these kids who refuse to open a book. Breaks their hearts. Life is so full of irony, isn't it?"

Lauren nodded.

"What about you, Lauren?" Cassie asked. "Any latent desires for children?"

"No. Never considered it." Lauren turned her gaze toward Faith and raised her voice. "Besides, Faith is like a big kid. I mean, I may as well have a child. Santa Claus and the Easter Bunny come to our house every year. If anybody would indulge her, she'd be out trick or treating on Halloween."

Faith, understanding that she was being drawn into the conversation, grinned at them, but said nothing. The waiter appeared at their table, hoping to interest them in a fourth round.

"No, thanks," Lauren told him. "We're done for tonight."

Faith turned her attention back to her postcard and started to write as the others shuffled around, getting ready to leave. Lauren pulled the cap off and handed it back to Cassie.

"Do you think we could keep in touch?" Cassie asked. "It's been so nice getting to know you and Faith."

"Oh, yes!" said Lauren, taking hold of Cassie's hand in both of hers. "We should have talked about this already. Absolutely. We feel the same way. We'll exchange all our information tomorrow before we leave."

Faith looked up and said good night to Cassie with a wave. As Cassie left, Lauren came and peered over Faith's shoulder, hugging her around the neck. "How are you doing here?" she asked.

"Just about done." She signed, simply, "Faith" at the bottom of the card. She had decided it would send the wrong message to withhold a card, especially after Emma had been so excited about the idea of Faith going to China. And if she made it breezy enough, impersonal even, it was an opportunity to reinforce the idea that Faith thought no more about Emma on this vacation than she did about anyone else in her address book.

She reread her message silently to make sure it had the right effect, realizing Lauren was reading over her shoulder.

"Dear Emma, we saw the hanging coffins as planned.

Fabulous! Going on to Shanghai tomorrow. You must come here if you ever get the chance. So many astonishing things to see. Faith."

Lauren still hung around her neck. "Emma?"

"My graduate student. You remember. She gave me that watercolor from her trip to Alaska, the one in my office at school."

"Oh, right. The northern lights. Sorry, I can't keep track of your students."

Faith pressed one of Lauren's hands to her lips. "No reason you should, darling. I can barely keep track of them myself."

# CHAPTER TWELVE

Faith was waiting in the ship for a porter to bring her suitcase. Lauren was down on the dock already, sitting on a bench, making notes in her journal, waiting for the others. A few feet away, the ship lay anchored on the bank of the Yangtze. Everyone was leaving, saying goodbye. Some were continuing their China tour, like Faith and Lauren, and others were going home, like Cassie and Jennifer.

Lauren was trying to capture some of the sensory details of the day, the way the ship's windows glinted with sunlight, the cry of gulls, a gray smell in the air like smoke and a haze over Chongqing—simple, old-fashioned pollution caused by the burning of coal. On their earlier trip, they had been shocked at the layer of smog that clung to the sky around every city. They weren't used to that in the United States, at least not in Oregon.

The new dam, hated by many, would flood the hanging coffins of the Bo, but it would help clean the air for the people still living.

As she was penning these thoughts, Lauren looked up to see Cassie and Jennifer coming up the gangway, rolling their luggage behind them. She closed her journal and stood, waving to them. When they made it to the dock, she hugged them each in turn.

"The bus is here already," Jennifer said, pointing to the street where a sleek, modern tourist bus stood with its engine running. "Why don't I take our bags over. You can stay here a minute."

Cassie nodded.

"Lauren," Jennifer said, "it was great meeting you and Faith. We had a wonderful time. Cassie tells me we'll be keeping in touch. Maybe you can come to Albuquerque for the balloon festival or something."

"That would be something to see," Lauren said. "Definitely a possibility. And Portland isn't a bad vacation destination either."

Jennifer gave a satisfied nod, then pulled the suitcases away toward the bus.

Lauren turned to Cassie, who was looking at her wordlessly, a joyless smile on her face.

"We saw Faith inside," Cassie said. "She'll be out in just a minute."

Lauren slipped a card out of her journal and handed it to her. "That's got everything on it. Our address, e-mail, phones."

Cassie took it, then reached into a pocket in her bag and handed Lauren a folded sheet of paper. "This is ours."

"Thanks." Lauren glanced at the paper without reading it.

"You're lucky. Your vacation isn't over. It's been wonderful. Better than I expected and I had high expectations. Well, you're partly responsible for that. I didn't count on meeting such interesting new friends."

"Nor did I." Lauren could see Cassie was beginning to feel the emotional impact of her leave-taking. She attempted to reassure her. "You'll hear from me first thing when we get home. After we pick up the cats. Maybe after we get the mail from the neighbor."

Lauren laughed an oddly hollow laugh. Cassie's sadness, which was growing, was infecting her.

"Promise," Cassie urged, taking hold of Lauren's hands.

"I promise." Lauren squeezed her hands to emphasize her words.

Cassie glanced over to the bus and frowned. Lauren looked in that direction to see Jennifer waving her over.

"Have a safe trip home," Lauren said.

Cassie threw her arms around Lauren and hugged her tightly. She held on until Cassie was ready to let go.

"Bye," Cassie said, then left rapidly.

Lauren watched her until the rattling of the gangway drew her attention. Faith was on her way up. When she arrived, she said, "You look like you're about to cry."

"Oh, you know. Goodbyes are always sad."

"You're such a softie," Faith said, clamping a hand on her shoulder. "Every ending is a tragedy to you. Let's get a taxi. We need to be at the airport in an hour for our flight to Shanghai. Nothing to cry about today. We're still on vacation. Adventures await!"

Lauren smiled, taking Faith's offered hand as Cassie's bus roared off down the street. Maybe Cassie didn't realize it, but Lauren, too, was anxious to continue their friendship. From her point of view, Cassie was a rare and wonderful stroke of luck. As soon as she was out of sight, Lauren started to miss her. A friend like this didn't come along often in a lifetime. At least not for Lauren. She wasn't like Faith. She didn't make friends easily. She didn't often feel a genuine connection with people she met and, for Lauren, that was a prerequisite to friendship. She demanded a lot from people, emotionally. She could already tell, though, that Cassie was capable of meeting those demands. She was honest and unafraid of her feelings. Lauren hoped there was some way they could maintain a friendship across so much geographical distance once they were each back home. It would be a challenge, but Lauren was committed to making the effort.

# PART TWO
Portland, Oregon

# CHAPTER THIRTEEN

As soon as Faith dismissed her Physical Anthropology class, several students crowded up to her to ask questions. The class was full, as it always was at the beginning of the semester, and chaotic. As she answered them one by one, she wondered again why they always did this, why they never asked their questions during class when she made a point of saying, "Are there any questions?" She had ten minutes between classes, so could usually not afford this delay, but today her two o' clock period wasn't a class. It was her weekly meeting with Emma. As Faith whittled the crowd down to just two remaining students, she saw Emma in the hallway outside the classroom. She gave a tiny wave through the glass.

As the last student left the room, Faith gathered her papers together and Emma came in. As always, she looked so well put together, her wavy ash-blonde hair styled just so, her clothes neat and perfectly coordinated down to the snappy brown flats on her feet. Even without heels, Emma was two inches taller than Faith, but looked taller still because of the trim lines of her body, the long slender legs, the slim hips.

"Hi," she said brightly.

"Hi. I'm just about ready."

"Would you like to go to Max's?" Emma proposed.

Faith zipped her briefcase. Max's was a restaurant near the campus they'd gone to before. Faith was determined to keep their meetings professional this semester.

"No, I think my office will do."

Emma followed her upstairs. Faith unlocked her office and left the door open as Emma sat in the visitor's chair. Sitting in her own chair under a row of primitive African masks, Faith said, "So, let's talk about your subject. I'm anxious to hear what you've come up with."

Emma crossed her legs. "I'm leaning toward the native tribes of the Pacific Northwest. I mean, why not? That's where we are, right?"

"Yes. Lots of interesting possibilities. I know you were awfully inspired by your trip to Alaska. Is that where you're going to focus?"

"A little broader, geographically, because I'm intrigued with the tradition of the potlatch. I mean, what an awesome concept, you know, getting everybody together to distribute wealth evenly among the tribe mates."

"Awesome, yes," Faith agreed. "What aspect?"

"Not completely sure."

"What interests you about it?"

"It's where we got the potluck, isn't it?" Emma shrugged playfully. "I'm a lesbian. It's a natural."

Faith laughed. "I hope you've got more than that?"

"Yeah." Emma turned serious. "I want to understand why the Christian missionaries and the early European governments considered it dangerous. Why was it banned? For the reasons given, that it was immoral, or were there political considerations?"

"I like it. Talk it out with me."

Faith leaned back in her chair and listened as Emma described her ideas for her thesis. She occasionally made a suggestion. A half hour later, it sounded like Emma had a solid handle on her topic.

"This is great," Emma said, excitement apparent in her clear blue eyes. "Thanks so much for helping me figure this out. I can't wait to get started."

"And I can't wait to see what you come up with."

"Do you think I could use that Nootka story you told in class last semester? It fits in nicely."

"Sure."

"Is it published anywhere? I can quote it from the published source."

"No. It's barely even written down. I'm afraid you'll have to quote me in person."

"Okay. No problem. Any particular reason you haven't written it up?"

Faith shook her head. "No. Just lack of organization. I'm notoriously disorganized. Sometimes I'm astonished I ever got that one book published. Even when I manage to get an article written, it languishes in my filing cabinet forever." It was only because of Lauren's help and encouragement, Faith knew, that the book ever did get finished.

"That's a shame. Maybe you need a secretary. An assistant or something."

"Yes, I suppose I do. Someone with the wherewithal to put a manuscript in an envelope with a cover letter and mail it off to some journal."

"Like me," Emma suggested.

Faith balked, worried that Emma was going to offer herself up as personal Girl Friday. "Yes," she said hesitantly, "like you. You definitely do have those skills. Perhaps someday when we're colleagues, we can collaborate on something and you can take care of the business end of it."

Emma smiled and stared directly into Faith's eyes. "I look forward to that. I think we work very well together. Like today. Look what great ideas we've come up with for my thesis. And our time isn't even up."

Faith glanced at the wall clock. "I guess we can knock off early, then."

"Oh, before I go, I have something for you." Emma reached into her book bag and extracted a small gift-wrapped box, which she thrust toward Faith with a sheepish smile.

Faith hesitated. "Emma, I don't think you should be giving me gifts."

"It's not anything, really. Just a tiny thing. Please accept it."

Faith reluctantly took the box. This was not the first time Emma had brought her something. Usually, it was food, something she'd baked, not something she'd purchased. The exception to that was the little watercolor that hung over her desk, a souvenir from Emma's trip to Alaska two years ago. Faith had accepted that as a thank you for encouraging Emma to make the trip.

Faith glanced at the watercolor with its greens and violets above a dim snow field, then opened the box. Inside was a pin, a parrot made of bright blue and red crystals in a gold-colored matrix.

"It's lovely," Faith said.

"I thought it would go well with your royal blue jacket. Dress it up a little. I saw it in the store and I thought of you immediately."

"Thank you, Emma. But, you know, this makes me feel a little uncomfortable."

"Why?"

"Well...you don't give your other teachers gifts, do you?"

"No. But you're not just a teacher to me. You're a friend. I mean, we've known each other for a few years now. And you've been such an inspiration to me. You're the reason I'm an anthropology major, as you know. And now you're my thesis advisor. You're hardly just another teacher." Emma leaned forward and spoke earnestly. "Faith, you're very special to me."

"Thank you," Faith said, uneasily. She was at a loss for words, not really wanting to talk about what she saw as a growing problem. She stared at the pin for a moment, trying to think of something to say. When she looked up, she saw that Emma's expression was serious and intense.

"I feel really close to you," Emma said quietly. "I feel like we have a real connection."

In some ways, Emma reminded Faith of Lauren. She had the same inability to be casual about anything. She threw herself wholly into everything and she experienced her feelings deeply. It was why she was such a good student, so passionate, but it also made her difficult in a case like this where she had fixed her affections on someone who wasn't available to her.

"I don't want you to get carried away with that idea," Faith said gently. "You know I like you too. You're an intelligent woman. You've been a joy as a student. I want you to succeed. I want to help you succeed. I'll do everything I can to help you... professionally."

Emma pressed her lips tightly together, then looked down at her hands in her lap. "I understand what you're saying," she said without looking up. "And I know why you're saying it. I'm sure you know how I feel about you. I mean, you're so perceptive and it has to be obvious, doesn't it?"

*Yes, it's obvious, but you should keep it to yourself anyway.*

"I think you're brilliant," Emma continued. "And kind and generous. Wise. Strong. Such a role model. I guess I've got sort of a crush on you." She laughed nervously.

Twenty-year-old girls have crushes on me, Faith thought. A thirty-four-year-old woman has something else. Emma was waiting for her response. Faith wondered what she expected. Surely she didn't expect Faith to welcome this "news."

"I imagine you'll get over that," she said. "Crushes are usually short-lived, based as they are on illusion."

Emma smiled, an ironic smile that made it clear she knew she had no school-girl crush. "I don't think I'm delusional." Her voice had now acquired a hint of the seductress. Definitely no innocent young girl. Therefore much more dangerous. Now that she had voiced her feelings, Faith felt obligated to address them.

"You should take this back," Faith said, handing her the gift box. "Seriously. No more gifts. Our relationship has got to be strictly professional."

Emma looked disappointed. "I guess I'm making you nervous."

"Yes, you are."

"That wasn't my intention. I just wanted you to know how I felt."

"Why?" Faith asked bluntly.

Emma looked confused, as if the whole concept of keeping one's feelings to oneself was unimaginable to her.

"What do you want me to say?" Faith asked, exasperated. "You know I'm with Lauren."

"Yes, I know. Love isn't rational. I can't help it."

Faith laughed, realizing it came out as extremely cynical. "That's a cop-out. A lot of harm in the world has been done by people saying they couldn't help themselves. You can help yourself. And you will. You're a mature woman. And I'm not available to you. Do the smart thing and talk yourself out of it the same way you talked yourself into it." Faith stood and picked up her briefcase. "Because if you don't, working together is going to be a problem for us. And I sincerely don't want to see that happen. I've been rooting for you since your first semester and I want to see you through to the end. Don't go this route, Emma."

Faith held a hand toward the doorway and Emma obliged her by standing and walking out. Faith followed her into the hall, then shut and locked her office door, steeling herself against the defeated slump of Emma's body.

"I'll see you next week," Emma said. "And don't worry. I understand. Strictly professional."

Faith nodded. "I appreciate that."

She felt herself soften at the sadness in Emma's eyes. Faith's heart wasn't hardened to Emma. For some time now, she had felt a tenderness toward her. For a while, she had thought they would be friends, eventually colleagues, and enjoy a long, rewarding relationship. Now, she didn't know how this would turn out. Maybe Emma would wise up and give up the notion of romance. Faith hoped so, but she also knew that women rarely talked themselves out of loving someone, no matter how prudent it was to do so.

She put her arm around Emma's shoulders to give her a heartening squeeze. "See you next week."

# CHAPTER FOURTEEN

Faith's eyes were getting tired. She removed her reading glasses and rubbed them, then decided to take a break from reading student papers to check her e-mail. She went to the den to use the computer. She heard the familiar static and modem tones as it attempted to dial up the online service, then reported there was no dial tone. Lauren must be talking on the phone, Faith reasoned, then went looking for her. Following the sound of the TV from the family room, she found Lauren sitting in front of the TV, the laptop computer open on the coffee table, a lengthy telephone cord snaking across the carpet to the phone jack on the back wall. The VCR was on and on the television, Miss Jean Brodie was in the middle of filling Mary McGregor's head full of impractical ideals of courage and self-sacrifice.

"What are you doing?" Faith asked, coming up behind the couch.

"I'm watching this movie. Cassie's watching it too."

"So what are you doing on the computer?"

"Chatting with her. We're watching the movie together."

"What?" Faith said, looking at the laptop screen where an open chat window showed a running commentary between Lauren and Cassie.

A soft ding announced a new message. "That woman is deadly!" appeared in the chat window.

"I can't believe this," Faith said.

"Since Jennifer's working tonight and you had papers to grade, Cassie and I decided we'd have a movie night. We both rented *The Prime of Miss Jean Brodie*. She loves Maggie Smith as much as I do. Do you believe that?"

"Do you want to pause the movie?" Faith suggested.

"No! It took us fifteen minutes to get in synch to begin with. We can't pause unless we both pause at exactly the same time."

"Oh," said Faith. "I guess you couldn't log off for a few minutes either so I can check my e-mail?"

"Can it please wait until the movie's over? It won't be that much longer."

Faith sighed. "Yes, it can wait. I'm not done with the papers anyway."

"Thanks, hon."

Faith leaned over the back of the couch and kissed Lauren's cheek. She took one more look at the chat window on the laptop screen and shook her head as Lauren rapidly typed a reply. "No good can come of this!"

She went back to the dining room table where her work was spread out, smiling to herself. Lauren and Cassie had become cyber-buddies. Ever since they'd returned from China, the two of them communicated daily. It was not unusual for dinner conversation to center around something Cassie had told Lauren that day in an e-mail. They were as likely to talk about Cassie's students as they were Faith's.

Lauren was getting used to Cassie's presence in her life, maybe a little too used to it. One day Cassie's e-mail service had gone down, so no messages. Lauren was genuinely upset, imagining all sorts of catastrophes from Cassie's death to, even worse, Cassie's indifference.

This went on most of the day until Faith suggested Lauren call Cassie on the phone and ask her if she was okay. At first, Lauren had balked. That wasn't how they communicated, but then she had called anyway and Faith had listened to her delighted laughter as she discovered the real cause of Cassie's silence.

Faith wasn't surprised at the passion of Lauren's relationship with Cassie. Casual friendships never maintained her interest, which was the primary reason, Faith had decided long ago, that Lauren had few friends. She demanded emotional honesty and depth of feeling from her relationships, and most people were unwilling to make that sort of investment in anyone other than their family members. Apparently Cassie wasn't afraid of Lauren's intensity. Perhaps she was a similar type. She seemed as dedicated to this friendship as Lauren was.

Less than two months after China, they were planning an in-person visit. Cassie and Jennifer were coming to Portland for a week in the spring. Lauren was excitedly making arrangements to show them everything worth showing. She was very happy and Faith was happy for her, though occasionally she did wonder if Lauren was becoming too involved, too preoccupied with Cassie. But, really, she thought, watching a movie together long-distance was actually very inventive and sweet.

Lauren came into the dining room. "Movie's over. How's the paper grading going?"

"I think I've had enough for tonight," Faith said. "I'm too tired to read any more of these. They're all sounding the same."

"Then let's just go to bed." Lauren took Faith's hand and led her to the bedroom.

"How was your movie?"

"It was a lot of fun. Next we're going to do either A *Room With a View* or *The Lonely Passion of Judith Hearne*."

"Is it a Maggie Smith marathon, then?"

"Don't know. Maybe. That would be fun."

"Well, let me know when you get to Harry Potter."

Lauren snorted.

"You know," Faith said, pulling down the bedspread, "I think I'm too wound up to go to sleep."

Lauren reached over and unbuttoned the top button of her

shirt, her eyes turning mischievous. "Who said anything about sleep?"

"Oh," Faith said with a small whimper of delight. She put her hands around Lauren's waist as she unbuttoned the rest of the buttons.

"I think I might be able to unwind you," Lauren said, then let her lips graze Faith's collar bone and slide lower, kissing the curve of her breast above her bra. Lauren slipped the shirt over Faith's shoulders and down off her arms, letting it fall to the floor.

Faith fell back onto the bed, pulling Lauren down on top of her. Looking into her eyes, she said, "I love you so much. Was there ever anybody as happy as we are?"

Lauren shook her head, then accepted Faith's kisses with enthusiasm.

# CHAPTER FIFTEEN

"I think you're still romanticizing your subject," Faith said, Emma's manuscript in her lap.

Emma sat in the visitor chair, her long legs clad in winter white linen, crossed at the knee, her lively eyes trained unwaveringly on her mentor. They were well into the fall semester, rapidly approaching Thanksgiving, so the rainy season had begun and both of their raincoats hung dripping by the open door.

"Sometimes you write like an English major," Faith continued, "painting a scene with an eye to artistic beauty. In other words, you're a good writer, but this isn't about creating an evocative scene. Anthropology is a science."

"I'm just trying to make it sound interesting," Emma said, the side of her mouth curling up slightly.

She's a beautiful woman, Faith thought, then slid on her glasses to turn her attention back to the manuscript.

"There's nothing wrong with that," she said. "As long as you don't color the perspective or lose objectivity. Like this description of the Salish dance. It sounds like a first-person account, as if you're writing fiction."

Emma smiled, though Faith was rebuking her. She tended to smile at everything Faith said these days, which made Faith more critical than she would have been otherwise.

"It's just a composite," Emma explained. "To give you a sense of what it was like. I was trying to make it seem like an actual incident."

"You did. It's just too—" Faith struggled to find the word. "Literary."

"I think I know what you mean. But *your* book is beautifully written. I'm just trying to do something similar."

"You have to keep your audience in mind. You're not writing for the general public and that makes a huge difference. My book was written for the layperson. This is for your colleagues, or your would-be colleagues."

"I'll try to objectify it a little more," Emma said.

"Yes, all right. As far as your research goes, you're doing very well. You've made some interesting points. I like this idea that the potlatch smacked of socialism to the European governments of the early Americas, that the objections to it could have been partly based on that ideological disagreement. The concept of free enterprise has always been valued by Americans. The idea of a community getting together and redistributing their possessions is too much like Communism, isn't it?"

"Yes. In the American tradition, we're all born equal, but that's where equality ends. Ambition and personal success are highly valued. The acquisition of wealth is what we all strive for. To give it away, to give everyone an equal share, is against everything we stand for. The idea that the lazy asses and dolts should all have as much as the industrious entrepreneur is just plain anti-American."

"I think that could be one of your main points, that the potlatch, in its purest form, was antithetical to Western political values. That may have had more to do with banning it than the reasons given by the American and Canadian governments at the time. I'd like to see this idea come more to the forefront of your study. That gives it something fresh and relevant."

"All right. I'll expand on that." Emma made a note in the binder she had open in her lap.

"But be careful you don't overshadow the fact that there were serious abuses and some very corrupted versions of the potlatch being practiced. There were legitimate reasons for outlawing it, at least from the viewpoint of the people who were opposed to it."

Emma nodded. "Objectivity, right?"

"Right. Which brings us to another passage I want to discuss with you." Faith turned several pages of the manuscript. "This is the one where you're describing a rowdy meeting that got out of hand, one of the incidents the missionaries often used as justification for the ban."

"Right," Emma said wryly. "The Tlingit bash of 1890."

Faith looked over the top of her glasses at Emma's grin, unable to suppress her own smile, then returned to her search. "Here it is. Several tribes got together, lots of revelry, drinking, etcetera, and somebody started shooting off a gun, wounding three people and killing a young woman of the host tribe, setting off an all-out feud."

"The Hatfields and McCoys all over again."

"Yes. But your description reads like fiction here too. And the part where you describe the young man stabbing himself in the heart is completely over the top." Faith read Emma's description aloud in a melodramatic style befitting the language. "'As the knife blade entered the tender flesh of his chest, he sunk to his knees, then pulled the knife free. Blood gushed from the wound, falling on his beloved and mingling with her blood in the dirt. His body dropped, landing with his lips so close to hers they appeared to be sharing one last kiss.'"

Faith looked up with what she hoped was not merely amusement, but disapproval as well.

Emma shrugged. "It was a romantic gesture. It called for romantic language."

Faith slowly shook her head.

"Okay, I'll rewrite it. Don't you think it's the ultimate

expression of love, though?" Emma leaned forward, her expression intense. "To kill yourself over your lover's body?"

"I think it's the ultimate expression of idiocy."

Emma tilted her head, obviously amused. "The great poets didn't think so, though, did they? I mean, look at Romeo and Juliet."

"I think you're forgetting that Romeo and Juliet were teenagers." Faith set Emma's manuscript on her desk. "And therefore idiots."

Emma laughed. Her light eyes twinkled with delight. She adores everything I say, Faith thought with dismay.

"You're just not a romantic," Emma teased.

Unfortunately, she could no longer have a discussion with Emma without this flirtatious undercurrent emerging. Once Emma had confessed her "crush," she apparently thought she had given herself permission to openly flirt. The fact that Faith sometimes secretly and guiltily enjoyed it made the situation even more difficult. And more pressing.

Faith didn't know what to do about Emma, but she knew something had to be done. Though she'd told Emma she had no feelings for her, she wondered if Emma could sense the truth. The last couple of months, she had felt herself growing more and more attracted to her. She had been looking forward to their weekly meetings with an exhilaration she recognized as perilous.

Just this morning, perhaps subconsciously aware she was seeing Emma today, she'd awakened with audible cries of passion from a vivid sex dream which had left her embarrassed and worried. Lauren had reached out with comforting arms, asking if she'd had a nightmare. Yes, she'd lied. Well, it wasn't entirely a lie. A dream in which Emma had made passionate love to her was a nightmare of sorts. Even now, gazing at Emma's face, she recalled how her mouth had been so ripe and anxious in the dream.

Faith shut her eyes tightly to block out the image. What did Emma know about any of this? What could she sense in subtle gestures and expressions? Did she know how distracting that extra open button on her blouse was? She probably did know. That was probably why it was open.

"I need to get home," Faith said. "I'm sure Lauren has prepared a fabulous dinner and I wouldn't want to make her wait."

She stood. Emma followed her example.

"I'll see you next week, then," Emma said. "If not sooner."

Standing close in the cramped office, Faith felt trapped. Emma moved closer and embraced her in a warm hug, her new way of saying goodbye, which Faith knew she should never have allowed. There was nothing sexual in the gesture, but Faith's body responded anyway to the pressure of Emma's breasts against hers and the smell of her hair, faintly herb-like. For just a second, her fingertips ached to take hold of this woman and possess her. But she stood immobile, her hands at her side, willing herself to resist.

Emma stepped back and smiled, her lovely face full of affection. "Have a nice weekend," she said.

As she turned to retrieve her coat, Faith reached out and grabbed her arm. "Emma!" she said, hearing the desperation in her voice.

In that instant, as Emma turned to her with a questioning look, Faith had no idea what she was about to do or say. That surprising uncertainty terrified her. She realized she was acting totally on impulse. Whatever that impulse had been, she immediately turned it to her purposes and said, "I can't continue as your advisor."

# CHAPTER SIXTEEN

Faith arrived home to find the kitchen full of tantalizing aromas. Something was in the oven and something was simmering in a saucepan on the stove, but Lauren was nowhere to be seen. Faith set the bouquet of autumn flowers she'd bought on the counter and took a vase from the cupboard. As she filled it with water, she saw Lauren in the back yard in her herb garden, a handful of green sprigs in her hand. Faith put the flowers in the vase just as Lauren came back inside.

"Hi, honey," Lauren said, leaning in for a quick kiss, clinging to her bunch of herbs.

When she stepped back, she saw the flowers and looked surprised.

"For my darling girl," Faith announced.

"Oh, how sweet! What's the occasion?" Lauren put her herbs on the cutting board and wiped her hands on a kitchen towel.

"The occasion is, uh, let's see...Friday."

Lauren smiled and kissed her again, more intensely this time. "Thank you. They're very pretty. Why don't you get changed. Dinner's almost ready."

"What are we having?"

"Something I haven't done before. It's a chicken tagine with preserved lemons and artichoke hearts."

"A chicken what?"

"It's a Moroccan dish. Served over couscous. It's supposed to be cooked in a special kind of pot called a tagine. But I'm using an ordinary casserole dish. Still, it should taste fairly authentic because of the preserved lemons. I made those myself. You remember?"

"You mean when you stuffed those lemons in a jar of salt?"

"Right. They've been magically transforming ever since and now they're ready." Lauren lifted her eyebrows enticingly.

"Lauren, my God, you are astonishing! And all of this on a weeknight."

"No big deal. Just a chicken in the oven when it comes right down to it. It's just the herbs and spices that make it special."

Faith went to the bedroom to change. Lauren really was a wonderful companion. I should bring her flowers more often, Faith thought. Not just when I'm feeling guilty for being attracted to another woman. As she pulled on a T-shirt, she recalled Emma's shock when she'd told her she could no longer be her advisor. Of course she had demanded an explanation. But what could Faith say that wasn't an admission of her own weakness? She couldn't say she didn't trust herself. She couldn't admit her attraction. Anything like that would have been far too dangerous. It would have given Emma hope, encouragement even. So there was no question that Faith couldn't say those things.

"Your feelings about me are getting in the way," Faith had told her. "Even though I've told you I can't reciprocate, you're still pursuing me. Working with you is uncomfortable."

"But you can't just drop me. This is my last year. This is my degree we're talking about."

"I'm sorry, Emma, but I've asked you to give this up. I told you it was a problem."

Emma had become agitated. "What do you expect me to do? I can't stop myself from loving you. I can't turn these feelings off."

"That's why we can't work together. I'm not happy about this, but I don't see any other answer."

Then, with Emma still objecting, Faith had left, upset with herself and the situation, especially upset that she had laid all the blame on Emma. At the same time, she also felt an enormous sense of relief.

It was all Faith could do to get off campus without bursting into tears. The last she saw of Emma, she had been sobbing. So Faith felt guilty both for what she'd done to Emma and what she'd felt for her.

She sat on the edge of the bed to take off her shoes and then just sat there staring at the wall instead, feeling several conflicting emotions—remorse, sorrow, hope and gratitude. Most of all gratitude. Nothing like a threat to make you appreciate what you have, she thought. Then she sighed deeply, feeling like she had just escaped a catastrophe.

She was roused out of her thoughts by the vibration of her cell phone. She didn't answer, but after taking off her shoes and socks, she listened to the voice mail message from Emma.

"Faith, I hope you'll reconsider working with me. I really need your help. Please call me. Let's talk. We can work this out. I can try harder. I promise it will be just business. Please give me another chance."

She erased the message, feeling sorry all over again for a situation she should have been able to avoid. It was too late for just business between them, but Emma couldn't know that. Faith was relieved to think she didn't know. She didn't know that even being alone together in the same room was now too much of a temptation for Faith.

Lauren appeared in the doorway. "Dinner's ready."

Faith turned to face her, and just for a second wanted to tell her about Emma. But she stopped herself—she would have to admit she'd made a mistake, that she'd been less than vigilant. Lauren probably couldn't imagine that. It would undermine her belief in the two of them, in the absolute rightness of their relationship. Faith wanted to protect that, Lauren's resolute belief, like a parent maintaining the illusion of Santa Claus. How ironic that Lauren considered her the childlike one. Although she certainly found joy in children's pleasures, it was Lauren who was much more likely to believe in fairy stories. At least this particular story, that for everyone in the world, there is just one person they are meant to be with, like the archetypal prince and princess.

No, Faith thought, I can't take that from her. It's one of the sweetest things about her, that she truly believes we were meant for one another, preordained by God or the stars or some other magical power. People live by such beliefs, and always have, very happily and successfully.

What Emma had said earlier, that Faith wasn't a romantic, that was true. A romantic was someone who casts a softening lens over reality, but she was the most pragmatic of realists. She didn't even care for the Romantic poets. She loved Lauren more than anything or anyone, but she knew their being together was merely a lucky happenstance. Chance was in charge of Faith's world, not Fate.

"Is something wrong?" Lauren asked, peering at her uneasily.

Faith shook her head. "No, nothing. I'll be right there."

# CHAPTER SEVENTEEN

Lauren's younger brother Jim took one more spoonful of sweet potato casserole as the rest of the group sat contemplating the sin of gluttony. Jim, who was thirty-three, was still able to eat like a young man without gaining weight. Faith eyed his thin frame enviously.

"This stuff is unbelievable," he said, slapping a big spoonful on his plate. "Super job, as always, Sis. Cranberries and walnuts in the Brussels sprouts—damn, that was inspired. You manage to get all the traditional flavors, but like…so original, you know?"

"I'm glad you like it," Lauren said. "You have an adventurous palate. Of all my brothers, that's why only you get invited."

"Oh! And I thought it was because you loved me best."

She laughed at his pouty face. "Well, that too!"

Faith sat back in her chair, savoring the last sip of wine in her glass, thinking this was one of Lauren's better Thanksgiving productions. The dining room was beautifully decked out in autumnal colors and the guests were a congenial bunch of friends plus just two relatives, Jim and Faith's frail, willowy father, who looked like he was about to fall asleep on his plate. Next to him, Faith's friend and colleague Natalie put her fork down with a formal gesture of finality.

"Well," she said, returning to a subject they had just finished, "it sounds like your trip to China was totally successful, then."

"It was," agreed Faith. "We could just keep going back and never exhaust it, though. It's such a big country. So much history."

Dave, who sat across from Faith's father, said, "Your trips are all so interesting because you don't just do the touristy things. Hanging coffins? I mean, come on!"

His partner Jason, who looked like he could be a twin brother, said, "It's true. The rest of us visit the Great Wall."

"Oh, we did that too," Faith said. "On our first trip. We try to do it all. Which is impossible, I know, no matter what country you're talking about. There's just so much fun to be had in this world, you know?"

"Where to next?" Natalie asked.

"We haven't decided." Faith glanced at Lauren. "Lots of choices. I'm leaning toward the Congo for next summer."

"I take it that wouldn't be strictly a pleasure trip?" Natalie shot a knowing glance at Lauren.

"Depends on your idea of pleasure," Faith replied. "Fortunately, I love my work. And even more fortunately, Lauren does too."

"I do," Lauren affirmed. "Though I am longing to go to Tuscany some day. Just for pleasure. What a novel concept, I know. A pleasure trip!"

"And we shall go to Tuscany," Faith assured her, as usual, then turned back to Natalie. "So, yes, the Congo would be a working trip. There's this tribe there with an interesting tradition of smoking their dead."

"Smoking?" Dave asked. "You mean like mincing them up and putting them in a pipe?"

Jason sputtered with distaste and wrinkled his handsome face at Dave. "I'm glad I'm done eating."

"Well, I'm not!" Jim said, putting his fork down.

Dave shrugged apologetically.

"Dinner conversation in this house," Natalie observed, "tends toward the macabre."

"Not that kind of smoking," Faith said, "though that reminds me of this other tribe that grinds up the bones of their dead and mixes them with their food. One of many rituals that involve ingestion of the dead. Now that's a whole other topic we could spend hours on."

"But we won't," Lauren said firmly. "We definitely don't want to go off on a cannibalism tangent before dessert."

"No, of course not," Faith agreed. "Back to the Congo. The smoking I was referring to is the sort where the body is smoked like cured meat, to remove the moisture. You end up with something like jerky."

"And then they ate him?" Dave asked, sticking out his tongue.

Faith shook her head, suppressing a laugh. "No."

"I know," Jim said, raising his hand and bouncing in his chair like a schoolboy. "They turned him into shoes for the family so they could take him along wherever they went."

"That's not far off. They stood him in a corner of the house and left him there. It was a preservation method, so the dead member of the family could hang around, watch the kids grow up."

"Now that could be a problem," Jim observed. "If you did that long enough, pretty soon your house would be crammed full of relatives."

Jason laughed. "But they wouldn't eat much."

Lauren rose from her chair. "I'm going to start coffee."

"I saved some room for dessert," Jason said, patting his stomach. "Lauren's desserts are to die for."

"If I eat another bite," Dave said, "I *am* going to die."

"You can take some home," Lauren said, walking toward the kitchen. "We don't want anybody dying here. Somebody's liable to smoke you and stand you in a corner so you'll be here for all the holidays yet to come."

"I've got to leave this table," Jim said, pushing back his chair. "Or I'll never stop eating."

Natalie leaned toward Faith. "What is dessert, by the way?"

"Let's see if I can get this right," Faith said, knowing she probably wouldn't. "Pumpkin mousse with apple pie-spiced whipped cream and toasted pumpkin seeds. And there's this lacework thing she did, dripping strands of hot sugar on some wax paper. Some sort of garnish."

Natalie's mouth fell open. "Are photos allowed?"

"Encouraged, I would think."

Faith noticed her father's nose was dangerously close to touching a pool of raspberry sauce on his plate. She couldn't see his face, just the top of his head where his cottony white hair didn't fully cover his tender pink scalp. He seemed to have gotten ten years older since her mother died a year ago. He was wearing his hearing aids, but whether they were turned on or not she didn't know.

"Dad," she said in her loud commando voice. He didn't respond, so she stepped it up. "Dad!"

His head lifted slowly and his eyes opened. He looked around, confused.

"Dad, why don't you go sit in the recliner in the living room. You'll be more comfortable. If you fall asleep, I'll wake you for dessert."

"Fall asleep?" he asked, looking indignant. "Why would I do that? It's nowhere near my bedtime. I go to sleep every night at ten o' clock and get up every morning at five. Been doing that for forty years. Seven hours every night."

Plus the five or so hours napping, Faith thought, but said nothing.

When Jim returned to the dining room, he had Yorick in his hand. "Look who I found trying to crash our party," he said, holding the skull up next to his head. "Grandpa Keegan."

Dave let out a curt, girlish scream and Faith laughed. Jim thrust Yorick toward the Brussels sprouts and spoke in a gruff voice, apparently his version of an old man. "Where's the turkey and mashed potatoes? You know Grandpa wants his meat and potatoes. What is all this frou frou food?"

From the kitchen, Lauren said, "Put that down and clear the table."

Jim waggled the skull in Lauren's direction, then set it on a shelf and proceeded to stack plates. The phone rang as Faith stood to help bring in the dishes. She glanced at Lauren, who held up a hand to indicate she'd get the phone.

"I'm going to take this in the bedroom," Lauren said after checking the caller ID, then dashed down the hall.

After ten minutes, during which the coffee finished brewing and the table had been cleared, Faith began to wonder why Lauren hadn't come back.

"Coffee's done," Jim said. "Should I serve it?"

"Not yet. We can't serve dessert without Lauren. All those fancy garnishes."

"Right."

The two of them stood in the kitchen looking at the irregular shards of hardened caramel on a sheet of waxed paper. They looked like diminutive amber trellises. Jim picked up a small piece and ate it.

"Between you and me," Faith said, "I wouldn't mind if, just once in a while, we had a plain old pumpkin pie with Cool Whip. Just occasionally, you know."

"You can say that because you get this sort of thing routinely. To you, maybe a plain old pumpkin pie would be special. For us, not so much. I want the pumpkin mousse with the spiced whipped cream and the fancy doodad."

Faith gave his shoulder a pat. "So how's the rest of your family?"

"Oh, the same, more or less. Harlan's wife just had gall bladder surgery. She's doing fine. Mom and Riley are spending their retirement in front of the TV. They're all having Thanksgiving dinner at the old house."

"Except you."

"I'll be there for Christmas. Today, I want to support Lauren. You know."

"Yes. I know she appreciates it too."

"We had the same old argument this year," Jim said, lowering his voice so the group in the other room couldn't hear. "Mom says Lauren is always welcome to come . . . when she renounces her evil ways. And, as usual, you are *not* invited."

Faith nodded. "I didn't imagine anything had changed. They're still blaming me for corrupting their innocent little girl."

"Yeah." Jim looked sheepish.

"I'm sure they need to blame somebody, but from what I've heard about Lauren as a child, it seems she was well on her way to being gay long before she met me."

"Oh, God, yes! Well, there was Stormy, for one thing. I don't know what Mom made of that, but I had no doubt what Lauren and Stormy were doing out in the tool shed."

"You could imagine things like that as a kid, huh? You were a teenager by then, I guess."

"Yes. But I didn't have to imagine. When I saw them go in the shed, I peeked through the window and watched. The window was mostly blocked by tools and stuff, but I could see enough to know they were making out. If it was a cold day, though, it wasn't long before the inside of the window was all steamy and I couldn't see a thing."

Faith clucked at him disapprovingly. "I guess at that age you really had no choice but to watch."

"Right. But even before that, before Stormy, she had all the signs. Nothing girlish about her. It was like living in a house with all boys. She did everything we did. She'd pick up frogs and snakes with no problem. And, man, could she throw a punch." He winced, feeling his jaw. "But around other people, she was really shy. She always hung back, avoided people. I think she knew she was different all along and that's why she was so introverted. She read all the time. Escaped into books. She was smarter than all of us."

"Cuter too."

"Oh, sure, much cuter!" He grew serious. "But, you know, Mom had such a lot of dreams about her only daughter. I think it really broke her heart that she turned out to be gay."

"It breaks Lauren's heart that her family has rejected her," Faith pointed out, knowing that Jim, alone among his family members, understood.

He picked up another piece of caramel. "That's why I keep having this argument with them. But they won't budge."

"Nor will she. She's very angry at her mother. And her other brothers. It's probably best not to bring this up with her. It will just upset her and hurt her feelings."

He nodded. "I won't. I'd only bring it up if something had changed. Like Hell froze over."

"It's sad. Your mother could have had her daughter all along. Lauren is a kind and loving woman. She'd make a devoted daughter. She could have given your mother so much."

Jim nodded with a look of gloomy resignation.

"Hey!" called Dave from the dining room, "what's the holdup?"

Faith waved a hand toward them. "I'll go get Lauren."

She scooped Yorick from the dining room shelf and detoured into the den to return him to her desk. On her way down the hall, she could hear Lauren laughing delightedly from the bedroom. She was talking to Cassie. Faith could always tell. There was something about the way she laughed without restraint.

She walked into the bedroom to see Lauren lying on the bed, phone to her ear, grinning. She waved. Faith stood beside the bed purposely until Lauren said to Cassie, "Just a second." Then she covered the receiver and looked attentive.

"Dessert?" Faith suggested.

"Oh, sure. I'll be right there."

As Faith left, she heard Lauren say, "Cassie, I have to go. I'll e-mail you later. I want to hear what you thought of my article."

Faith stopped in the hallway, turned and walked back to the bedroom where Lauren was hanging up the phone.

"What article?" she asked.

"You know, the one I've been working on, the French colonial period influence on modern Shanghai cuisine."

"Yes, the one you want to sell to an in-flight magazine. Sure. I didn't know you'd finished."

"More or less. Ready for a critique anyway. I sent it to Cassie yesterday. She has some suggestions. I'm sort of anxious to hear them."

Faith was surprised. "Why didn't you ask me to read it?"

"You've been so busy with midterms and everything lately. I knew you didn't have time right now."

Faith tried not to sound hurt. "I would have made time. You know I'm always interested in your writing."

Faith could tell by Lauren's tender expression that she had not succeeded in hiding her hurt feelings.

"I know that," Lauren said softly, putting a hand on her arm. "And I do want you to read it. You're my best critic, always. Your advice is spot on. I figured you could read it this weekend, once the whole Thanksgiving thing is over. I'm sorry. I didn't think it would matter if I got her opinion first."

"No, I'm sorry." Faith felt suddenly foolish and wanted Lauren to understand her irrational response. "You're right. It doesn't matter. It was just a momentary feeling that you were going to her for something you used to go to me for."

Lauren shook her head. "No. Not at all. I had every intention of having you read it, as soon as we had a chance."

"I know. Like I said, just a momentary feeling. It was silly. The more readers you have, the better. And Cassie is uniquely qualified, isn't she?"

"Yeah. An English teacher." Lauren laughed. "I'd be an idiot not to take advantage of that. In addition to, not instead of, your help. I value your opinion above all others."

Lauren kissed her sweetly, a gentle, slightly lingering kiss, meant to mollify.

Faith felt ashamed she'd even brought it up. She realized with dismay that she was beginning to feel jealous. She'd never been the jealous type. But this wasn't the first time she'd felt it lately, a vague uneasiness over the way Lauren and Cassie entertained one another so well. Like how Lauren would burst into laughter reading an e-mail from Cassie or how she couldn't wait to repeat something Cassie had said, something she deemed incredibly witty. Faith had been struggling with herself, trying hard not to feel diminished by the joy this friendship gave Lauren. That was such a petty way to react. She was above that kind of behavior. She wanted to be, anyway. She had managed, up until this moment, to avoid expressing any such feeling to Lauren. But now she had said it. Or she may as well have said it: "I'm jealous of Cassie."

Lauren was a smart, perceptive woman. She would know. She already knew. Faith could see it in her expression and hear it in her reassuring words.

*What will she do now that she knows I'm capable of jealousy?* Faith hoped it wouldn't drive her underground, cause her to keep things to herself. That would be the most natural response, to avoid triggering this reaction. Faith resolved to try harder to be happy for Lauren, not to make her feel guilty for having found a friend.

"Come on," Lauren said, taking her hand. "Let's serve dessert. I'm expecting a loud volley of accolades for this one."

Faith smiled. "Don't worry. There's no way it could miss, especially as you've upped the anticipation by making everyone wait so long."

# CHAPTER EIGHTEEN

Just as Lauren shoved the lasagna back into the oven with its new layer of mozzarella, she heard the garage door open. Her level of excitement was already so high she was alarmed to note it getting even higher. So that's what that weird expression means, she thought, about jumping out of your skin. She pulled the oven mitt from her hand too quickly and knocked the flour over. A cloud of white dust splashed across the countertop tile. No time to do anything about that, she realized, because she could hear them talking as they approached the back door.

For months, for seven months to be precise, she and Cassie had been planning and talking about this visit. Since two days after their return from China when Lauren first proposed it, they had been in constant contact. During those months, there were very few topics they had not discussed. They'd shared stories about their childhood and compared views on religion and politics and television shows and cheese. Everything! Lauren knew Cassie took her coffee black, that her favorite color was green, that her father had red hair, that she preferred Almond Joy to Mounds. Or, in her words, that she "always felt like a nut." And she knew similar things about Lauren too.

Now that they were about to be facing one another, she was full of anxiety. Why did I tell her all those things, she wondered. I barely know this woman. Had Cassie been entertaining Jennifer with Lauren's personal revelations? Did they laugh over her foibles? What she cared about more than embarrassing revelations, though, was whether or not this deepening friendship would survive a week of close proximity. It was one thing to carefully measure out every word, edit and rewrite, given the luxury of e-mail and their mutual skill at writing, but this week would be completely different. She was filled with dread to think that the in-person visit would taint or even destroy what they had both come to cherish, that other presence, distant but on call and reliably sympathetic. Cassie had rapidly become her best friend. But there was something about the medium of e-mail that made her seem a little like an invisible, even imaginary, friend. Their online relationship had been going on much longer and was much more intimate than their few days in China. Now, her imaginary friend was coming through the door of her kitchen, laughing, in the flesh, and she could barely contain herself.

Faith held the door open and Cassie rushed into Lauren's arms, hugging her exuberantly. When their long hug was over, Lauren reached out to Jennifer to hug her too.

"It smells so good in here," Cassie said, hooking her hair behind her ear. "At last we're going to get a sample of your cooking. I've heard such wonderful things about it. All from you, of course."

Cassie laughed and Faith did too.

"I can't believe you're finally here," Lauren gushed.

"I know," Cassie agreed. "It seems like we've been planning this trip for years."

"It's only been seven months since China," Jennifer pointed out, a period of time that apparently seemed like a trifle to her.

Jennifer looked the same as she had seven months before, but Lauren realized she'd remembered her inaccurately. She was a good looking woman, but over the last few months, Lauren's memory had changed her somewhat to resemble a scowling troll more than a swimsuit model. She was far closer to the latter.

Cassie, though, looked the same as the image Lauren had held in her mind—bright, delighted eyes behind her glasses, toothy smile, dimples. She stood with the easy lank posture Lauren immediately recognized as her signature stance. The familiarity gave her optimism for the rest of the visit. They were going to like one another just as well in person as they did long distance. She was suddenly sure of that.

Faith led them on a tour of the house, during which Lauren heard a high-pitched scream that sounded like Cassie in some kind of delightful discovery. When they returned, Lauren asked, "What was the scream about?"

"Yorick!" Cassie exclaimed. "I saw him in the den."

"Oh, yes."

"Other than that," said Jennifer, "your house is very nice."

They brought in the luggage while Lauren put dinner on the table. The lasagna had turned out perfectly and everybody had seconds. They were a loud, animated group at the table. Faith and Cassie dominated the conversation, which was what Lauren would have anticipated. Faith talked about other vacations they'd taken. Lovely trips to Europe and Asia, Africa and Australia.

"Our trip to Australia," Faith explained, "was my aborted attempt to get to Sky Island. You remember that story?"

"Yes," Cassie said. "The mountain where the islanders took their dead to ascend into heaven."

"And get eaten by vultures," Jennifer added.

"Right. At least I got to a couple of the larger islands and was able to interview some old timers there about the tradition, hear the stories first-hand. I got some good information. It was hurricane season. The weather was too bad. Unpredictable. No one would take us to Sky Island."

"Thank God!" Lauren said, bringing coffee to the table. "As usual, Faith would have gone out in a typhoon in a dinghy if anybody would let her."

"Too bad you didn't get to see it, though," Cassie said.

"Some day," Faith said, taking the offered cup from Lauren.

Lauren handed a cup to Cassie. "Just black for you, I know. And, Jennifer, how do you take your coffee?"

"Black," she answered.

Jennifer seemed more relaxed than she had in China. Lauren was glad to see it. She wanted them both to enjoy their visit, the first of many such reunions.

Once everyone had coffee, Lauren served dessert, a frozen praline cheesecake with a crushed nut crust, a twist on the traditional pecan pies she knew Cassie loved.

"Oh, my God, Lauren!" Cassie said with her mouth full, "this is so good. It's like ice cream and pecan pie and cheesecake all in one. This has just become my favorite dessert of all time."

"It really is good," Jennifer agreed. "Everything was so good. Did you ever go to cooking school?"

"No. Just picked it up as I went along. I enjoy it. Cooking's a stress reliever for me."

"Not for me," Jennifer said. "It causes me stress to even think about cooking. But, seriously, you could be a real chef."

"I did consider it, actually," Lauren said, "as something to do later, in retirement. Either that or travel writing."

"Travel writing about food," Cassie affirmed. "That's your angle. Combine the two."

"Yes," Lauren said. "That's the idea."

"As long as it keeps you engaged," Cassie said, "keep at it. You're a good writer. That article on Shanghai was great. Really brought the place to life. Very colorful."

"Thanks," Lauren said.

"I agree," Faith said. "I'll be surprised if it gets rejected. You sent it to Southwest, didn't you?"

"Yes. I'm still waiting on that."

It seemed to Lauren there was a subtle competition going on between Faith and Cassie, but one that only Faith was participating in. All evening she had made a point of saying things that made it clear she was actively involved in Lauren's life, that the two of them were intimate and happy. Which they were. There was no need to make a point of it. It wasn't often apparent, but every once in a while in the last few months, Lauren had sensed Faith's insecurity over Cassie. Lauren had felt the need to reassure her occasionally that there was nothing to be concerned about. They were just good friends and Lauren was hopelessly in love with Faith and ecstatically happy with her life. All of which was true.

Lauren was aware that she was captivated by Cassie beyond the bounds of ordinary friendship, but she attributed that in part to the artificiality created by geographical distance. She had never admitted this to Cassie and only barely admitted it to herself. In the same way she expected Faith's fears to be eased by Cassie's proximity, she also expected her own fascination to be tempered by the real-life woman. She considered her image of Cassie to be an illusion, a fantasy. As such, it would certainly be dispelled by a dose of reality. Lauren was looking forward to that, to her own disillusionment, which she had no doubt would be forthcoming. Once Cassie became a real person to her, with irritating habits and jarring shortcomings, they could fall into a comfortable, ordinary friendship with one another. What she'd felt toward Cassie up to now was just the opposite of comfortable. It was excessive. It was too happy, too excited, too anxious. It was too emotional, so she was very much looking forward to the calm which she was sure was just around the corner.

"Speaking of alternative careers," Faith said, addressing Cassie, "have you given any more thought to law school?"

"Still thinking about it."

Jennifer frowned, then said, "That's just not realistic. If Cass went to law school, she'd have to give up her job. She might be able to get something part-time, but it wouldn't even come close to paying what she makes now. I mean, why give up a good paycheck for something so uncertain?"

"Why uncertain?" Faith asked.

"Well, you know, law school is hard. The bar exam is hard. A lot of people don't pass it. And then what? Cassie's the type who wants to give it all away for free anyway. She'd spend so much time doing pro bono work we'd starve. Okay, not starve. I make enough to feed us. But there would be no more trips like China. And nothing like the kitchen remodel we're doing right now."

Lauren looked at Cassie, who smiled self-consciously before taking another bite of her dessert. In their discussions of law school, Cassie hadn't mentioned that Jennifer was so set against it.

"You're remodeling your kitchen?" Faith asked.

"Yes. We're going with cherry cabinets and this faux granite countertop. Like granite, but harder, less porous. The ceiling will have recessed lighting and the backsplash is going to be...." Jennifer turned to Lauren. "You know all about this already, don't you?"

"Uh, huh," Lauren said. "I've seen photos of all your materials."

"Hell," Cassie said, scraping the last of her pie off the plate, "Lauren picked out the floor tile."

Lauren saw a brief look of surprise on Faith's face before she laughed and said, "Well, I haven't seen any of it."

"Oh, don't worry," said Jennifer, "you'll get to see it when you come visit us this fall."

Faith was taken by surprise again, Lauren realized, and remembered she had not yet mentioned this proposal.

"We've just been talking," Lauren offered nonchalantly. "We might run down later in the year. I've never been to Albuquerque. Lots to see there."

"Right," Faith agreed, graciously. "I'm sure we'd have a wonderful time."

"We thought October because of the balloon festival," Cassie said.

"Oh!" Faith brightened. "I've always wanted to see that."

"One of our main attractions," Jennifer remarked.

Did Faith think it was odd they were planning their next visit with Cassie and Jennifer before this one had even concluded? She was being very agreeable about all these surprises being sprung on her. There'd been so many times Lauren had felt she was talking too much about Cassie, so she'd held back. But now she realized there were some things that would have been better discussed, like their trip to Albuquerque, a trip that, despite the casual way she was talking about it now, was so well formulated between herself and Cassie that the dates were set and Lauren had already put in her leave slip at work.

She glanced at Cassie, who gave her a tiny smile of complicity. Lauren felt like a teenager sharing a secret with her little sister at the dinner table. Faith, cast in the role of indulgent mother, stared calmly at Lauren over the rim of her coffee cup.

"What are we doing tomorrow?" Jennifer asked.

"Touring Portland," Lauren answered. "We'll take in some of the sights here first, then head out to the Columbia River and drive along that. It's very scenic. Lots of waterfalls."

"What's the one with the bridge across the middle," Cassie asked. "You see it all the time in postcards. Will we see that?"

"It's Multnomah. We'll definitely see it. Maybe we'll stop there for dinner. There's a lodge and restaurant. Then, after we've done Portland, we thought we'd drive down the coast. Lots to do there. We booked a hotel, so we can take our time, drive down nearly to California. Then drive back up the next day."

"Sounds wonderful," Cassie said.

"No graveyards?" Jennifer asked. "No coffins, skeletons, devil statues?"

Faith laughed loudly. "No. This is your vacation, not mine. But if you really want to see something along those lines, I might be able to dig something up."

Cassie flung herself back in her chair and laughed without reservation. "Dig something up!"

"No, thanks," Jennifer said while Cassie continued laughing.

Her laugh was wonderfully carefree. Lauren watched her admirably. It was so good to have her here in the flesh at last.

# CHAPTER NINETEEN

On the way south from Astoria to the California border, they explored the aquarium in Newport, the sea lion caves, the Oregon dunes and various waterfalls and lighthouses. As the afternoon grew toward evening and they neared their destination for the night, they stopped at a long beach to watch the surf and explore the tide pools. Cassie and Lauren sat together on a rock with their toes in the sand, talking, while Faith and Jennifer tracked down limpets and anemones.

The visit was going wonderfully, Lauren decided. The fears she had held a few days ago had been completely unfounded. Everything had been perfect. She turned to look at Cassie and their eyes met. They both smiled.

"I think you and Faith complement one another well," Cassie said.

"How do you mean?" Lauren looked at the ground where her toes were drawing circular patterns in the sand.

"You fill in one another's gaps. I'm basing that partly on what you yourself said over the last several months. But, you know, she sees the big picture and you see the details. She can be reckless and you're the voice of caution."

"Years ago we went on a picnic that ended up defining our roles very aptly. We have this saying about it. She remembers to bring the wine and I remember to bring the corkscrew."

"Well, that sure sums it up!" Cassie laughed. "She's sort of a dreamer, isn't she?"

Lauren considered that for a moment, then said, "Yes, she is. Her imagination tends to go only upward, skyward. I think she'd fly right into the sun if she had wings."

"That's what I meant. She's impulsive. Sort of fearless."

"It's because she never thinks anything bad can happen."

"And that's a great way to live, don't you think?"

"I do." Lauren looked over to where Faith was crouched over a tide pool, peering down with rapt attention. "But bad things do happen."

"Yes, but they're going to happen whether you worry about it or not. I think her approach is better than living with a sense of dread."

"I agree."

"I finished her book, by the way. I was hoping to have some time to discuss it with her."

"What'd you think?"

"Riveting." Cassie sighed. "I had no idea there were so many ways to approach death. It was really an eye-opener. A wonderful book. I've loaned it to a friend and raved about it to several other people." Cassie shook her head. "Some of those stories are so bizarre."

"Yes, they are. But all true. No embellishment."

"It sort of makes you wonder. If every culture believes in an afterlife, maybe it's because there really is one."

Lauren smiled. "Maybe. But then you have to wonder, which one is it?"

"Well, I hope it isn't the one where we turn into snakes and spend eternity trying to escape the jaws of the Great Jackal."

Lauren laughed and bumped playfully against Cassie.

"Something I noticed about the book," Cassie said, "was the writing style. Sometimes it seemed very similar to yours."

"Oh, sure. I'm her editor. Unofficially. We worked on that book together. I mean, she wrote it and I helped her polish it for the layperson. She tends to be too technical sometimes."

"That's nice that you can work together like that."

Lauren nodded. "She helps me with my articles too. We're very involved in each other's work."

"That's wonderful, really." Cassie sounded wistful, then squinted and asked, "Do you ever feel eclipsed?"

"Eclipsed?" Lauren glanced over at Faith, thinking about the various ways in which she glowed so much brighter than most people. "No. I would only feel eclipsed if I wasn't getting what I wanted."

Cassie smiled, then slipped her arm around Lauren's and hugged her close. Lauren wasn't normally comfortable with people touching her, but she was comfortable with Cassie, even from the first day. It felt natural and easy, like they were good friends already, like she had known her, even loved her, all her life. Like a sister, she reminded herself.

"Why did you ask me that?" Lauren asked.

"When I first met you, you seemed, uh, I don't know how to describe it. You were quiet, in the background sort of. You didn't stand out. But I was drawn to you right away, anyway. You didn't say much, but when you did speak, you were so clever. Once I got you to myself, I discovered what an interesting, fun, vibrant woman you are. Faith's just such a strong personality. When the two of you are together, you seem to fade a bit. Sort of like a tiny diamond next to a big old quartz crystal. The diamond, when it's not in the company of the quartz, is exquisite."

Lauren studied Cassie's face, wondering at this line of questioning. There was a subtle, implied criticism of her relationship with Faith, something she'd never heard from Cassie before.

"Do you really think of me as so small next to her?" Lauren asked.

"Not exactly. I think you're content to sit back and let her shine."

"I think you're right. I'm perfectly happy not being in the limelight. I get a lot of pleasure watching her forge her path through the world. I don't feel like I'm giving up anything or compromising myself, if that's what you're getting at."

"Yes, that's what I was getting at. I was just wondering if you felt that your own needs had to be secondary."

"No," Lauren said firmly. "If there was something I really wanted, I'd know how to ask for it. As it is, I'm very happy. I feel enriched being with her, not diminished. Not in any way."

Cassie stared into Lauren's eyes momentarily, then smiled. "Good. Well, you look happy. You both do. You look happy together. I'm glad you are."

Faith was still some distance away. She was standing in a rocky area with a couple of kids, gesturing in a way that suggested she was giving them a lesson in shoreline ecology or something. Maybe she was explaining how sea stacks were formed or why it was important not to touch the tiny creatures in the pools. Whatever she was telling them, they were listening attentively. Faith was a commanding presence. Those children wouldn't be able to ignore her, not until she turned her back, at least.

"I love the ocean," Cassie said, holding her face up to the sun and closing her eyes. "And I'm particularly loving this day. Your coastline is very beautiful. Not just the ocean, but the little towns and the countryside. The fishing villages remind me of watercolor paintings. What was the name of that one town we stopped in for lunch?"

"Coos Bay."

"Coos Bay. Right. I could have stayed there for hours. Actually, I can imagine living there. It just had that feeling about it. That I'd be content to walk those streets and say howdy to the townspeople for the rest of my days."

Lauren laughed. "It isn't Mayberry!"

"You're right. But I would like to retire someplace like that some day."

"Would Jennifer want to live in a place like that?"

Cassie smiled absently. "I don't know."

Lauren decided not to pursue that subject because she knew that on some level Cassie believed she and Jennifer would not stay together for the long term. She hadn't said it directly, but they'd come to know one another well over the last several months and Lauren had been listening carefully. Cassie and Jennifer were growing apart. Their lives were taking divergent paths, the gap between them widening, gradually, in a way they themselves didn't yet acknowledge. Not openly anyway and not to one another, but Cassie, Lauren was sure, at least suspected they were heading toward a break-up. They were still living as if they were happy and in love, having fashioned all of their habits around a truth that might no longer be true.

Cassie did sometimes openly express her frustration. Like when Jennifer went out drinking with her coworkers instead of coming home, or acted impatient when Cassie tried to talk about her day. These disappointments were either becoming more frequent or Cassie was allowing herself to express them more liberally. Lauren was resolved to be there with unreserved support when the time did come for the two of them to break up. If it did. There was always a chance they would work through their problems, one of which was Jennifer's youth, a problem that would resolve itself naturally in time. It didn't seem hopeless. For one thing, Lauren was certain Cassie really loved Jennifer. Whether the reverse was true or not wasn't as clear. Lauren barely knew Jennifer. What Lauren had detected in Cassie of late was a feeling of loneliness, though she knew Cassie wouldn't have admitted that outright. The two of them, though, had developed a sensitivity to one another so acute that even from their distance, through only a few neutral, written words, they could sense one another's moods.

Today, though, everything was right. Cassie was happy and Jennifer was agreeable and the four of them were completely, fabulously in the moment. To Lauren, living in the moment seemed like the key to a happy life. If there was any one thing she could have singled out as the main difference between herself and Faith, that would be it. Faith knew how to live that way. It seemed to come naturally to her. Lauren could almost never manage it.

Suddenly Lauren noticed Faith standing several feet away, aiming the camera at them, apparently having just taken a photo.

"Hey, you two," she called. "Come out here and take a look at this sea star. It's worth seeing."

Cassie released Lauren's arm and they followed Faith to the tide pools where they picked their way carefully over the wet rocks trying to avoid stepping on anything living.

Faith led them to a pool with a tiny sea star, brilliant red, but only an inch across. "Isn't that cute?"

"It's precious," Cassie agreed, leaning over the pool.

Faith went to join Jennifer further along the beach. Lauren and Cassie both lay down on their stomachs on the rocks to peer into the pool at the diminutive sea star. There were scads of interesting things in this pool. The longer she watched, the more Lauren saw. Several small snails crawled across the surface of submerged rocks. Two green sea anemones, only slightly larger than the sea star, occupied sheltered crevices. A few limpets the size of dimes clung securely to their bases. Every couple of minutes a rush of foamy water came flowing in, then drained back out, leaving the pool calm again.

Lauren turned to smile at Cassie, who did the same. She watched Cassie's face as her gaze turned solemn and dropped briefly to Lauren's mouth before she seemed to rouse herself and push up with her hands to a sitting position. She leapt to her feet and ran off down the beach. Lauren turned over and sat up, watching Cassie plow through surf toward Jennifer, who was standing waist deep in the ocean. They embraced one another in the waves.

Lauren shivered involuntarily. That was the first evidence she had seen that Cassie felt it too, the pull that Lauren had been pushing aside all week. The attraction she felt for Cassie was becoming more insistent, was threatening to burst over the boundaries by which she had defined it. What she had been telling herself, what she had told both Faith and Cassie, was that she loved Cassie like a sister. It was a phrase she kept foremost in her mind—*like a sister*. Every time she looked at Cassie's face and felt herself softening with affection, before that affection could turn to desire, she repeated this phrase, reminding herself that she was a mature woman with the ability to direct her emotions. She was not some undisciplined adolescent subject to the spontaneous whim of physical urges. She could control herself.

But if Cassie was struggling against the same current, that was a complication Lauren hadn't considered. She'd thought this was her own private battle.

As she watched Cassie splashing in the surf, she was aware of a powerful anxiety creeping over her. It wasn't the first time she'd felt it. It had actually been going on for months, her secret feeling of dread that sometimes overtook her joy. In fact, it usually appeared at precisely the most joyful moments, as if the joy itself were cause for fear. That wasn't new for Lauren. Being happy invariably led her to worrying about losing whatever it was that was making her happy. After fifteen years with Faith, though, she had gradually learned to be more optimistic, in general.

But this new anxiety was nothing to do with Faith. It was Cassie she was afraid of losing now. The sense of doom had become more intense than ever. It was the kind of feeling you get when you start something knowing how it will end, knowing that every action you take is leading you toward a disastrous conclusion and nothing you do will make it come out differently. It was like driving a train on a track to a washed out bridge, unable to turn, unable to stop. You know there's nothing you can do but continue toward your fate, and so, after an initial panic, you resign yourself and watch as a bystander might, as you hurtle toward oblivion.

# CHAPTER TWENTY

Jennifer popped the cap on her third Michelob Light just as the Giants scored another run and the three men at the bar fell into a round of hissing and cursing at the big screen TV in the corner. All of them were Dodger fans, as was Jennifer. Faith was the solitary Giants fan in this group. She and Jennifer sat at one of the tables watching the game and playing checkers. Jennifer shook her head in dismay at the TV.

"What the fuck!" shouted the short guy at the bar. "What the fuck! Why the fuck didn't he throw that ball? He could've thrown that motherfucker out."

"Hey, fellas," cautioned the bartender, "watch your language. Ladies present."

All three of the men at the bar turned to look at Faith and Jennifer, then, as if they had forgotten. The short guy looked apologetic and mumbled, "Sorry."

Jennifer waved a hand in their direction. "What the fuck," she said.

The guy laughed and slapped a hand on his thigh before turning back to the game.

"Your move," Faith said.

Jennifer moved one of her checkers, then took a swallow of beer. Faith was drinking 7-Up tonight. She was tired after their long day of sightseeing, perhaps more than the others, since she'd been driving. As soon as the ball game was over, she decided, she was going to bed. Lauren might be up for hours yet. She was such a night owl. Faith hadn't seen her since dinner when the four of them had broken up. Watching a baseball game was not Lauren's idea of a good time. Faith could rarely talk her into watching. It wasn't Cassie's cup of tea either, apparently. Jennifer, though, had leapt at the idea of an evening of sports. Much preferred, no doubt, to talking about books she hadn't read or science she didn't know or any of the subjects they invariably veered toward when Cassie and Lauren were together. One thing that was becoming obvious to Faith was that Cassie was starved for an intellectual equal to talk to, and it was partly that gap Lauren had been filling for her. Given that Lauren had Faith to talk to, though, Faith wasn't really sure what need Cassie was fulfilling for Lauren.

Faith jumped two of Jennifer's checkers on her next move. So far, she had won every game. Jennifer wasn't very good at this. Or maybe she just wasn't paying attention. By the time the bottom of the ninth inning started, Faith had won the checkers game. And the Giants were about to win their game as well.

"That's enough," Jennifer said. "Let's watch the end of this disaster over here."

Minutes later as the Giants emerged victorious, the guys at the bar cursed, more mildly this time. Jennifer did the same.

"I think it's time for me to call it a night," Faith said.

Jennifer turned up her bottle and finished what was left in it. "Me too."

Faith stood and pulled on her jacket. "Where do you suppose Lauren and Cassie are?"

Jennifer stood and stretched her hands over her head.

"Probably up in the room fucking."

Faith stared at Jennifer, who appeared indifferent. "Why'd you say that?"

Jennifer shrugged. "I wouldn't be surprised. Don't you think they want to?"

Faith didn't know how to answer that because if she were totally honest about it, she would have to say yes. Or at least maybe. Not that she thought they actually would. In fact, she suspected that any physical attraction on Lauren's part was entirely subconscious. She didn't believe Lauren would be actively cultivating a romantic relationship with another woman. Especially not right in front of her partner. The two of them made no attempt to hide their affection for one another, openly touching, even holding hands. They apparently thought it was innocent, which meant it was.

"No," Faith said. "That's ridiculous. They've formed a close friendship. I think it's sweet."

Jennifer threw her jacket over one shoulder, swaying as if she might tip over. "Sweet? Yeah, right." She sounded cynical and resentful and slightly drunk.

They walked together out of the bar and across the lobby of the hotel. Faith scanned the area quickly.

"Maybe they're outside," she said.

"I'm telling you," Jennifer insisted, "they're upstairs going at it. You want to go together or do you want each of us to check our own rooms and see which one of us hits the jackpot?"

"You don't really believe that. If you did, you wouldn't be so calm."

Jennifer shrugged again. "Like I said, I wouldn't be surprised." Faith began to feel angry at Jennifer then for planting that idea in her mind. Now a little doubt was playing around the edges of her consciousness. Not that the idea hadn't already occurred to her, at least the idea that Lauren and Cassie were becoming too affectionate. But she had never thought they were acting on it.

Every night this week, the two of them had stayed up into the wee hours talking, as they were now, presumably, completely preoccupied by their fascination for one another. Faith watched with a mixture of wonder and uneasiness at Lauren's involvement with Cassie, at how happy she appeared, at how much she looked like a woman falling in love.

If she were falling in love with Cassie, did she know it? Lauren was insightful and self-aware. She never ceased analyzing herself. So what did she think was happening? How did she explain this to herself if she didn't recognize it as infatuation? Did they talk about that during their endless conversations? Did they talk about their feelings for one another? If they did, what conclusions did they reach?

Faith had been asking herself these questions as the days passed, as she observed, as coolly as she could, and reassured herself that Lauren was totally committed to her. She knew she could ask Lauren these questions. She hesitated to say anything, though. She knew that if she asked, she would get an honest answer. So far, she had shied away from that. Faith had never been very good at confronting strife. Or even acknowledging it. So far, she and Lauren had encountered very little strife in their relationship. She hoped that wasn't about to change.

"I'm going to check outside," she told Jennifer.

She pushed through the courtyard doors into the mild night air, followed by Jennifer. The pool was a shimmering rectangle of cool blue light under a starless sky. No one was in it. Under one of the poolside umbrellas, Lauren and Cassie sat across from one another at a table. Faith glanced at Jennifer with an I-told-you-so, then walked over to them.

"Hi," Lauren said. "Is the game over?"

"Yes. Giants won."

"What've you two been doing?" Jennifer asked.

"Just talking," answered Cassie. Then she yawned. "What time is it?"

"After eleven," Faith said. "I'm going to bed."

Lauren stood. "I'll come up too."

Cassie shoved her chair back and got up. "It's getting kind of cold out here anyway."

The four of them walked back through the lobby to the elevators.

"What time do you want to leave in the morning?" Cassie asked as they rode up to the fifth floor.

"Early," Faith said, "but not obscenely. Let's try for eight."

"Okay. See you at breakfast."

Cassie took Jennifer's hand as they exited the elevator and the doors closed behind them. Faith and Lauren continued to the sixth floor.

"What were you talking about all that time?" Faith asked.

"Oh, you know. This and that. Nothing important." They left the elevator and walked to their room. "It just keeps amazing me, though, how much we have in common. It seems uncanny sometimes."

"You've become awfully fond of her, haven't you?"

"Yes," Lauren answered without hesitation. "Though I can't really say the same for Jennifer. I mean, she's okay. On occasion, she can even be endearing, but I do sometimes wonder what Cassie sees in her."

"Are they happy? I mean, is their relationship strong?"

Lauren slid her key card into the lock and pushed the door open. "They've got some problems."

"Well, every couple has problems." Faith shut the door and turned the dead bolt.

"We don't." Lauren tossed her jacket on the end of the bed.

Faith hesitated, reluctant to open up a difficult subject, before asking, "Don't we?"

Lauren looked momentarily puzzled. Then she approached Faith and kissed her tenderly. "No. As far as I know, we have no problems whatsoever. We're fantastic."

Faith held Lauren loosely. "Then we're very lucky, aren't we?"

Lauren nodded, looking happy and worry-free. Faith was peeved all over again at Jennifer for putting negative thoughts in her mind. There was obviously no need for concern. Lauren wasn't capable of the kind of duplicity necessary to look the way she was looking—affectionate, lighthearted—and to be secretly longing for another woman. As if to prove it, Lauren pulled her closer and kissed her with a lingering passion, her body full of need.

"I think we do have a problem," Faith said when Lauren released her.

"What?"

"You're very frisky and I'm very tired."

Lauren smiled, then released her and swatted her hard on the ass. "Sweet dreams, my love."

# CHAPTER TWENTY-ONE

"I'm going to make an ice cream run," Faith said, jumping up from her chair.

"I'll go," Jennifer chimed in, raising her hand. "Cass, what kind do you want?"

Cassie stood beside Lauren at the kitchen sink, drying dishes. "You know my tastes, Sweetie."

Jennifer nodded. Faith grabbed her keys and kissed Lauren on the cheek before leading Jennifer out to the garage.

This was their last evening together. Lauren was sad, thinking about Cassie leaving in the morning. She was trying hard not to succumb to that emotion, but was having only marginal success.

As the Indigo Girls CD finished, the next one in the carousel began to play. Cassie raised her eyebrows at the music, a wordless question.

"Schubert," Lauren answered.

"Well, that's fine with me, but Jennifer's not going to be able to listen to that."

"Let's find something else, then. Come on."

Lauren hauled out a stack of CDs from the music rack and placed them on the coffee table. They sat on the couch and started looking through them.

"I have this one too," Cassie said, holding up k.d. lang's *Ingenue*.

"Sure. Don't we all?"

As they went through the CDs, they made a pile of those that would appeal to all four of them and another pile of rejects.

"Oh!" Cassie shouted, holding up one of Lauren's most recent acquisitions, *The Best of Jane Morgan*.

"I bought that just a couple of months ago, you know, because you remembered her recording of 'Fascination' so fondly. You remember; they played it on the ship."

"Can we play it?"

"Sure."

"Quick before Jen gets back. She hates these old songs."

Lauren put on the CD and returned to the sofa as the first song, "Strangers in the Night" began to play.

"Nice," Cassie said. "What track is 'Fascination'?"

"Fifth or sixth."

They continued to sort through the music, looking for something that Jennifer wouldn't object to while Cassie hummed along to the Jane Morgan songs, most of which were old romantic standards they both knew well.

"That was an incredible dinner," Cassie said. "You've impressed me every time you've served us food. Even breakfast."

"I'm trying to impress you," Lauren confessed.

"Oh, sure, I know that. I know you don't eat like this all the time."

"I want you to enjoy your visit. I want you to come back some day."

Cassie laid her hand over Lauren's and squeezed it reassuringly. It seemed she was always offering reassurance. Why did this friendship seem so fragile? Lauren wondered.

She'd always felt that way, from the day she knew she really cared about it, that last day in China as they said goodbye. Even then, she'd felt nearly hopeless about the chances of this long-distance friendship.

"What flavor ice cream do you think they'll come back with?" Cassie asked.

"Well, Faith will hover over strawberry, coffee and rum raisin."

"None of those are going to appeal to Jennifer. She'll go for chocolate or something with nuts, like butter pecan."

"Maybe we'll end up with vanilla."

Cassie laughed with abandon in the way she typically did when she was happy and relaxed.

"What's this?" she asked, holding up a John Denver CD.

"Oh, that's one of Faith's. Put that in the reject pile."

"Gladly. It didn't seem like you. I mean, one thing we do have in common is music."

"We have a lot of things in common," Lauren said.

"True. Sometimes I feel like you're my alter ego or something. I'm still amazed at how close we've become, so quickly."

Lauren smiled and looked up from the CDs on the table. "I feel the same way."

How easy it would be, Lauren thought, to say "I love you" to Cassie. Whenever those words formed in her mind, which had happened several times during this week-long visit, she pushed them aside. She had signed her Christmas card "Love Lauren and Faith." She had signed, "Love Lauren" on a couple of special-occasion e-mails. But sitting here face to face with Cassie, she cautioned herself to avoid that word. She didn't want to go over the line, a line she was finding it harder and harder to even recognize.

"Do you want some coffee?" Lauren asked.

"If it's decaf."

"It is." Lauren went to the kitchen and poured two cups of coffee, stirring some milk into hers. As she returned with Cassie's cup, "Fascination" started playing. Cassie sprang up from the couch and stood listening, a brilliant smile on her face. Lauren set the cups on the coffee table.

134

"It's just as I remember it," Cassie said, breathless. "Oh, Lauren, I feel like I'm ten years old!"

Cassie's eyes suddenly filled with tears. Then she shook herself and wiped them away, smiling again. "Thank you so much for playing that."

"You're welcome," Lauren said, amused at the dramatic reaction.

Cassie approached and they held one another in a close hug as they had often done. Lauren put her hand tenderly on the back of Cassie's head, aware of a stillness that had overtaken them as they stood together, unmoving, barely breathing, frozen in the awareness of their bodies touching. Simultaneously, they each turned their heads to face one another. Cassie's mouth was a mere two inches from her own. She tilted her head slightly as their mouths came together. Lauren wrapped Cassie into a tighter embrace as the kiss deepened and continued, slow and soft and sensuous. She closed her eyes and parted her lips, urging Cassie deeper. As their mouths grew more insistent and she felt Cassie's body pressing urgently against her, Lauren began a passionate freefall.

She knew now that she'd been wanting and waiting for this every day since Cassie's arrival. The way she was responding made it clear it had been the same for her. There was nothing tentative about this kiss. It was full of hunger and the joy of winning something long desired. It filled Lauren's body with heat and an aching need.

By mutual consent, they moved apart at last and stood looking at one another, wordless, for a long moment. Then Cassie swallowed hard and looked away.

Oh, my God, Lauren thought. *What have I done?*

"Uh," Cassie said, looking flustered, "I—"

She didn't finish. Instead, she rapidly left the room. Lauren sank to the couch, her skin on fire, and stared at the covers of the CDs on the table as they began to swim, the colors all blurring together. She was roused finally by the sound of the garage door opening. In a moment, Faith and Jennifer bustled in, laughing. Lauren struggled to overcome her distraction.

"What'd you get?" she asked, standing to greet them.

"Butter pecan," Jennifer announced.

"Strawberry," Faith said, holding up her purchase.

"Ah, so no compromise, after all."

"You know what I say," Faith said. "Why not have both?"

"Yes, you do say that." Lauren was immediately struck with the awful irony of that sentiment.

Cassie came in from the other room. "Butter pecan for me," she said.

Lauren tried to read her mind, but Cassie avoided her eyes.

"I don't think I'll have any tonight," Lauren said. "But don't eat all the strawberry. Save me some."

Faith nodded. The song currently playing was "Only One Love." God, that Jane Morgan is so full of mockery, Lauren thought bitterly. She escaped to the bedroom as the others dished up ice cream amid the clatter of bowls and spoons. Already she could feel doom descending like a heavy blanket over her. She lay in bed for at least an hour, just lying there wide awake and keeping her mind blank. Eventually, Faith came to bed and curled up around her in the dark.

"Are you feeling okay?" she asked.

"Yes, I'm fine. Just tired, I think. Worn out."

"Did you have a good day?"

"Yes. It was a wonderful day. I think everyone enjoyed it."

"Oh, sure. On the way to the store, Jennifer was chatting non-stop about the botanical garden. And that meal you made, it was remarkable, as usual."

"I think the whole trip went really well."

"Just about perfect."

From behind, Faith slipped her arm around Lauren's waist.

"And tomorrow they go home," Lauren said.

"Yes. I hope you're not going to be too sad."

"It's always hard when somebody goes away, especially when you've had such a good time."

Lauren turned to face Faith, then kissed her briefly. Faith stroked her face in a way that told Lauren she was trying to offer comfort, but Faith couldn't know just how devastated she was, or why.

# CHAPTER TWENTY-TWO

Lauren knew Faith sensed something was wrong, though both Lauren and Cassie were doing their best to keep themselves afloat, pretending, even to one another, that nothing had happened. Cassie and Jennifer were packed and their bags were in the car. Lauren had declined to ride with them to the airport. She couldn't bear it.

"What's wrong?" Faith asked in a private moment.

"Nothing," Lauren answered. "Everything's fine."

"You and Cassie didn't have a fight about something?"

"No. Not at all." Lauren touched Faith's cheek tenderly. "Saying goodbye is just hard on everybody."

It wasn't hard on Jennifer, though. She was full of energy and cheer this morning.

When it was time to go, Cassie gave Lauren a brief, pointedly platonic hug in the doorway, then shot her one last look, a look Lauren read as deep regret. Lauren couldn't hold back her tears any longer and started crying as Faith grabbed her raincoat and kissed her cheek.

"Cheer up, hon! Just a few months and we'll see them again. No time at all."

When they'd gone, Lauren sat down and cried in earnest. She already knew there would be no autumn trip to Albuquerque. Maybe she had always known. The look on Cassie's face as she left proved she knew it too. They both understood without a word what had happened and what now had to happen as a result.

This sequence of events began almost immediately after Cassie arrived home when she sent an e-mail, a note that would have looked ordinary, even cheerful, to anyone but Lauren.

"We had a great time," Cassie wrote. "Just lovely. I adored your beaches. And the little coastal towns. You two were perfect hosts."

"We loved having you," Lauren replied. "It was so much fun. Such good luck too that the weather was so cooperative."

For the first time ever, their notes were superficial. Before, Cassie and Lauren wrote to one another three or four times a day, every day. Now, after the initial pleasantries, they backed off to just a couple of notes in the week following the visit. And then there was nothing. Logging into her account and seeing no note from Cassie day after day was physically painful to Lauren. But she knew this was how it had to be, so she resisted her own urge to write.

Cassie had been a constant presence in her life for months, a source of joy. All of that had been so stupidly destroyed. Lauren couldn't believe she'd let it happen. Yes, she had felt it many times, had known on some level that she wanted Cassie in that way. But she didn't have to act on it. Acting on it had been the unforgivable part. She couldn't be blamed for her feelings, after all. If she could have resisted, over time it would have been manageable, it would have subsided and they could have been the best of friends. Probably. Maybe. Lauren ached to take back the moment she'd let her body betray her.

She knew her friendship with Cassie was over. There was

nowhere to go together but in a direction Lauren would never go, not with anyone. She held a deep conviction that Faith was her one true love, the person she was destined to be with.

After two weeks without a single note between them, one appeared. Startled but overjoyed, she opened it immediately. "I miss you so much!" she read. That was all it said.

With tears in her eyes, Lauren hit Reply and wrote, "I miss you too. I don't want to give you up. Isn't there some way we can—" Then she stopped herself, took a long, deep breath and closed her eyes. After a minute, she opened them again and discarded the message without sending it. She sent no reply.

She didn't hear from Cassie again. Whatever Cassie was or could have been to her, it was over.

## PART THREE
Ten Years Later

# CHAPTER TWENTY-THREE

Arriving at her gate in the Denver airport, Lauren scanned the banks of hard plastic chairs for a semi-private spot to continue her phone call, though she would have been glad for an excuse to end it. After a week with Charity, she'd had enough sisterly love to last her a long time. She smiled, thinking how ironic that was, considering how badly she had once wanted a sister of her own.

"Lauren," Charity instructed, "you be sure to call me first thing when you get home. I want to be sure you make it safely."

"I'll do that," Lauren assured her, taking a seat removed from other passengers. "My brother's picking me up at the airport in Portland. Don't worry. There's nothing to worry about."

She glanced at the flight schedule, verifying her gate and departure time. She was early. She had forty-five minutes to wait. The crowd lining up at the gate was for an earlier flight. She squinted to make out the destination: Albuquerque.

"We're so glad you came," Charity said. "I hope you enjoyed yourself. Ron and I were both so happy to have you."

"Of course," Lauren said, distracted by someone in the boarding line.

She stared harder at a woman carrying a navy-colored flight bag and dressed casually in sneakers, jeans and a long-sleeved shirt. She was about Lauren's height and wore glasses. Her hair was straight and thin, dark brown in color and quite short.

"I want to thank you again," Charity said, "for Grandma's ring. I'm wearing it right now."

Charity's voice broke and Lauren feared she would start crying again.

"No need to thank me," Lauren said. "I was glad I finally got it to you."

*Could it be?* she wondered, looking intently at the Albuquerque passenger in profile, at the shape of her forehead and chin. Was it possible that was Cassie standing over there, waiting impatiently to board her flight?

As the woman turned her head slightly, revealing her face, Lauren became even more convinced it was Cassie. Besides a general softening of her features, ten years hadn't changed her much. She was two years younger than Lauren, so she would be forty-five now. She shifted her bag to the other hand. The line she was in wasn't moving. They were still pre-boarding her flight.

"Bob wants me to tell you how much he loved that casserole you made last night," Charity said. "You didn't have to cook for us, but after all the bragging we heard from Faith over the years about your cooking, we were hoping you would. Bob wants me to get the recipe. It's not a secret, is it?"

"No, it's not a secret. I'll be happy to send it to you."

With the Albuquerque flight about to board, Lauren realized she had to decide quickly what to do. Should she run over and say hello? She wasn't completely sure it was Cassie. Even if it was her, maybe Lauren was the last person on earth she wanted to see. There hadn't been a single word or even a Christmas card between them in all these years.

Then the woman appeared to notice her, which surprised

her, even though she was staring unabashedly. As their eyes met, Lauren saw her expression change. She looked curious for a second, then surprised, an emphatic sort of surprise accompanied by a jaw-dropping gape. Through the glasses, Lauren couldn't see her eyes well, but could tell by her expression that Cassie recognized her. That expression, so familiar, also verified it was Cassie. No doubt.

"Well," Charity accused, "I know how you serious cooks are. You leave out that one special ingredient so nobody's dish ever comes out quite as good as—"

"Charity," Lauren said brusquely, "I've got to go. I'll call you when I get home."

She ended the call and stood, raising a hand in a tentative greeting. Cassie broke out of her line and they walked toward one another as an indistinct loudspeaker voice announced the Albuquerque plane would now begin general boarding.

"Lauren?" Cassie asked, her face breaking into a warm smile complete with dimples. "Is it you?"

Lauren nodded, recognizing with relief the familiar versions of Cassie's face as a range of emotions played across it. The hair below her temples was mostly gray now and a spattering of gray through her bangs was also new. Lauren thought it looked good on her, this touch of age. On her face too, the creases on either side of her mouth and the crinkles at the edges of her eyes—all of those lines deepening at the moment because of her unreserved smile—looked entirely natural and appealing.

They hugged one another with the sort of relentless hug Lauren's maternal grandmother used to give her, the sort of hug a child recoils against and can't wait to be free of. When that long hug was over, Cassie stood looking into her face with an expression of joyful disbelief. Lauren supposed her own expression was similar.

"My God, this is incredible!" Cassie said. "How are you? What are you doing here?"

"I'm on my way home."

"Me, too. I've been at a convention in New York. This is just a pit stop."

A convention in New York, Lauren briefly pondered, seemed

143

like an odd thing for a high school English teacher. She wondered if Cassie had moved into administration.

"Your hair's so short," Lauren observed. "I like it. It's cute."

"Thanks." Cassie tousled her hair. "It's been this way for a while."

"Wow! Where to begin," Lauren said, overwhelmed. "Are you and Jennifer—"

Cassie waved a hand. "No. We broke up eight years ago. She still lives in Albuquerque too, with her new wife. And their kids. Yes, she's got two little ones. We're friends, but we don't see each other often. And you? Still with Faith, I'm sure. How is she?"

Lauren hesitated to answer out of consideration for Cassie's feelings. She hated telling people about Faith. Sometimes, if it was someone she didn't know that well, someone she wouldn't run into again anytime soon, she lied and said, "She's fine, fine. Just great." That was probably a terrible thing to do. She hadn't done it often, but she had done it. It was so much easier and sometimes it cheered her a little. In this case, though, she didn't consider it. She and Cassie had been too close for that.

"Actually," she said, "Faith passed away two years ago."

"Oh, Lauren!" A look of genuine pain crossed Cassie's face. "How? What happened?"

"Cancer. Ovarian cancer."

"Oh, my God!" Cassie said. "You poor thing. She was so full of life. It's so hard to believe."

"I know. For me too. Hard to remember sometimes."

Cassie took Lauren in her arms again to give her a more purposeful hug this time, after which her right hand slipped down to Lauren's and held it firmly. She remembered how Cassie had held her hand before, just like this. It had comforted her then too. It had made her feel like a young girl with a best friend. It was one of the warmest feelings she'd ever had as an adult and she had often been sorry this innocent kind of affection between them couldn't have been maintained. A best friend would have been a tremendous asset to her during the last ten years. Especially the last few.

Cassie glanced back at the line she'd been in to see that it had nearly disappeared into the plane.

"Shit!" she said. "Now I feel like I should miss my flight so we can talk."

"Don't do that. You know what kind of problems you create when you miss your flight."

"Right. Still, I wish we had more time. I've been in this damned airport for the last two hours with nothing to do but read a ponderous old novel by Trollope for my stuffy book club. Have you ever read Trollope?"

"No. I'm more of a Sue Grafton type."

"Yes, of course. I remember. I think I need to find a new book club or just assert myself and insist on something deliciously trashy." She smiled a quirky smile that Lauren remembered like yesterday. Then her eyes turned sad. "You must have been through hell."

"I'm doing okay."

She looked skeptical.

"Really," Lauren said. "I'm fine. It's wonderful to see you again. You should probably go, though."

She nodded. "It's good to see you too. Honestly, Lauren, you've never been far from my thoughts all these years. I'm so sorry about Faith. I wish I didn't have to go. Damn!"

Cassie opened her carry-on and fished out a business card, handing it over. "Call me. I want you to. Seriously."

Lauren nodded.

"I mean it," she said, giving Lauren's hand a shake. "I know how you are. You'll talk yourself out of it. Send me an e-mail if you'd rather. It's on there too. Please promise me."

Lauren nodded again, feeling as though this scene was an echo of another from the past. "I will. I promise."

"Okay. Bye, then."

With another quick hug, she was gone, moving fast toward the gate, where she handed an attendant her boarding pass, then turned to glance back one more time and wave.

When she was gone, Lauren sat down again, feeling disoriented. It felt so familiar—her voice, her face, her hand—and yet so strange after all this time. A few minutes passed before she remembered the card in her hand. "Cassandra A. Burkett," it read. "Attorney at Law, Albuquerque, New Mexico."

Oh, my God! she thought, looking up again at the boarding gate Cassie had disappeared through. Apparently, a lot had happened in the last ten years, for both of them.

# CHAPTER TWENTY-FOUR

"There it is!" Lauren declared triumphantly as she found Cassie's business card in the pocket of her green jacket. She looked at it momentarily, then set it by the phone as she finished loading the washer. What if I'd washed that? she thought. *I'd have rediscovered Cassie only to lose her again.* Then she realized she was being melodramatic because Cassie, a practicing attorney in Albuquerque, would be easy to find, even without that card.

Seeing her in the airport had been such a surprise. A shock, really, like seeing a ghost. It wasn't that she hadn't thought about her in the intervening years, but Cassie had become someone so thoroughly relegated to the past that she hadn't thought of her going on about her own life independently. Seeing her ten years older, too, had been yet another surprise, as if she might have been suspended in time at the moment she last saw her, as if her life hadn't continued in the same way Lauren's had, once they were out of one another's view.

She'd been home three days and hadn't seriously searched for that card yet because things were so hectic as she got back into her routine. But she had been on the lookout for it, regularly talking herself into and then out of calling Cassie. Seeing her again, so full of life, after having had nothing but indistinct memories and static photos for so long, had seriously tugged on her emotions.

Lauren got the laundry started and put her suitcase in the guest room closet alongside her larger, serious, going-out-of-the-country-for-a-while suitcase which had not been used in a few years and wasn't likely to be used any time soon. Cocoa, her bulky long-haired mutt of a cat, tried to slip into the closet unseen, but Lauren was onto him, so she pulled him out before shutting the closet door. He looked up at her with his vaguely Persian blackish mug.

"Come into the kitchen," she urged. "Maybe I can find you a treat."

Cocoa followed her to the kitchen. It was his habit to follow her around the house, so she knew he would. He had never followed Faith around. Lauren assumed that was because she was the food provider in this house. All good things in the mind of a cat came out of the kitchen. Cocoa had liked Faith, though, and had sat beside her for hours on the bed during her illness, resting his chin, and occasionally one paw, on her, keeping her company with a resolute vigilance. Lauren had often found them thus when she came into the bedroom, Cocoa with a paw on Faith's thigh, Faith with a hand on Cocoa's back, a comfortable pose while she watched TV or read. It wasn't unusual to find them both asleep in that position, especially during recuperation from some surgery or in the aftermath of chemotherapy when Faith was easily tired.

Lauren opened a can of tuna, gave Cocoa a hunk of it in a bowl on the floor, and then mixed the rest with lemon juice, celery and parsley for her lunch. She took her sandwich to the living room and turned the TV to a baseball game. The Braves were playing the Indians today, a quirky pairing that made her laugh. Beyond that, she knew the game wouldn't hold her interest, but the familiar sounds provided a soothing backdrop.

As she ate her sandwich in front of the game, she contemplated calling Cassie. It was Saturday and there was a good chance of actually getting hold of her on a weekend, she imagined. Once she'd made up her mind to do it, she immediately began wondering if Cassie had been sincere. Was she just being polite? No, Lauren told herself, she could still read Cassie, even after a ten-year hiatus. She really had been delighted they'd run into one another.

It was during this discussion with herself that the phone rang. Illogically, Lauren's first thought was that it was Cassie calling her. She leapt for the phone and immediately saw that the unrecognized number was local.

"Hello," said a pleasant female voice. "Is this Lauren Keegan?"

"Yes," Lauren answered somewhat reluctantly.

"Oh, good. This is Emma McKinley."

Stunned, Lauren dropped to the stool beside the phone, recognizing the name with disbelief.

"You may not remember me," Emma said, "but I was a student of Faith's years ago. She was a tremendously influential person in my life. She was my mentor, in fact."

Emma's voice was hesitant, as if she were choosing her words carefully. Lauren wasn't surprised. What she knew of Emma McKinley was mostly through the letter that had been returned as undeliverable right before Faith died, the letter that was sitting at this moment in the bottom of the drawer of her bedroom nightstand where she'd left it nearly two years ago.

Emma continued. "I was devastated to hear about—it was shocking. I'm so sorry."

Emma waited and Lauren realized she was expected to say something. "Thank you," she said, unable to think of anything else to say.

"It's sort of ironic because I've just returned from sabbatical with the idea of calling Faith to ask to see some of her work on Alaska. I've been living up there for the last several months, doing research."

"You're an anthropologist," Lauren said, not asking so much as reminding herself.

"Yes. I've been teaching at the university in Eugene for several years."

Lauren tried to gather her thoughts, to take advantage of this unexpected opportunity. After reading that letter, she'd been left with so many questions.

"Did you keep in touch with Faith?" she asked.

"No. I haven't spoken to her since grad school."

That would explain why Faith didn't have a good mailing address, Lauren thought. They'd had no contact, a comforting fact.

"Now," Emma said, "I feel really bad about that. I wish I'd taken the time to look her up again. I wish I'd known she was sick. I would have liked to have told her—"

Emma stopped. What? Lauren thought. *What would you have told her?*

Talking to Emma now, the real person, as strange as that seemed after so long thinking of her as some mysterious unknown entity, Lauren felt guilty all over again for having read the letter Faith had never meant her to see. That letter, as lovely and thoughtful as all of her farewell letters, would probably have meant something special to Emma. But Lauren wasn't feeling particularly charitable toward Emma, despite the sincerity in her voice.

"You said you wanted to talk to Faith about some of her research?" Lauren asked.

"Yes. I remembered she'd done some work on the tribes in British Columbia and Alaska. Some of the sites she visited, there's just nothing there now. And the people she interviewed, they're gone too, most of them. They were old people even then."

Emma sounded intelligent, reasonable, not at all like a woman who had nearly destroyed her education by recklessly falling in love with her professor.

"Can you tell me what happened to her papers?" she asked.

"They're still here. I'm intending to donate everything to the university. I just haven't gotten it all organized yet."

"Would it be possible—" Emma began, sounding unsure. "Would you mind if I looked through them?"

Lauren fought her first impulse, to deny Emma's request, which she recognized as immature, and tried to focus on what Faith would have wanted instead.

"I don't know," Lauren said. "I don't really know you. Maybe if I knew more about your work and what it is exactly you want to do with Faith's research—"

"Yes. I understand. I'd be happy to explain. Would you like to get together somewhere and talk about it?"

This was yet another unanticipated opening. Lauren hesitated, struggling with her conflicting emotions. "Okay," she finally said. "I'm actually free today if you are."

"That would be perfect. I'm in Portland this weekend visiting my parents, so today would be easy. Wherever would be convenient for you."

Home turf advantage, Lauren advised herself, and proposed that Emma come to her house. They agreed on three o' clock.

In addition to straightening up the house, there was one other thing she needed to do in preparation for Emma's visit. An unpleasant chore, but she felt it was necessary because she hadn't read that letter in a long time.

She went to her bedroom and dug down through some magazines to the bottom of the nightstand drawer to pull out an envelope with its red "Undeliverable" stamp on the front.

Faith had spent many hours composing these letters. It hadn't been easy for her to find the right things to say to people and she'd been determined to say just the right thing to everyone. She wrote to old friends and distant relatives, to colleagues and mentors, people she had loved and people who had touched her in one way or another. For some of them, this was how they found out she was ill. For others, it was a final, formal farewell they could hang on to. It was a thoughtful, although painful, thing to do. She was frequently in tears as she wrote those letters, recalling old joys and sorrows, and knowing the person she wrote to would probably be in tears as well, reading her words.

Since Lauren had taken the letters to the post office, she knew who received them, including Emma McKinley, a former student who had apparently made an impression on Faith. There were several of those, the special students whose lives and careers had been more than marginally influenced by their association with her.

Lauren hadn't read most of the letters. They were very personal and she felt no need to intrude. Sometimes when Faith was writing to some old friend, she would stop and tell Lauren about an incident she remembered, some memory the letter writing had triggered. These were usually happy memories. This process of saying goodbye was Faith's way of reliving the joys of her life. They were beautiful letters, by all accounts. Lauren had seen a few of them, later. People had shown her. Like Faith's sister Charity during her recent visit. Despite all of their disagreements, Faith had written about their childhood together and the special bond of sisters. She had managed to fill that letter with love and humor. The way Charity spoke now, it sounded as if she had completely forgotten the two of them had ever quarreled.

The letter to Emma had been returned only days before Faith died. Lauren had set it aside without mentioning it, something to be dealt with later. With everything else that was going on, it wasn't important. At least, that had been Lauren's assumption. Just another student. Not worth troubling Faith over. And then she'd forgotten about it for a while.

A couple months later when she rediscovered the letter, she decided to track down a current address and mail it, but she'd opened it and read it instead. In those early days, she was desperate for any reminder of Faith, and her familiar handwriting on the outside of that envelope was easily enough to overcome the ethics of reading someone else's mail. It would be like hearing her voice again. Who wouldn't open it, she rationalized, under the same circumstances?

But she'd been completely unprepared for the words Faith had written to Emma. The letter had sent her into a tailspin and she'd put it away, unable to face it. She sometimes thought about it, but hadn't looked at it since.

She took the letter into the family room and sat in her recliner. Unfolding the pages, Lauren swallowed hard, hoping it wasn't as shocking this time around.

*Dear Emma,*

*It's been so many years since we spoke, but you've often entered my thoughts, as you do today as I prepare to go, as Dylan Thomas euphemistically put it, "into that good night." I have terminal cancer and not long left now. So I'm saying goodbye to those who touched my life significantly. I'm not sure you ever understood how thoroughly you were one of those.*

*I hope you're content with whatever gifts your life has brought you, personally and professionally. I hope you found someone who makes you as happy as Lauren has made me. I've had such a good life with her. She's been the perfect companion. Our adventures together have been thrilling. We celebrated our twenty-third anniversary last month. Not bad, don't you think? Frankly, it makes me furious to think what I'm doing to her. She doesn't deserve to be left like this. If there were any god or devil to make a pact with so I could keep from leaving her, I would do it. But neither gods nor devils have ever spoken to me, as you know.*

*The main reason I'm writing you is that I'd like to apologize for what happened between us. I feel responsible and I hope you can forgive me. If I'd been stronger, you wouldn't have lost that year of your education. I also want you to know that it wasn't just because of your feelings that I sent you away. Other students came to me, before and after, with their hearts in their hands. Life continued and we all survived without much of a tremor to the planet. But it was different with you. It was because of my own feelings that I sent you away. I didn't trust myself. I didn't know what else to do. I was so sorry I couldn't tell you, then, how I felt, but I'm telling you now because I want you to understand how important you were. I sent you away because I was afraid of you and what you could have meant to me. I cared more for you than circumstances allowed me to admit.*

*I'm so glad you were able to recover and finish up, which says a lot about your determination and strength of character. I've always been extremely proud of you. I've watched you from afar in your professional achievements, blossoming and gaining confidence. I've read everything you've published. Despite my cautions to you early on, I love your literary voice. It reminds me of my own style, and how could I not love that? You're such a careful researcher, so thorough and controlled. I've often wished we could have worked together as you originally imagined. It would have been such fun and I'm certain my own work would have benefited greatly from your conscientiousness.*

*I know you'll continue to make remarkable contributions to our science. I wish I could be around to see them. I really did love anthropology. The human animal has always fascinated me. Such a complicated creature. So complicated, in fact, we never complete our studies of even our own selves no matter how long we live. There is enough mystery in just one human being to confound universes of scientists and philosophers.*

*Enjoy unraveling the mystery. I did.*

*Love,*

*Faith*

Lauren let her hand fall to her lap and leaned her head back against the headrest. It didn't have the same shock value this time, but, of course, she had known what to expect. After reading this letter the first time, she'd tried to remember anything she could about Emma McKinley, anything at all that might explain the contents and the apparent truth that Faith had been so attracted to this student she'd been unable to continue working with her.

But it had been too long ago and all she could remember was the occasional mention. She wondered if she had just not been paying attention or if Faith had purposely never talked about Emma. Lauren had met other graduate students now and then, eager young people who admired Faith and did their best to prove their worth to her. She couldn't imagine Faith ever falling in love with any of them, or even thinking herself capable of it. What was so different about this one? Lauren wondered.

That was one of the reasons she'd agreed to meet Emma. She wanted to find out. She also wanted to know the rest of the story. The letter didn't make it entirely clear what had happened between them. She was both afraid and determined to know.

# CHAPTER TWENTY-FIVE

When Emma arrived, right on time, Lauren extended a hand to her and she immediately moved past that to hug her warmly and for several seconds. It was the kind of hug people give you to express sympathy. Lauren had gotten many of them in the last two years. But in this case, she had the feeling the expression of condolence was as much for Emma herself as for Lauren.

"Lauren," she said, standing back, "I'm so glad to meet you."

Emma was a poised and attractive woman with thick hair flowing in loose curls over her shoulders. She was tall, wearing tan pants and a tailored jacket. Her face was thin and pale. Her light blue eyes were intelligent and unreadable. Lauren had expected a younger woman, someone around thirty, but Emma was clearly older. Because of that, Lauren's whole concept of what had happened ten years ago started rapidly revising itself.

"Come in," she said, standing aside.

"Your rhododendrons are gorgeous!" Emma said, coming into the living room. "Such a profusion of blooms."

"Yes, we usually have a good show this time of year." Lauren realized she had said "we" out of long-established habit, but decided not to correct herself. "Would you like some coffee?"

"If you have some made, yes, I would." Emma remained in the living room as Lauren went to the kitchen.

"Not too surprising that your flowers are exquisite," Emma called from the other room. "You're an expert in soil, agriculture, that sort of thing. Isn't that right?"

Lauren carried in a tray with coffee, sugar and cream and set it on the table between the couch and chair. Emma was standing in front of the fireplace, looking at the photos on the mantle.

"I was. I'm retired now." Lauren wondered how much this woman knew about her, how personal her knowledge was.

"I remembered that," Emma said, looking briefly over her shoulder. "Faith talked about you all the time."

"Really?" Lauren heard how cold her voice sounded.

"Yes. Oh, not in the classroom. Just between the two of us."

*What am I supposed to say to that?* Lauren wondered, walking over to the fireplace.

Emma was looking at the photo of Faith and Lauren at their commitment ceremony, Faith holding her hand as she slid the ring on.

"She looks incredible!" Emma said, then turned to look at Lauren. Her expression, which had been one of delight, rapidly dissolved as she said, "You look gorgeous too. That's a wonderful picture."

"Yes, I've always liked it. I don't photograph well, but that was a rare case where we both looked really happy."

Emma returned her attention to the mantle, moving past the vase containing Faith's ashes, which stood directly in the center between two matching picture frames. On the other side was a photo taken at Faith's fiftieth birthday, an elaborate gathering

156

at Mount Hood where their group had taken up a good chunk of the lodge and loudly dominated the restaurant, ski lifts and lounges for three days. As much trouble as it had been to plan that event to fit in with everyone's schedules and book all the facilities, it had been worth it. Faith had been so happy with all the attention. In the photo she was standing on skis, wearing a heavy parka and knit cap, laughing at Lauren who had fallen and was half buried in snow. Lauren was laughing too. Nobody had known it at the time, but that was Faith's last milestone birthday, which made Lauren more grateful than ever that she'd managed to arrange a bona fide celebration.

"This one's very good of you both too," Emma commented.

Lauren forced a smile and led the way back to the sitting area where they sat across from one another over the coffee table. Emma took her coffee and stirred a spoonful of sugar into it.

"I want to say again how sorry I was to hear about Faith's passing," Emma said. "I'm sure I would have heard about it sooner if I hadn't been living in Alaska. It's a different world up there."

"I've been there," Lauren said, examining Emma's features and mannerisms, trying to understand what it was that had appealed to Faith. "How old are you?"

"Forty-four," Emma said without hesitation.

She was only three years younger than Lauren. She would have been ten years younger than Faith.

"Can you tell me about your project?" Lauren said. "How you want to use Faith's material?"

Emma spoke about her work haltingly at first, but she soon became less self-conscious and more animated, allowing her enthusiasm to guide her discussion. She sounded knowledgeable and professional, a serious scientist with a passion for her work. Her area of expertise was the myth and magic of the whaling tribes of the Pacific Northwest. Lauren listened without comment. Emma was aware of the research Faith had done on the Nootka tribe of Vancouver Island. She was hoping to reference that.

"She used to talk about a burial site where several chieftain skulls were collected as a power center for the whale hunt rituals. I don't recall all the details, but I'm sure she would have kept records. There were other, similar stories. I'm basically hoping to see whatever she had. I've been through all her published papers. Nothing about the Nootka there."

"No," said Lauren. "That one didn't find its way into print. But I remember that site."

"Oh, you were there?"

"I went on most of the research trips. Faith liked to make vacations out of them. Some people never did comprehend why all my vacations were centered around human skeletons and burial grounds. But I had a good time. We had a lot of fun."

"It's wonderful that you were so involved in her work." Emma paused to swallow a mouthful of coffee, then set her cup down. "Hey, did you go to China with her too, the Yangtze River trip?"

"The hanging coffins of the Bo," Lauren recalled. "Yes, I did."

Emma seemed to bounce on the couch, slapping her hands on her knees gleefully. "Oh, I wish I'd seen that! No chance now, not after the dam was built. Oh, you're so lucky. That was my last year at Oregon State. I would have given anything to have gone on that trip."

"It was a great trip," Lauren said. "I've got a photo album. There are a few pictures of the coffins. Would you like to see them?"

"Oh, my God, yes!"

Faith's disorderly nature had had no impact on the photo albums. Those were in Lauren's domain. The photos were neatly catalogued, chronologically, and everything was labeled, so it was no trouble to find the album containing their China trip.

"This young man," Lauren said, sitting beside Emma and pointing at a photo of Joe, "was our hired guide. These two were friends, Cassie and Jennifer. And here are the coffins."

Emma examined the photos Cassie had taken of the coffins while Lauren's eyes lingered on a picture of Cassie. She was standing beside one of the coffins making a funny face, as if she'd walked into an old Lon Chaney horror movie.

"Thank you for showing me these," Emma said.

Lauren closed the album and set it on the coffee table.

"You must have had some marvelous adventures," Emma sighed. "By the way, did Faith ever get to Sky Island?"

Lauren shook her head. "We were all set to go a few years ago, but then riots broke out in Guadalcanal and it was just too dangerous. We had to cancel. After that, there just wasn't time."

"She wanted to see it so much. I've always remembered that story. She told it in my first class with her, cultural anthropology. She made the whole ritual sound so beautiful and solemn."

"It was a favorite story. She told it often." Lauren stood. "Emma, before I decide about the research, I want to be assured that you'll give Faith the credit and respect she deserves."

Emma looked up in surprise. "Of course! Lauren, I feel so much gratitude toward Faith. I was sick when I found out she had passed. I want to do this partly for her. I want to do it to say thank you to her."

Lauren studied Emma's eyes, trying to read her thoughts. "Thank you for what?"

"For everything. It's because of Faith I became an anthropologist. She inspired me. She was that teacher, you know, the one who takes hold of your imagination and sends it to the stars. It was because of Faith I got my job too."

"In Eugene?"

"Yes. Without her recommendation, I doubt they would have hired me. After I had to leave Oregon State without finishing my master's—"

"You didn't finish?"

"No. I quit in the middle of my last year." Emma hesitated, appearing to be searching very deliberately for her next words. "A year later, I applied at Eugene and finished up. Then Faith recommended me for a teaching position there. It was very generous of her."

"Was it?" Lauren asked. "She did that sort of thing for her students, her best students."

"Yes, I know she did. She was such a wonderful woman. Such an inspiring teacher."

"She was more than just a teacher to you," Lauren said coolly. "Isn't that right?"

Emma stared at her, her eyes revealing nothing. "What do you mean?"

Lauren hesitated, then decided to be direct. "You were in love with her."

Emma dropped her gaze, then said, "I didn't know you knew."

Lauren held her breath, hoping Emma would feel like talking.

Emma looked up again. "That was a long time ago. She put me in my place, believe me. She even resigned as my advisor. Essentially shut me right out of the program. Even after I finished my degree, she was very firm that I wasn't to come back to State. She would help me get on at Eugene, she told me, but she would do everything she could to prevent me from getting on here. That had been my original plan, to teach here. My family's here. This was my home, but I understood why that wasn't going to happen."

"Because she didn't want you working on the same campus."

"Right. At the time, it really hurt. Now, though, I see how right she was. If I had come back, it would have just started up again. I mean, I would have— It would have been difficult. A couple years later, I met someone else. I fell in love again. It all worked out." Tears were forming in Emma's eyes. "Oh, you were so lucky to have such a woman! I thought so then, not always kindly. I hated you, to be honest. She loved you so much. She told me that. She told me I was a beautiful, smart, sensitive woman. But, she said, her heart belonged to you, all of it. All she could give me was friendship. Which she did. But I wasn't satisfied with that. I pushed her."

"And that's why she had to distance herself."

Emma nodded. Lauren handed a box of tissue across the table. Emma took one and wiped her eyes.

"She never gave you any encouragement?" Lauren asked.

Emma shook her head. "Oh, no. She tried all the time to discourage me. I should have listened, but I was, oh, well, younger. What can I say? No, Faith was completely uninterested in me that way." Emma spoke rapidly, nervously. "She was totally into you. Not that she shouldn't have been. That was very admirable. She was admirable in all kinds of ways. I admired her. It just sort of evolved from there. But entirely one-sided, really. It's embarrassing to think what she must have told you about me back then. I'm sure she found me completely foolish and annoying."

Lauren took a deep breath, relieved to hear that Faith had kept Emma at arm's length.

"When exactly was that?" she asked.

"Um, that would have been ten years ago. My last year at State. What would have been my last year. I think everything came to a head around November, when she'd finally just had enough. I do know that by Thanksgiving, I had dropped out."

Ten years ago? thought Lauren, realizing that had been the year they'd gone to China, the year Lauren had met Cassie. Oddly, they had both weakened their defenses that year, allowing someone to move closer to their hearts. Why was that? Had they come to some vulnerable point in their relationship without being conscious of it, some thinning of their devotion, like an old sheet with one threadbare spot that, if pulled on just a little too hard, will tear apart? Or was it just another strange coincidence that both of them had attracted the attention of an outsider that same year?

Emma was sobbing now. Lauren wasn't sure why. Because she had loved someone who was unavailable to her? Because the person she had loved was gone? Because she was no longer the woman who fell in love with her teacher? Faith had always said you never fell in love the same way twice. Lauren assumed she meant you never fell as *deeply* in love the second, third or fourth time around. When questioned, though, Faith just said it was "different" each time, that one grew wary of one's own undisciplined passions. Maybe that's what Emma was crying about, her lost youth.

Lauren felt herself growing more compassionate. Emma was just a woman who had fallen in love, after all. Then she remembered the letter and how Emma had been under a misconception all this time that Faith had had no feelings for her. Lauren considered showing her the letter, but then changed her mind.

When Emma had composed herself, Lauren said, "I'll show you the den. All of Faith's research is in there, though it may not be organized as you'd like. It's going to take some time to go through everything."

Lauren felt slightly guilty at the appreciative look Emma gave her.

# CHAPTER TWENTY-SIX

After Emma had gone, Lauren sat silently in the living room thinking, Cocoa sleeping beside her. She was relieved to learn nothing had happened between Emma and Faith, nothing physical anyway. But the episode must have been troubling for Faith, considering the information provided by the letter. In the midst of that crisis, Faith had chosen not to confide in her.

And she herself had done the same, she thought, staring at the photo album on the coffee table. They had both weathered these threats to their relationship on their own. Communication had never been their strong suit, not when it mattered. Even when Faith was told she had cancer, she'd kept it to herself for over a month. Lauren had been furious with her for that. Or perhaps she'd just been furious at the cancer. But it had hurt her,

Faith's decision not to share the pain and fear of that. It wasn't out of character, though.

Maybe she was just trying to protect me, Lauren thought, returning to the subject of Emma. That had been her reason for silence in the case of her illness. She always did think she had to shield Lauren from the hard lessons of life.

When they met, Lauren was so young. Faith never got over thinking of her as a wide-eyed innocent, ill-equipped to face the world by herself. So Faith had never said a word about Emma. And Lauren hadn't said anything about Cassie either, not until three years ago when Faith had pointedly asked her.

Lauren picked up the album and turned past the Yangtze River trip to the photos from Cassie and Jennifer's spring visit the following year. There was a picture of Lauren sitting on a rock beside Cassie, engrossed in conversation with her, both of them with the tops of their heads cut off, neither of them aware their picture was being taken.

Lauren hadn't looked at any of the albums since Faith had died. They'd gone through them together after she got sick, though, reminding themselves what a fabulous life they'd had together. They weren't thinking at the time that Faith would die. At least Lauren wasn't. It seemed like such a remote possibility... at first. Looking at these same photos of Cassie and Jennifer, Faith had said, "They were fun. That trip to visit them, that never happened. Why not?"

"Oh, you know," Lauren had replied with a dismissive wave of her hand. "Everybody's busy. People just never get around to things like that."

"But the two of you were so happy to have found one another. You said she was like the little sister you never had. What happened? Why did you cut it off?"

"Cut it off?" Lauren had asked, startled. Faith's expression was solemn and Lauren knew she wouldn't let her brush this aside. She wanted an explanation. She knew about Lauren and Cassie. Knew enough anyway, from watching them together, from photographs like this, their arms intertwined, their heads close together like girls in collusion.

"Why didn't you ask me about it then?" Lauren had asked.

"At first, after they'd gone home, I didn't realize something had happened. Once I did realize it, I think I was just afraid to deal with it. You were so sad. You were in mourning. That's how it seemed to me. Whatever made you decide to end it, I was afraid of doing anything that would make you change your mind. It seemed smarter to be quiet and still, like a cornered animal, and wait for it to pass."

Lauren stared at her. "So you knew?"

"All I knew was that you had strong feelings for her. It seemed like it was mutual. And then, suddenly, after that visit, it was over and you didn't mention her again. There wasn't another word about visiting them. There wasn't any explanation. She was out of your life. It wasn't a gradual drifting apart. It was a deliberate termination. So what else could I think but you had stopped it because it was a threat? To us. And how could I know how hard or how easy that was for you, that decision to choose me over her."

"You should have asked me. Actually, I should have told you. You had nothing to worry about. I never would have chosen her."

"But you were in love with her," Faith said.

"It didn't get that far. Once we recognized where it was going, we stopped it. Both of us stopped it."

"That must have been difficult."

"It *was* difficult," Lauren admitted. "But I didn't consider doing anything differently. Nor did she. Neither one of us ever wanted more than friendship." Lauren looked Faith in the eye. "That's why I was so sad. Because I lost her as a friend. It wasn't because I wanted to leave you."

"I'm sorry I didn't talk to you about it at the time." Faith took hold of her hand. "I should have. I knew you were in pain. I was just afraid. Your feelings seemed so intense. Sometimes your intensity scares me."

"Sometimes it scares me too."

"Still, we should have talked about it. You must have felt very lonely."

Yes, Lauren now thought, that's exactly what she had felt. So alone. She had lost her best friend and she couldn't ask her lover for comfort because she felt too guilty for feeling that way about another woman.

165

"I got over it," she had said. "And, eventually, I was very happy with how I handled it, how we both handled it. It might have gone differently. It might have destroyed people's lives."

"You never saw her again?" Faith asked.

"No. I never heard from her at all after that spring."

"And you never regretted your decision?"

Lauren shook her head vigorously. "Not at all. I've been in love with you every day since we met."

"Every day?"

"Every single day. Even those days when you were yelling at the TV with a can of beer in your fist like some yahoo from the sticks."

Faith laughed. "Baseball!"

"We all have our faults. But, seriously, my love, I was never for a moment tempted to leave you. We've been very happy together. I know a good thing when I've got it."

Lauren had kissed her then and they had said no more about it.

Apparently, they had both had secrets. No matter how close you are to someone, there are things about her you'll never know. She wasn't thinking just about other women like Emma and Cassie now. She was thinking about the feelings and thoughts you keep from one another, to avoid hurting each other.

But what she'd said to Faith that day had all been true. She had never considered leaving, as much as she had been drawn to Cassie. There wasn't a woman anywhere on earth who could have taken her away from Faith. She felt lucky to have found her true love when the time was right for both of them. She also felt lucky they were able to spend so many joyful years together. She was grateful for that the entire time. In the last ten years, she'd also been grateful to herself for turning away from the temptation of Cassie. Faith had been the right woman for her, then and always.

A lot had changed since she and Cassie had known one another. She had changed. Cassie must have changed too. Maybe the mistake they had made ten years ago could be put behind them after all. Lauren went to the phone and dialed Cassie's number.

"I'm thrilled you called!" Cassie said after Lauren identified herself.

"We've got so much to catch up on," Lauren said, settling into the deep cushions of her couch. "So you're a lawyer. How did that happen?"

"Honestly, Lauren, it's because of you."

"Because of me? How can that be?"

"The way you kept telling me I was smart enough and how if I didn't do it, I'd regret it later. Just the pep talks about pursuing your dream."

"I guess I was right, then."

"I loved law school from the first day," she continued. "I really blossomed. Not surprisingly, that was the beginning of the end for me and Jennifer. She was threatened by my new ambitions. She'd always said, and I believed her, the reason she didn't want me to go to law school was that our income would suffer so badly for a while. But I began to understand that wasn't the real reason at all."

"She was intimidated?"

"Yes. Somehow just talking to her about school made her defensive, so I quit talking to spare her feelings, but then she felt left out of my life. And, realistically, she was."

An hour ticked by as Lauren listened to Cassie describe her life. She had dated sporadically, but was not in a serious relationship, not since Jennifer. She'd devoted herself to her work and had a small practice with one other attorney. It sounded like she was involved in her community and doing good work. She spoke of it with love and enthusiasm.

When it was Lauren's turn, she told Cassie she had taken an early retirement. "I decided to quit working when Faith got sick so I could stay home with her. It was the right decision because there was a lot to do. Then, too, we had that year together."

"That must have been a lot to handle. I hope you had some help."

"Yes. There were friends. Faith had some wonderful friends. I was very grateful for them. And Faith's sister came out for three weeks during a rough patch. We managed."

"What have you been doing since then?" Cassie asked.

"I've continued writing. That's going pretty well, actually."

"I'm so glad to hear that. So we're both doing what we wanted to do." After a brief pause, Cassie said, "Hey, here's something you don't know. Remember that day you and Faith drove us down the Oregon coast? I just adored Coos Bay, if you recall."

"I do. You said you could imagine yourself living there. I remember you really enjoyed that day."

"I bought a place there!" Cassie announced joyously.

"In Coos Bay?"

"Near it. A little house with an ocean view. It's my vacation home. Aren't I the pretentious bitch? Vacation home!"

"No, I think that's wonderful. When was this?"

"Couple of years ago. I've been out there several times. It's the perfect place to run away to."

"Are you going to retire there?"

"That's the idea, yes. It's a small town, but Oregon is fairly liberal and who's going to care about a harmless old dyke living alone with her cat anyway?"

"From what you've been telling me of your life in recent years, I can see you heading up the first annual Coos Bay pride parade."

Cassie laughed. "If I did that, it'd be just me, my cat, and a couple of guys who live on a houseboat at the marina. A very sparse parade."

Lauren was enjoying talking to Cassie so much she didn't want the call to end, but it had already been an hour and a half. She recognized this feeling as the same one that had led them to plan their second vacation together only two days after coming home from their first. Even then, in the days following the China trip, she'd thought they missed one another too much. They were too happy together for an ordinary friendship, then. Lauren didn't feel that now, though. Her joy at talking to Cassie again was tempered by a lot of living in the last decade. As glad as she was to be reconnected with Cassie, she didn't feel like jumping up and down with glee. Glee was no longer part of her repertoire.

"Why don't you drive down?" Cassie suggested, proving once again they were thinking in concert. "Take a little holiday. I could meet you there. Or you could just have the place to yourself if you'd rather. It's very restful."

"Sounds nice," Lauren said nonchalantly.

"I'm serious. Let's get together. It'll be fun."

"I don't know."

"Lauren, I think we should. The way things happened before...."

Oh, Lauren thought, so we are going to talk about that. She wouldn't shy away from it. She'd always felt free to say anything at all to Cassie. It was sort of a surprise, really, that they hadn't discussed it at length right after it happened. That had been an anomaly for them.

"Yes," Lauren said. "I've always felt guilty about what happened. It was so self-indulgent and stupid of me. It ruined everything."

"What? You're blaming yourself?"

"For kissing you, yes. That's what you're talking about, isn't it?"

"Yes, but it was *me*. I kissed you. I was the one who did it."

"Really? Is that what you think?"

There was a brief silence, then Cassie said, "I think we should definitely get together and talk."

# CHAPTER TWENTY-SEVEN

Lauren drove down from Portland on a warm summer day with white, fluffy clouds drifting overhead. It had been three weeks since she and Cassie had agreed to this visit. They had reinstated their e-mail correspondence, although the notes tended to come along every other day rather than three times a day like they once had. They wrote mainly about what had happened during the ten years of silence, and sometimes they shared interesting facts about their days.

Lauren had learned that Cassie's son Eric had gone to college, had majored in sociology and had married two years ago. Cassie's legal practice was successful and kept her busy. She had specialized in family law and actively courted the gay community to specialize even further in issues surrounding children—adoption and child custody cases. Lauren was glad she was doing something she was passionate about.

Once she reached Coos Bay, she consulted her GPS receiver to guide her to Cassie's house. It was a single-story modern structure on a bluff overlooking the ocean, set back away from the cliff at least a thousand feet. It wasn't a large house, but it was a handsome one. The front, the side facing the ocean, was one long wall of high window panes framed in dark wood. Lauren pulled into the driveway and verified the address one more time. She'd have the place to herself for a few days, as Cassie wasn't arriving until the weekend.

She was looking forward to seeing her, but she was also looking forward to the peace and isolation of this place. She knew being alone here wouldn't be lonely in the same way being alone at home was.

Stepping out of her car, she stretched and breathed in the ocean air, cool and briny. The house had a small front yard and no lawn, just hardy native plants, some of them in bloom, adding a spot of color to the greenish gray background of the coastal scrub along the rest of the bluff. The nearest neighbor was at least a half mile away.

This cost some money, she thought. Jennifer's fear that Cassie would give it all away for free had apparently been groundless.

Lauren lifted her suitcase out of the trunk and walked up to the front door, feeling lighthearted. The front door key, she had been told, would be buried under a thin layer of dirt in a planter holding a silk palm tree. She scraped lightly around the base of the plant until she found the key in a slim plastic box. She turned it in the lock, unbolting the door. The room inside was bright, filled with light streaming in from the wall of sea-facing windows. It was a living room, a big open space with seating, a large screen TV and an entertainment center. Lauren was startled to hear the stereo playing a cool jazz instrumental. Was it possible Cassie had changed her mind and arrived here first to greet her?

Then, with a jolt, Lauren saw a young, naked woman standing at the entrance to a hallway on the other side of the living room. She was a brunette, slim, with a sleek and sexy body that made Lauren's mouth fall open. Her suitcase slipped from her grasp, hitting the floor with a hard *clunk*. She wouldn't have been surprised if Cassie had arranged a welcome gift for her, but she would have guessed a fruit basket or maybe a box of chocolates.

Lauren blinked hard, thinking she might be seeing things, but hallucinating naked women wasn't one of her usual eccentricities. When she opened her eyes, the woman was still there, grabbing a pillow from the sofa to cover herself. She appeared as shocked as Lauren was, so obviously she wasn't here to be her sex slave after all. Or, if she was, she was already playing out some fantasy of the shy, innocent girl encountering the experienced older woman who would seduce her ruthlessly and perhaps with one of those deep-toned evil laughs. *Bwaa-ha-ha!* she silently practiced. *Am I capable of that?*

Before she could consider her answer, she heard someone coming in from the right at a gallop. A young man, also completely naked, bounded into the room. Lauren stared, wide-eyed. It had been quite a while since she'd seen a naked man. This one was definitely intriguing in an art class kind of way. He had a full black mustache and thick dark eyebrows, luxurious black hair, deep-set eyes and a pale, nearly hairless chest. His genitals appeared fully functional.

His eyes were on the naked woman across the room. "Ah, there you are!" he called playfully.

As he started toward her, she pointed wordlessly at Lauren. He let out a short, high-pitched yelp that any gay man would be proud of, and covered himself with his hands.

With a series of sputters, he backed hurriedly out of the room. Lauren turned her attention back to the young woman, who crouched behind a recliner, presenting only her head and shoulders.

"Are you in the right house?" she asked tentatively.

"I hope so. I'm a friend of Cassie Burkett. She invited me."

At the mention of Cassie's name, the girl behind the chair nodded. "You know what? Let me just get dressed and then we can talk."

"Okay."

She smiled uncomfortably. "Can you turn around for a sec?"

"Oh, sure," Lauren said. "Sorry."

What an amusing turn of events, Lauren thought, smiling to herself. Now that she was alone, she examined the room more carefully: a modern, open floor plan, tastefully furnished with muted, complementary colors—gold, sage and light blue. A series of three photos on the far wall drew her over. They were all of the same boy, a ten or eleven year old version of the man she had just "met." She recognized his eyes and eyebrows. His expression, though smiling, was tentative in each of the photos, as though he felt awkward in front of a camera. Lauren could sympathize with that feeling. She hated having her picture taken. Her smiles, with rare, astonishing exceptions, all came out looking like someone was giving her a wedgie.

She walked into the kitchen, a bright, high-ceilinged space with white cabinets and black counters. There was an oval island in the center of the room and impressive, upscale appliances. Lauren ran a hand over the curve of a red Kitchen Aid mixer. She studied the gas range and its stove-top grill with envy. Whoever had designed this room had a fairly serious chef in mind. That wasn't Cassie. Though not helpless in the kitchen, she was not particularly inspired either. Not unless she had changed considerably since Lauren knew her. Opening a couple of lower-level cupboards, she discovered all of them had inserts that slid out on glides. A recycling tote in the corner contained several cans and bottles. These young people must have been here at least a couple of days.

Just then, the young man appeared in the doorway wearing khaki shorts, Teva sandals and a forest green T-shirt with a large gecko on the front. With clothes on, he looked strikingly handsome.

He held out his hand. "I'm Eric Hutchins."

"You're Cassie's son." She shook his hand.

"Right."

"I'm Lauren, a friend of your mother's. I'm sorry for intruding. I understood it would be just me here, at least until the weekend when your mother is scheduled to arrive."

"It's my fault. She doesn't know we're here." He leaned against the counter. "I have an open invitation to use this place, which I do now and then. It makes a great weekend destination because we can be up here in about seven hours."

"And the girl, that was your wife Adele?" Lauren laughed nervously. "I hope."

He smiled. "Yes, that was Adele. Sorry for the unconventional welcome."

"I sort of enjoyed it, actually."

He snorted lightly. "Have you been here before?"

"No."

"Then I'll show you around. And if you don't mind sharing the place tonight, we'll take off in the morning."

"You don't have to go. I feel badly about interrupting your... vacation."

"We can talk about that over dinner. We were just going to barbecue some chicken, if that would be okay. You're not a vegetarian, are you?"

"No. That would be great. But now I feel like I'm intruding."

"No way! You're the one with the invitation."

He smiled warmly, a smile that reminded Lauren of Cassie, the shape of her mouth and the dimples. That smile made her feel welcome, made her feel that Eric's friendly demeanor was sincere.

Once he had shown her around, she put her suitcase in the guest room and washed up in the adjoining bathroom. As she was putting her clothes in the closet, her phone rang. It was Cassie.

"You're there?" she announced, her voice full of excitement.

"I'm here! Wonderful place. Not quite the little cottage you described."

"I need to give you instructions. How to turn on the water heater, for instance. Where to find that special bottle of scotch."

"The water heater is on. Turns out your son and his wife are here."

"Oh. I had no idea. Sorry about that."

"It's okay. I was actually glad to meet them. They've offered to clear out, but I think I might ask them to stay until you arrive."

"Whatever you prefer. I thought you'd like a couple days alone to relax, maybe do some work."

"I have a lot of alone time these days, so I think I might opt for the company. Besides, a young, straight couple. What a novelty!"

Cassie laughed. "Okay, then. I'll see you on Saturday. I'm so excited. I can hardly believe you're there in my house."

"Me too. See you soon."

Lauren slipped on a sweater and joined Eric and Adele on the patio where the chicken was already on the grill and Adele was seated at a glass-topped table. She was dressed in a long-sleeved blouse, capris and flip-flops. Her long brown hair, which had been loose before, was now pulled back and restrained with a large clip. An open bottle of shiraz, a large and colorful salad, and a stack of three plates were there as well, but Adele's glass contained only water. Eric, who was tending the grill, had a glass of wine.

"The chicken smells wonderful," Lauren said, taking the chair next to Adele.

"Do you drink?" Adele asked.

"I wouldn't mind a glass of wine."

"Oh, good," Eric said cheerfully. "Somebody to drink with. Adele's pregnant, so none for her."

Lauren looked more carefully at Adele, recalling her svelte body from earlier, and concluded she was not very far along. She smiled, a little uncomfortably, it seemed. Did she guess Lauren was thinking about her naked?

Lauren poured herself some wine. "So Cassie's going to be a grandmother."

"Yes," Adele said. "In seven months."

"How exciting. Does she know?"

"No," Eric said, turning the chicken with tongs. "I don't think we've talked to her in a while, not since Christmas. Has it been that long, hon?"

"Not since Christmas, yes, I think that's right."

They had not gotten close, then, Lauren realized, with some misgiving for Cassie's sake. As an only child, Cassie had no siblings either, so her family was very much on the lean side.

"You can tell her on Saturday," Lauren suggested.

"If we stay." Eric shut the lid on the grill.

"I'd like you to. If your plans allow it. It's just two more days."

Eric turned a questioning look toward Adele who said, "I don't see why not. We can stay and see your mother. But I don't expect her to be all that interested in the idea of a baby."

"Why's that?" Lauren asked.

"She's just never been much for kids."

"Not even her own," Eric said matter-of-factly. He sat at the table and poured another glass of wine. "My mother didn't raise me. I lived with my father and stepmother."

"Yes, I knew that. But if she didn't like kids, why'd she become a high school English teacher?"

"She liked English," he said.

Adele looked at her stomach briefly, then said, "I can't even imagine giving up my child. I mean, not being there to watch him learn things and grow and turn into a human person."

"Some women don't have the powerful mother instinct you do," Eric said, taking her hand. "We both love kids. We're planning a big family."

It was interesting to hear someone other than Cassie talking about Cassie. Her version of this story was that she had given up her child for his sake, not because she didn't want to raise him or didn't have a maternal instinct.

"I work in a preschool," Adele said. "I should be able to keep that up until the baby is born and then I'm going to stay home for a while. At least a year."

"Sounds like the perfect arrangement," Lauren said. "Don't you also work with children, Eric?"

He nodded. "I'm a special investigator with Child Protective Services."

"You look into child abuse cases, that sort of thing? Take kids out of dangerous homes?"

"Well, we try to keep them in their homes. It's the best thing, to leave them with their parents and siblings. Then give the family counseling and whatever help they need to keep the family together. It's heartbreaking to see what some of these kids have been living with. Sometimes we have no choice but to remove them. But no one wants to take children from their parents."

"It's a powerful bond," Lauren observed. "The link between a parent and a child can survive a lot of injury."

"Yes, it can," he agreed wistfully. "I love my job, though, despite how hard it is to see what goes on in some homes."

"It's important work." Lauren wondered what part, if any, Eric's broken home had on his choice of career.

"So tell us about yourself," Adele suggested brightly.

Lauren fingered the stem of her wine glass. "I live in Portland. I'm a retired civil servant. Department of Agriculture."

"Retired," Eric said. "You don't look old enough."

"Actually, I retired early. I'm now working as a freelance writer. Travel articles. For lifestyle magazines and newspapers. You know, where to go for a romantic weekend getaway. That sort of thing."

"You could write an article about Cassie's beach house." Adele laughed at her joke.

Eric went to take the chicken off the grill. When Lauren tasted it, she was genuinely impressed.

"This is really good." She took another bite. "What did you put on this?"

"It's a dry rub," Eric said. "Cumin, garlic powder, lemon pepper, some thyme, and just a tiny bit of cayenne."

Lauren stopped eating to stare at Eric. "Nice. I'm surprised Cassie has such a well-stocked spice cupboard."

"Oh, she doesn't. I brought that with me. Mixed it up at home. I knew we'd be grilling quite a bit. When we're here in the summer like this, we eat outdoors a lot. Don't like to waste the view."

"Eric does almost all the cooking in our house," Adele said, smiling fondly at him. "He's so much better at it than I am. My mother can't get over how lucky I am to have found a man who likes to cook. She cooked all her life and hated every minute of it."

"She's jealous," Eric smiled that smile again that reminded Lauren of Cassie. He turned to her and asked, "How do you know my mother?"

"We met on a cruise on the Yangtze River."

"Her trip to China," Eric said, "that was years ago. She was with Jennifer then, right?"

"Yes. It was ten years ago, actually. Then last month I ran into her by chance in the Denver airport. It was such a surprise, after all that time. I found out she had this place, that she was within driving distance. We decided to meet here and catch up."

"So you haven't seen her in ten years?" Eric asked.

"Other than the few minutes in the airport, no. I'm really excited about seeing her again."

Adele stared, her expression one of delight and surprise. "Oh, my God," she blurted, "this is such a romantic story!"

Since Lauren's mouth was full of chicken, she shook her head and waved her fork before she was able to speak and say, "Oh, no, no, it's nothing like that. Cassie and I are just friends."

"Oh," Adele said, clearly disappointed.

"Sorry," Eric said. "We thought you were meeting her here for—" He stopped, looking embarrassed. "I thought you two were—"

"We think of this as the love shack." Adele giggled self-consciously.

Lauren didn't know what to say. So they had assumed she was here for an amorous rendezvous.

"I'm sorry, Lauren," Eric said. "We're being childish and stupid."

"Cassie and I are just friends," she repeated firmly, knowing it wasn't necessary. But it was something she had been telling herself too and she felt it needed to be reinforced for all of them.

Lauren had no intention of anything romantic developing between Cassie and herself. The feelings she'd had once were long gone. But she realized for the first time that she didn't really know anything about Cassie's feelings. She'd assumed Cassie too had moved past all of that and the two of them could finally have the friendship they should have had all along. Ten years, she thought, was surely long enough to erase one kiss.

# CHAPTER TWENTY-EIGHT

The following day, Eric and Adele went sightseeing and Lauren declined to go with them, preferring to spend the day at the beach house. She volunteered to cook dinner, eager to prepare a meal in Cassie's beautiful modern kitchen. After the young people left, she walked down to the beach, negotiating a weathered wooden staircase that let her out onto a narrow stretch of deep tan sand, deserted except for several white gulls riding sideways on the cold wind. She arbitrarily chose to walk south. In occasional calm lulls, the climbing sun spread a feeble warmth over her before the breeze kicked in again.

This wasn't a beach for tide pools or shell collecting. There were only tiny pieces of shells, smashed up by the grinding of the waves, and some glistening hanks of seaweed churned up and dropped by the tide. Far out on the horizon, a cargo ship glided slowly by, heading north. On the inland side was the eroding cliff, undercut by waves at high tide. Further back were homes, spaced far enough apart to give everyone the feeling of being someplace special, perched on a lonely finger of wind-ravaged headland, remote and Brontë-esque. *Brontë-esque*, Lauren repeated silently, with a private smile. She would try to remember to tell Cassie that.

Despite the impression, though, this place wasn't the least bit remote, as she was reminded when a woman came by walking her dog. Like Lauren, she was wrapped securely in a coat and scarf. She nodded as they passed one another.

It's too cold for a walk on the beach, she thought. That's why it was nearly deserted.

As she continued walking, she came upon a milky beige shell protruding from the sand. As she pulled it free, she saw that it was whole, a snail shell of some sort, three inches long, coiling into an elongated spiral tip. There wasn't even a nick around the fragile edge of the opening. It was perfect. How extraordinary, she thought. How did it manage to remain whole like this? It didn't seem possible considering the violent pounding of the surf. The living creature this had once been was long gone. Just the sanitized exoskeleton remained.

I've seen my share of skeletons, Lauren thought. Usually human. A skeleton always implied a living creature. It was the only tangible thing left of those once living. What was left after death that wasn't tangible? she asked herself. Was there anything?

She held the shell tight against her ear and listened for the sound of the waves. It was faint, but it was there. *It remembers the sea.* What's left when you're gone are the echoes of your life, the memories you leave with other people.

It was so hard to think of someone as dead when she was alive every day in your mind and in your heart. In your dreams at night, she spoke to you and kissed you just like she always had. The concept of death was so difficult to comprehend. That's why people have invented so many ways to deny it.

She slid the shell into her jacket pocket, still wondering how it had escaped destruction. Faith would have said, "There are cases that defy the odds. Some people would call them miracles.

Others would call it luck." There was no question which view Faith had subscribed to.

Too cold to continue any further, Lauren made her way back to the house.

Cassie's house was not what she had expected from a beach house near Coos Bay. She could see this was more suited to Cassie's style, though. She had pictured one of those intimate bungalows with three rooms and a trundle bed and knotty pine paneling and creaky floorboards. The kind of place you could decorate to look cute and cozy with quilts and deep-cushioned chairs and miniature lighthouses. This house was nothing like that. It was modern and bright with lots of white surfaces. The blond hardwood floors gleamed around tasteful earth-toned throw rugs. The art on the walls was simple and graceful, not kitschy or cutesy. There wasn't a lighthouse in sight. Lauren preferred this contemporary style. She felt comfortable in this house.

She inspected the CD collection by the stereo and found a lot of favorites, as she expected, knowing that Cassie's musical tastes resembled her own. What she didn't expect was the shelf of old records, a stack of inflexible disks she assumed were seventy-eights. She shuffled through them quickly, noting several songs by Nat King Cole, some Judy Garland, Vera Lynn and the song that had been their undoing ten years ago, "Fascination" by Jane Morgan. Lauren wondered if Cassie had ever listened to that song in the last ten years. She herself had not. Looking through the components of the audio rack, she didn't find a turntable. *Still nothing to play them on, Cassie?*

She settled on a Vivaldi CD for background music to accompany her work, and spent the next couple hours in the bright living room with her laptop, doing more gazing out the window at the sea than typing. It should have been the perfect setting for working, but Lauren was distracted, as she so often was these days. She had yet to find the peace of mind that led to sleeping through the night and focusing on a task for more than a few minutes at a time. But the ocean was beautiful to watch, especially from the warmth of the house, and it did leave her feeling calmer than usual.

As the afternoon grew late, she sorted through the raw materials in the refrigerator and pantry and settled on making a salad with some of the leftover grilled chicken. She stood in the kitchen  slicing a cucumber when Eric and Adele arrived, shattering the quiet mood of the day with their laughter, a welcome disruption.

Their meal was simple but satisfying, the salad and a bottle of sauvignon blanc they had picked up during their day's adventure. The three of them sat for a long time at the dinner table and ended up finishing the wine while Eric and Adele talked about their hike to a fire lookout.

After dinner Adele suggested they play a game. Looking through the choices in the hall closet, they settled on Yahtzee. Lauren felt a little odd having them spend their last evening playing a table game with a middle-aged woman, but they seemed agreeable and it wasn't like they had a houseful of kids to go home to. They could extend their romantic holiday at home if they chose.

Eric opened another bottle of wine, a syrah, and insisted Lauren taste it. "You'll like it," he said. "It was the best thing we tasted. Well, Adele barely tasted it. She had to spit."

So Lauren assented, but took only a small splash. "You're right. It's very good."

The three of them chatted amiably while they played. Lauren was enjoying herself with Eric and Adele. It wasn't just that they were young and optimistic, although that was part of it. It was also because they were interacting with just her and not something they knew about her. They weren't like friends and relatives who treated her like a person in mourning, who, whenever they saw her, were reminded that Faith had died. These two knew nothing of that. It felt good to just be Lauren and not Faith's widow.

"Did you see those old records?" Adele asked, gesturing toward the stereo.

"Yes. I believe those belonged to Cassie's grandmother."

"I'd like to hear them," Eric said. "Especially that one called 'Mairsy Dotes.' What's the deal with that?"

Lauren laughed. "There's no turntable. And I'm not entirely

sure a modern turntable would play them anyway. I've never seen records like that myself."

"How old are they?" Adele asked.

"Forties, fifties. I barely remember records at all. When I was young, we had cassette tapes. Now obsolete too." Lauren shook her head. "It's scary to think about how fast things are changing."

"Not just for you," Eric said, taking his turn with the dice. "Sometimes I think about what kind of world my kid's going to live in. He, or she, will probably never wear a watch or roll down a car window or buy a paper map or carry a wad of cash in his front pocket."

Lauren was reminded of something Faith had said during her illness, once they both understood she wasn't going to make it. "The thing that bothers me most is that I won't be around to see what crazy stuff people come up with next." Being an anthropologist, she had a keen interest in what stuff people came up with. But she would have felt that way whenever she had died, at whatever age, because people do just keep coming up with crazy stuff.

"Our son or daughter," Adele remarked, "will live in a world so different from ours, we can't even imagine it."

"Have you picked out names yet?" Lauren asked, taking the dice.

"No," she said. "Not really. We're still thinking about it."

"Kevin," Eric said firmly.

Adele shot him a warning look.

"If it's a boy," he clarified, his voice not entirely steady.

"I've told you I don't think that's a good idea," Adele said. "Besides, let's not talk about that now."

Apparently there was a lot more to this than a simple disagreement over a name, Lauren realized. Despite Adele's tone and threatening expression, Eric did not back down. Lauren suspected he was by now feeling the effects of more than half a bottle of wine.

"I don't know why you won't even consider it," he said.

"Yes, you do. We've talked about this."

They may not have forgotten her, but neither of them was

looking at Lauren. They were leaning into one another with the posture of people preparing for a fight. Very awkward, she thought, setting the dice down silently on the table in front of her.

"We could at least do that much," Eric insisted, his voice noticeably quavering now.

Adele jumped up from her chair, her expression severe. "I am not naming my son after your dead little brother and that's final!"

Staring up at his wife, Eric looked disconsolate. He got up and left the room. Adele glanced at Lauren in exasperation, then she followed him out.

Deciding she would have another glass of wine after all, Lauren poured it, then left the game table and sat in the living room by herself. She heard nothing from the master bedroom. She tried not to speculate what this was about, hoping someone would explain. If not tonight, then maybe Cassie would tell her when she arrived.

Adele eventually returned and sat beside her on the couch, smiling reassuringly. "He's watching TV in the bedroom," she said.

Lauren nodded.

"I don't know if you know anything about this," she said.

"No. I didn't know he had a brother."

"He didn't. I mean, the baby was never born. It was a miscarriage. There never really was a Kevin. That was just what Lucas, Eric's father, told him they were planning to name the baby."

"This baby—are we talking about Cassie or was this later?"

"Cassie. She was still married to Lucas. Eric was just over a year old when this happened. But it's sort of haunted him all his life, this little brother he never had. He had a hard time. He didn't make friends easily and he was very lonely as a child."

Lauren recalled Cassie saying Eric was a bookish boy, not into sports. "But he would have been too young to have remembered anything about this."

"Right. But his father told him about it. Lucas took it hard too. It was right after the miscarriage they got divorced. I don't know what part that played. I do know that Lucas blamed Cassie for losing the baby. The whole thing was apparently very sad and hurtful."

"Why did he blame Cassie?"

"Look, I know she's your friend and I don't want to say anything bad about her. And of course I didn't know her then."

"Neither did Eric," Lauren pointed out.

"You're right. Obviously, he's gotten this from his father. But that happens in divorces. There's a lot of resentment. It spills over onto the kids." Adele sighed. "The way I've heard it, it wasn't a friendly process. Lucas was still in love with Cassie. He didn't even want a divorce. She's the one who wanted out of the marriage. She had a—" Adele hesitated, looking uncomfortable.

"Girlfriend?" Lauren asked.

Adele nodded. "That was another reason it turned out so badly. Cassie was at a confusing place in her life when all of this went down. She was just starting to come out and it was hard on her and everybody else."

"It doesn't really make sense that Eric has this grief about this unborn baby. It isn't his grief. It's his father's."

"Right, but it's how he feels anyway. He feels like he lost a brother. Ever since I knew I was pregnant, he's been asking me if we could name our son Kevin. I didn't even know why at first. But I started asking questions because he was so insistent about it, and that's when I found out about this brother."

"Under the circumstances," Lauren said, "I can understand why you don't want to name your son Kevin."

Adele nodded and rolled her eyes. "Why would I want my son to be wrapped up in any way in this family mess? It's like some weird Greek tragedy. The son hates the mother because she killed his brother, emasculated his father, and fucked his babysitter."

Lauren swallowed hard, then, as Adele's eyes widened at her own indiscretion.

"Oh, I'm sorry!" she offered, leaning heavily on Lauren's arm. "I shouldn't have said that."

# CHAPTER TWENTY-NINE

In the morning, Lauren could hear Eric whistling cheerfully from the kitchen as she emerged from her shower. For him, perhaps, the evening's drama had been a catharsis.

"Waffle?" he asked when she approached the coffee pot in her bathrobe and slippers.

"Sounds great." She took her coffee and sat at the kitchen table in front of an empty plate.

"Adele's in the shower. She's already had breakfast."

"Sorry I'm so late. I didn't get to sleep until the wee hours."

"No problem." He slid a waffle onto her plate. "And I'm sorry I fell apart last night. Adele said she explained."

Lauren nodded, pouring a small pool of syrup on her waffle. "She did."

"Mother called. She'll be here around noon."

"Are we picking her up?"

"No. She's rented a car."

From his demeanor, Lauren surmised there would be no stabbings or beheadings or even tears, for which she was grateful.

"We're staying just long enough to say hello, then heading out. We have to take off right away to get home before dark."

While Adele and Eric packed, Lauren did the dishes and cleaned up the kitchen. By noon, they were all just waiting. Eric seemed happy about seeing his mother, which was hard to reconcile with what appeared to be a deep and painful anger. But that's how family relationships are, Lauren reminded herself, thinking of her own complicated relationship with almost everyone in her family.

When Cassie arrived, there were smiles and hugs all around. She was animated and clearly overjoyed to see her son. After the flurry of greetings, Eric carried in her luggage and the four of them sat in the living room, talking. Lauren hung back in the conversation because of Eric's upcoming departure. She and Cassie would have plenty of time to talk later. She asked Eric about his job and his new house and then asked Adele about her job. She seemed genuinely interested in their lives. As they talked, Lauren kept thinking about the scene from last night and about the deep-seated resentment Eric was keeping to himself. Did Cassie know about that?

"Anything else new with you two?" Cassie asked.

"We're going to have a baby?" Adele announced.

Cassie shrieked and leapt from her chair, throwing her arms around Adele. Then she stood in front of her, holding both her hands. "When?"

"Seven months."

"Congratulations! Lauren, did you hear?"

"Yes, Grandma Cassie."

The entire hour between Cassie's arrival and Eric's departure went much like this. There was laughter and lively conversation and then another round of hugs and kisses as the young people prepared to depart. There was no sign of tension. The mood was lighthearted and jocular. Lauren suspected this was normally how Cassie and her son interacted. No conflicts. No controversy. And no real communication.

As their car rolled down the driveway, Cassie turned to Lauren and sighed deeply, then held out her arms. Lauren went to her and accepted her warm embrace. Now that they were alone, the mood shifted to a calmer and more intimate tone.

"I like your son," Lauren told her. "He seems serious and thoughtful. He's very polite."

"He always has been. What about Adele?"

"I like her too. They're a delightful couple."

"Yes, they are. I think he's made a good choice."

Cassie stood staring at Lauren with a goofy smile on her face. "I'm so happy you're here. This is going to be so much fun."

The next hour was spent talking, and then they moved to the master bedroom where they stripped the bed and put on clean sheets.

"So I'm going to be a grandmother," Cassie said, snugging up the mattress pad.

"How do you feel about that?"

"Old." Cassie hooked the elastic corners of the bottom sheet into place.

"But, I mean, do you think you'll be involved? It sounds like you rarely see them."

"I don't see them much. Once a year, maybe. This was a rare treat. So, no, I doubt this child will even know he has two grandmothers."

"Does that make you sad?" Lauren snapped the last corner of the bottom sheet over the mattress.

"Sure. I'd love to see my son being a father. I've often wished I was more involved in Eric's life. But I made that choice way back when."

"When you gave custody to Lucas?"

"Right. Eric and I have never gotten to know one another that well."

"What was that all about, Cassie?" Lauren tossed the top sheet across the bed and they each took one side. "Giving up custody. You told me once you did it because it was best for Eric. Why would you think that?"

"I wasn't always so together as I am now, Lauren. At the time, I had a lot of problems." Cassie bent over to tuck the base of the sheet under the mattress, then stood up and looked serious. "I was a young married woman with a baby and I was having all these feelings for women. I fell in love with the babysitter, for Christ's sake. I was confused and scared and sometimes I just wanted to die."

Lauren felt like giving her a hug, but held her place, smoothing the sheet with her hand. "You had an affair with your babysitter?"

"No. I was in love with her. Well, I thought I was. She wasn't even a lesbian. She was just a stupid girl, same age as me. I never even touched her. Just fantasized about her. But Lucas was convinced there was more to it than that. He fired her. That sent me into a fury, which he took as proof she was my lover. I was so miserable after that. That's when I started getting high and then things really went downhill."

"You never told me any of this."

"No. I'm not proud of it. I screwed up." She tossed over a pillow and pillowcase. "It was a painful time in my life. I hurt people and I made bad decisions. It was all much worse because of the baby. I didn't even know I was pregnant. Not the first two months. As soon as I found out, I stopped the drugs, cold. I'll never really know if I lost the baby because of the drugs or if it would have happened anyway." Cassie sat on the edge of the bed, her shoulders slumped. "Lucas blamed me, and that was the main reason I gave up custody of Eric. At the time, it seemed like the right thing to do. He convinced me I was an unfit mother. After all, I had killed my unborn child."

This time Lauren wasn't able to hold back. She moved over to Cassie, sat beside her and put her arms around her.

Cassie patted her arm. "Lucas never forgave me for that."

"Eric never did either."

Cassie looked at Lauren, her eyes moist. "I know. Once when he was visiting me, when he was twelve, he threw a tantrum over something. I don't remember what. Something unimportant. But in the midst of his tirade, he screamed, 'You killed my brother, you killed my little brother Kevin.'" She forced a smile. "I had never even heard the name Kevin before. But later I found out it came from Lucas. He had chosen it for our second son."

After a moment, Lauren said, "Did you ever consider renegotiating the custody arrangement? Joint custody or something?"

"Honestly, Lauren, that was a big part of why I wanted to become a lawyer. I went to see one when Eric was eight. I told him I wanted to sue for joint custody. By then, I was a college graduate. I had a good job teaching high school. I had my shit together. I hadn't touched drugs of any kind for years. He told me to let it go. He said it would be difficult and messy and would harm my child."

"Why?"

"Because I was a lesbian. He said I'd probably lose my job too. With the facts coming out in court like they surely would, my students' parents would find out I was gay and who knew what trouble that would cause. He made it seem impossible and I really didn't want to bring any more chaos into Eric's life. So I let it go. I mean, he had a good life. He wasn't in danger or anything. But now I can see how different things could have been with the right lawyer. Maybe. It's hard to say. If Lucas had fought me, you know how they would have portrayed me in court."

"Like he apparently portrayed you in his home."

They sat there quietly side by side on the edge of the bed.

"Thanks for telling me about this," Lauren said at last.

"It's always been very easy to talk to you."

"You know I feel the same." Lauren squeezed her hand.

"There's one thing we never did talk about, though, isn't there?"

Lauren understood she was referring to the kiss.

"It's ironic," Cassie said. "Such a big thing. An important thing. We never talked about it. Not a word."

"I thought it was because we didn't need to."

Cassie nodded. "Maybe so."

"Or maybe we were afraid to talk about it," suggested Lauren.

"Afraid? Why?"

"Because sometimes a declaration of love grants permission."

Cassie tilted her head, her face a question. "Permission for what?"

"To act. If we had talked about it, we might have been unable to turn away from one another like we did. It was hard enough as it was."

"It was," Cassie agreed. "Very hard. Maybe harder for me than for you. I was getting more and more unhappy. More lonely. If you had given me the slightest opening...."

The look in Cassie's eyes troubled Lauren. She stood, turning away.

"Fortunately, we were both mature enough to know how to handle it," she said. "Disaster averted."

Lauren picked up the comforter and tossed it on the bed. Cassie slowly rose to her feet and helped put it in place.

Anxious to lighten the mood, Lauren said, "Oh, I have to tell you the hilarious story of my arrival here the other day. You're going to crack up at this."

Lauren proceeded to tell how she had caught Eric and Adele *au naturel*, embellishing the tale with a storyteller's flair. It had the desired effect. They both ended up laughing themselves to tears.

# CHAPTER THIRTY

"Are you seeing anyone?" Cassie asked as they strolled along the bluff trail.

Lauren laughed as though it was an absurd idea, then realized that was rude. "No," she said.

"Not interested?"

"Right. Nobody interested in me either."

"I doubt that."

"Depends on who you count. There's Jaspar Henshaw, my neighbor. He's a widower, sixty-eight, has gout and wears his pants up to his tits. He makes lewd comments to me regularly and I suppose he would have me if I were interested." Cassie sputtered out a laugh. "And there's that cute postal carrier, Michelle. Now that she knows I'm home most days, she makes a gazillion excuses to come up to the door to personally deliver my mail. 'Looks valuable,' or 'too big and I didn't want to leave it on the porch,' or 'looks like a greeting card and I didn't want the humidity to warp it.'"

"Michelle, huh? Not a prospect?"

Lauren shook her head. "No. She's twenty years old. It's a crush. Lately I've taken to hiding in the back of the house when I see the mail truck coming."

"But if you were putting yourself out there, looking for someone, you would find someone appropriate."

"I'm not, though, because I'm not looking for someone. I have no interest in dating. The whole idea of it seems so unappealing. I'm content to be alone now."

"Sounds like you know what you want." Cassie studied her face briefly, then turned her attention back to the trail.

Lauren walked with her hands in her jacket pockets. It was chilly again today, even though the sun was shining and there wasn't a cloud to be seen anywhere. The trail followed close to the edge of the cliff. Some of it had crumbled away with the natural erosion of waves cutting into the base of the sandstone wall. The trail had been rerouted further inland in the worst of those places.

"Do you walk out here often when you're in residence?" Lauren asked.

"In residence? You make it sound like Queen Elizabeth at Windsor or something. I should put up a flag to let the commoners round about know that I'm here, shouldn't I?" Cassie's nose was red from the cold. "Yes, I do walk here quite a bit. Clears my head. After two or three days, I usually manage to achieve a sense of peace I never feel back home."

Cassie led the way off the trail to a rocky outcrop. They climbed to the top and sat close together with a view out to the ocean, waves crashing on bare rock fifty feet below.

"This is a good turnaround point," she said.

As they sat watching a brown pelican riding the air currents, Lauren had to ask herself how this was different from ten years earlier when she had sat beside Cassie watching the surf of this ocean. They were older, of course, and, if not wiser, then at least less confident about their power over the world. She didn't know about Cassie, but her own sense of helplessness and confusion had grown with time, especially in the last few years. Cassie didn't seem to have changed much. Lauren felt as comfortable with her now as she had then. It almost seemed as if no time had passed at all. They had slipped effortlessly into their old affectionate friendship. It was a nice feeling.

One thing that had changed, however, was that Lauren no longer felt any physical desire for Cassie. Back then, she'd found it impossible to fight off that hunger. But now it was completely absent. Maybe ten years really had been enough to erase that. Lauren felt relieved. In the absence of desire, they were such wonderful companions.

"You'd never know it was summer," Lauren observed.

"Not today. But you can't tell the seasons here by the temperature. We have warm and cold days year round. Maybe it will warm up tomorrow. I hope so. So tell me about this article you're researching. Where are we going while you're here?"

"I've got a list. We can get started tomorrow. There's an olive farm near Port Orford. The olive press is open for tours. Then there's a dairy on Highway 42 where they make small batches of brie and camembert that can only be purchased on site. And a Russian bakery in Reedsport where they reportedly have very authentic piroshkies, not to mention some unbelievable Russian rye."

Cassie laughed. "Just food, then!"

"Right. That's what my article is about, eating and drinking your way along the Oregon Coast."

"I have to say I like that idea. This is going to be fun!"

"I'm glad you think so. I know it'll be more fun for me having you along."

They watched the brown pelican again as it dove into the surf and came up empty. Returning to her earlier thoughts, Lauren asked, "Do you think I've changed?"

Cassie pursed her lips and squinted as though trying to decide. "Yes and no. You have a few gray hairs."

"You know that's not what I mean."

Cassie laughed shortly. "Yes, I know. You seem the same in a lot of ways. And different in the ways one would expect. You seem sad. Not moping. Not that kind of sad. But fundamentally sad. That's no surprise, though, after what you've been through."

"Anything else?" Lauren asked, sensing that Cassie had more to say.

"You seem less free. Less open. Like a turtle pulled into its shell. Not willing to stick your neck out. It's very subtle. Not a complaint at all. But I sense it. You don't seem to have aged much in obvious ways, but your soul seems older."

Lauren laughed shortly.

"Why did you laugh?" Cassie asked.

"Oh, it's just that word. 'Soul.' Faith and I had so many discussions over that word, over so many people's version of that thing we call the soul. She didn't believe in it, as you know. I've never had the conviction about anything that she had, and certainly not about something like that, something that seems completely unknowable."

"But you know what I mean by it, don't you?"

"Sure. I know what you mean. You mean the life force."

Cassie nodded. "Okay. I can accept that. That part of you was more adventurous when we knew one another before. Your life force."

"I'm sure that's true because Faith was the adventurous one, you know. If I was like that at all, it was because of her."

"No, I don't buy that. It was you. I knew you. You had a happy and fun-loving spirit. Her personality overshadowed yours, but that's not what we're talking about. It's still there, I'm sure, your joyful spirit. Just like a turtle. Not quite ready to poke out and take a look yet. Given time, though, I'm sure you'll resemble yourself again."

Lauren shrugged, not convinced. She knew she was still in mourning. "Maybe so."

Cassie smiled affectionately, then her expression grew serious. "I still can't believe Faith is gone," she said, turning to look at the ocean. "Was it really awful at the end?"

"It was awful in some ways. The hardest thing was to remain cheerful. I had to do that for her. Keep living in the moment, but it isn't my nature. I was always either reliving some past event or worrying about the future. Mostly, I was thinking about what the future would be like for me when I was alone. Some days I couldn't help feeling like she was already gone. So it was a real challenge not to completely fall apart around her. I didn't always succeed."

"But she must have known you were feeling that way a lot of the time anyway."

"Sure, she did. I think she was trying to be cheerful for me too. She was so worried about me, it sometimes seemed I was the one who was sick."

Cassie took hold of Lauren's hand and held it in both of hers. "She thought you wouldn't be able to go on?"

"She thought I would withdraw from life. She said, 'I don't want you to die with me. I want you to live for me. Do everything. Laugh and love and eat lots of lobster.'"

Cassie laughed. "Did she really say that?"

Lauren smiled. "Yes, she did."

"So, have you been eating lobster?"

"No, I don't think I've had any since...in a long time."

"Why not?"

"Well," Lauren pointed out, aiming for light-heartedness, "the thing about lobster is that they don't just wander into your kitchen routinely. You have to make a conscious effort to seek them out. I just haven't done that."

Cassie smiled appreciatively and nodded.

"But we had fun too," Lauren said. "It wasn't all gloomy. When her hair started growing back, it came in coarse and more gray than before, so I dyed it bright red and spiked it up for her. She loved that. And I thought she looked totally hot with that hairdo."

Cassie laughed. "I'll bet!"

"Every day we had together was another chance to share something nice. We did try to stay in the moment, and there were a lot of good days during that last year."

"Make every day count," Cassie said, echoing a thought she'd heard a long time ago.

"Right. We tried."

Lauren gazed at Cassie for a moment, thinking about how simple it was to talk to her. There was no one else she could be this open with. The closest was her brother, but their conversations never got this serious. Lots of people offered. *If you want to talk, Lauren, don't hesitate to call.* But she hadn't, wouldn't seriously consider it. Exactly the opposite, in fact. When people tried to talk to her about Faith, especially about her feelings, she changed the subject as quickly as she could without seeming rude. She'd thought she had no need to talk. What practical purpose could be served by talking? But at the moment she felt a great sense of relief to be doing just that.

"It sounds like she was very brave," Cassie noted.

"She was. She never felt sorry for herself. Just the luck of the draw, she said. And she didn't convert or anything at the end like people do sometimes. They start believing in heaven or reincarnation or something because they can't face the idea of nothingness. People would rather believe in hell than in nothing. But she didn't waver. That impressed me because she had a lot of stories to choose from, so many different versions of the great beyond, you know, that she might have latched onto for comfort. Some of them aren't all that objectionable, even to a scientist like Faith. But she was okay with the idea of nothingness."

"That seems ironic to me, that she didn't believe in some version of the hereafter, considering her work. You'd think something would have rubbed off on her."

"Maybe there were too many versions. So many different stories make it hard to believe in any one of them. Pretty soon they're all just stories." Lauren looked around for the pelican, spotting it as it prepared for another dive. "I sometimes wonder if all of it wasn't some sort of search."

"Search for what?"

"Something to believe in." Lauren shook her head. "If it was, she never found it. She was completely certain there was nothing else."

Cassie faced Lauren, her expression solemn. "What do *you* think?"

Lauren considered the question briefly, then said, "I hope she was wrong."

# CHAPTER THIRTY-ONE

Olive oil tasting is not as much fun as wine tasting, Lauren knew, so she promised Cassie a stop at a winery later. But Cassie wasn't complaining. Quite the opposite. She was making herself useful by serving as photographer, leaving Lauren free to concentrate on taking notes. They toured the olive orchard and presses, then spent half an hour in the olive oil tasting room. The different oils, several hues of green and gold, were served in shallow bowls.

Cassie laughed as she read the cards beside each oil. "Oh, my God, this sounds just like wine. Listen to this. 'High fruitiness, peppery, hint of citrus, clean finish.'"

"Believe it or not, the serious tasters do drink it from a glass just like wine. They sniff, swirl, and swallow."

"I'd like to see that," Cassie said, her eyes twinkling with delight. "I'm sure it's hilarious. Really, Lauren, I can't believe people do this, like a day out in the country. I mean, it's interesting and kind of a hoot, but who are all these people?"

She had lowered her voice to a whisper, jerking her head toward the other tasters gathered around their bread cubes and saucers.

"Foodies," Lauren answered. "We're a strange bunch, but we're growing in numbers. There are foodie tours all over the world nowadays."

"I remember you always wanted to go to Tuscany. Even I know food and Tuscany go together. Do you think that's where you'll want to go next?"

"Oh, I don't know. I haven't thought much about traveling." Lauren dipped a piece of bread into a murky, greenish oil. "It wouldn't be the same without Faith."

"No, it wouldn't be the same. But it would still be fun. You love to travel. You don't want to give it up."

Lauren stared momentarily into Cassie's encouraging face. This wasn't the time for a discussion of all the things she no longer felt any desire to do.

As they left the olive orchard, Cassie asked, "Now we go to the winery?"

"Not just yet. One more stop."

She unlocked her car doors with a chirp from the remote. "What is it this time? Fruit, nuts or berries?"

"Flowers. It's an organic flower farm." Lauren slid into the passenger seat.

"Sounds lovely, but I thought you were writing about food and drink spots only."

"I am. Edible flowers."

Cassie looked startled, then seemed to comprehend. "Oh, like sunflowers. Sunflower seeds."

"No. Like violets and roses and nasturtiums. Oh, you'll love it. They've got a little deli on site where they serve gorgeous salads. And desserts too, if you prefer, decorated with brilliant little pansies."

Cassie sat behind the wheel and stared for a moment. "I bet it was really hard for you to find ways to combine your research with Faith's. I mean, how did you manage to integrate artisan chocolates, for instance, with mummies?"

Lauren laughed shortly. "Believe it or not, it wasn't that difficult most of the time. Of course, the mummies and chocolates did require two different stops."

"Hey," Cassie suggested, "you could write a book about the best places to grab a bite whenever you're out raiding a tomb or digging up graves."

Lauren laughed.

"Limited audience, I suppose," Cassie continued. "Archaeologists, mainly. Anthropologists too, and the odd black market treasure hunter."

"And grave robbers and mad scientists," Lauren added. "Don't forget them."

"Yes! An unusual audience for a restaurant guide, I admit, but at least you'd be branching out from the West Coast foodie crowd. It's always a good idea to broaden your appeal." Cassie's grin relaxed into a warm smile. "Nice to hear you laugh," she said.

It was nearly dark when they arrived back at the beach house with their purchases, including a blossom-studded salad of baby lettuces, roasted yellow beets and chèvre. They sat at the kitchen table and popped open the plastic boxes. Cassie handed Lauren a fork and then sat staring at her salad for a minute without touching it.

"What's the matter?" Lauren asked.

"I don't know whether to eat it or put it in a frame and hang it on the wall."

"You haven't eaten since noon, so I'd say eating it would be preferable."

Cassie tasted a beet. "Now that's good. I've never had yellow beets before. I like them. Very earthy. I have to say, Lauren, a day with you is a day full of adventure."

"I'm glad to hear you say that. Faith always said each day should have something unexpected in it, to keep you interested."

"Well, today had several unexpected things in it, at least for me." Cassie dug into her salad with enthusiasm.

For me, too, Lauren thought, marveling over the day, at how much she'd enjoyed it. She'd had fun. More than expected.

She'd laughed a lot, just like she had ten years ago when Cassie had come for her spring visit. After ten years, she would have expected something to be different. She felt different, like a different person altogether sometimes, from that young woman who hadn't yet known the sting of life's indifferent brutality. She would have said, if anyone had asked, that that woman, with her happy, innocent heart, no longer existed. That was why she'd been surprised today at the sound of her own frequent laughter, at the effortless lightness of it.

"Cassie," Lauren said, "there's something I'd like to ask your opinion about."

"Sure. You can ask me anything."

"It's something I'd like you to read, actually."

"Oh, one of your articles? You want a critique?"

"No. More personal than that. It's a letter Faith wrote to someone before she died. She wrote letters to dozens of people. Telling them she was thankful for them. Saying goodbye. This particular letter was returned. The address was no good. I kept it for a couple of months after she died, intending to find the correct address and resend it."

"But?" Cassie prompted.

"But I opened it and read it instead." Cassie raised her eyebrows. "I know I shouldn't have done that. But at the time I was torn up pretty badly. Well, anyway, that's what I did. And it was disturbing what Faith wrote to this woman."

"Who was she?" Cassie looked concerned, then alarmed. "Did they have an affair? Did Faith cheat on you?"

"No. Not exactly. I mean, they didn't have a physical relationship, but— But it upset me anyway. This woman, her name is Emma, she was a student of Faith's, years ago. She was in love with Faith."

Cassie sputtered and waved her hand dismissively. "That happens all the time with students. No big deal."

"Yes, I know. It did happen. I mean, it happened several times. But this was different. Well, you can see that from the letter."

Lauren retrieved the letter and put it on the table in front of Cassie. She then sat across from her, folding her hands together to stop them from fidgeting, going through the letter's contents in her mind as Cassie read.

When she was done, she folded the pages and slid them back into the envelope, then looked up. "I don't really know why this bothers you. It sounds like Faith did the right thing."

"But she had serious feelings for Emma. She never even told me about her. It feels like she lied to me. Or at least kept something important from me."

Cassie breathed deeply, then said, "Lauren, the relationship with complete honesty doesn't exist. Everyone keeps something to herself. We do it to protect something. Ourselves or our lovers or our relationship. It doesn't mean she loved you less. It doesn't mean she regretted anything. Look what she said about you in this letter. She adored you. She loved her life with you."

"Then why did she fall in love with Emma?"

"You make it sound like she cheated on you."

"It feels sort of like that," said Lauren, feeling distressed. "That's how I felt over you, after all. I felt I'd been unfaithful, not even because we kissed, but because of the feelings I had. I had feelings for you I wasn't supposed to have. Even now, I don't understand why that happened. In so many ways, the emotions are more important, more powerful, than any act."

"I suppose that's true."

"I always thought I was 'the one' for Faith, you know, the person she was meant for. That there was no room in her heart for anyone else."

Cassie shook her head. "People come into your life, Lauren, people who have something to offer you. It just happens. What matters is how you handle it. Faith was faithful to you. And you were faithful to her. You chose to stay with one another. That's all that really matters."

Lauren took a deep breath, not feeling particularly comforted by Cassie's words.

Cassie stood, stepped over to her and put a hand on her shoulder. "You don't really believe in 'the one,' do you? That there's only one person for each of us?"

"I always did believe it. That's one of the reasons I was able to stop myself from wanting you. I thought Faith and I were meant for each other, that nobody else could possibly ever mean as much to me."

"Do you still believe that?"

"I still think it's true for me."

Cassie took her hand from Lauren's shoulder and turned away briefly, then said, "Lauren, the human heart isn't like a pie you slice up and give away till it's gone. It's unlimited in its capacity to love. It's infinitely renewable. Faith loved you. Maybe she also loved Emma. But she never did anything to suggest she wasn't happy with you and didn't want to be with you. There's nothing in that letter to give you any reason to think so. It's no wonder Faith kept it to herself."

"I guess that's the part that really hurts, that she didn't ever tell me. She didn't feel she could talk about it."

"She was trying to protect you, to keep from shattering your idealistic concept of what it means to love." Cassie knelt in front of Lauren and took hold of her hands. "You're a very lucky woman to have been loved as well as that woman loved you."

Lauren nodded weakly, feeling chastened. Cassie stood, releasing her hands.

"What are you going to do with that letter?" she asked.

"I don't know."

"It belongs to Emma. You should send it to her. Do you need help finding her address? Shouldn't be too hard. Lawyers can find anybody, unless they're really good at hiding."

"I don't need help finding her. She was over at the house the other day."

"Oh?" Cassie sat back in her chair. "Why's that?"

"She wanted to look at some of Faith's research. She called me. It was quite a surprise."

"And you didn't give her the letter?"

Lauren shook her head. "She doesn't know anything about it. She doesn't even know Faith... cared for her."

"And you don't want her to know?"

Lauren, feeling sheepish, nodded and stared at the table. "I know it's petty, but I feel like Faith's last 'I love you' would be going to another woman. That should be mine."

Cassie gazed sympathetically across the table, but said nothing.

# CHAPTER THIRTY-TWO

For the next two days, Cassie and Lauren knocked off the food tourist sites, visiting the places Lauren had scoped out and a few they happened across on their travels, like the U-pick berry farm where they'd spent an hour filling a bucket with blueberries. Cassie's mouth, stained purple, explained why her contribution to the bucket was so meager. After these adventures, they returned to the house each evening to assemble their purchases—fruit, nuts, bread, cheese—into a conglomerate dinner of some kind, usually a salad or sandwich.

On Thursday, it was Cassie's turn to plan their outing. They packed a lunch and walked south on the bluff trail under a clear blue sky. It had warmed considerably since Lauren's first day and they were both wearing shorts and T-shirts. After a mile walking parallel to the shoreline, they followed the trail as it dipped down to sea level through a ravine that cradled an ocean-going stream.

"We go inland here," Cassie said. "We'll follow the creek."

She led the way through dense brush and tree cover on a narrow dirt path. They were in shade now and it wasn't long before the sound of the crashing waves on shore had faded away. There was no noise other than their steps on the ground and the trickling of water in the stream to their right. Cassie paused to point out tiny wildflowers on occasion and once she stopped quite suddenly and held a hand out behind her. She pointed to the opposite bank of the stream where a doe and fawn stood in a sunny clearing. The doe was watching them with black eyes, her ears twitching. They waited, unmoving, for a couple of minutes until the deer walked gracefully into the brush.

"Have you been on this trail a lot?" Lauren asked as they continued.

"Three or four times. Any day now there'll be some ripe blackberries along here."

"Doesn't anybody else know about this trail? We haven't seen a single person."

"It's not a developed or maintained trail. Nobody but the locals come here. They'll be out here on the weekend, but it looks like we have it to ourselves today. How come you haven't asked me where we're going?"

Lauren shrugged. "I just figured we were going on a hike. Is there a destination?"

"You'll see."

Most of this trail was shaded, for which Lauren was grateful. As the sun climbed higher, the day got hotter, and the uphill climb left her with perspiration on the back of her neck. But it felt good to be out in the woods. She hadn't been on a hike for a long time. It reminded her of some wonderful adventures from the past.

The creek they followed had grown slightly larger and proportionately noisier. They stopped after a particularly rough climb to sit on a log and drink some water. Lauren tipped the water bottle up and chugged it, then handed it to Cassie, who had a goofy smile on her face.

"You look really beautiful this morning," she said, taking the bottle.

Lauren laughed. "You like your girls sweaty?"

"It's just the rosy glow. Lots of life in you today." She took a drink from the bottle, then returned it to her pack. "Not much further."

They walked along a fairly level path about fifty feet above the stream. Lauren began to hear a rush of water that grew louder as they continued. Suddenly, as they turned a bend, a waterfall came into view, a good forty or fifty feet tall, falling over a sheer cliff straight down in one thin, filmy tier to an emerald green pool below. The pool was wide and placid. At the lower edge, it spilled steadily into the shallow stream they'd been following.

Lauren gasped at the sight. "It's gorgeous!"

Cassie smiled, then turned onto a steep spur trail that descended to the edge of the pool. It was a small private slice of paradise with the sun directly overhead, glinting on the calm surface of green water and turning the waterfall spray into showers of sparkling crystals.

Cassie removed her pack and sat on a rock next to the pool. "Like it?"

"Perfect." Lauren sat on her own rock and took a drink of water from her bottle while Cassie unpacked their lunch. Out came the spoils of their recent junkets—a hunk of chewy sourdough bread, a wedge of gouda and a thermos of merlot.

"'A jug of wine,'" Cassie quoted, "'a loaf of bread and thou, beside me singing in the wilderness.'"

Lauren laughed. "How classic!"

"I do love the classics. You can't beat them, really."

They tore the bread, broke the cheese and passed the thermos of wine back and forth in an informal fashion ideal for the setting. Sitting beside the waterfall with Cassie and the rustic meal, Lauren felt calm and contented.

"I love it that you can appreciate this sort of thing," Cassie said. "I mean, a day like this and a lunch like this. And at the same time, you seem equally at home in a fancy restaurant with three forks."

"Truth be told," Lauren said, pulling a chunk of bread from

the loaf, "I think I like this best."

Cassie nodded. "Me too. Sometimes. You know, Jennifer would have never done this."

"Really? What part?"

"Any of it. She didn't like the outdoors. Too dirty and buggy for her. I think that hike in China was the last time she went for a walk that wasn't on a treadmill. She had a very limited idea of what was fun."

When Lauren had swallowed the bread, she asked, "What was it that attracted you to her in the first place?"

"Oh, you know, the usual thing."

"No, what do you mean? What's the usual thing?"

"Sex, of course."

Lauren laughed. "Oh, come on!"

"No, I'm serious. Well, you know. It was the typical lesbian thing. We met, went out, had sex, and the next thing you know, we're living together."

"How much time did all of that take?"

"Two weeks."

"Oh, one of *those* things."

"Yeah, one of *those* things. It's my belief that if two women go on a first date, they should be prepared to spend the rest of their lives together."

Lauren nodded. "You're right."

"By the time I got to know her, we'd been living together for months. We were in a committed relationship. And it had been going along pretty well, actually. Like I said, sex."

"All that sex in the beginning, it forms a powerful bond, doesn't it?"

She nodded. "But by the time we broke up, we hadn't had sex for a year. Well, I hadn't. Turns out she was sleeping with one of the other EMTs. Ambulances were one of their favorite places."

"Well, sure."

"I don't have any hard feelings toward Jen, though. We never should have been together. Not like you and Faith. You just worked so well."

"It was just luck, though. We started out the same way. Met, went out on a couple of dates, had sex."

"You do luck out sometimes," Cassie agreed. "But it's better not to leave it to luck. Better to be friends first, if you can. Take some time to see if you like someone, develop an affection based on something other than lust."

"The classic recipe for romance."

"Yes. The classics again."

Together, they both said, "You can't beat them," then laughed.

As they finished up, Cassie handed Lauren the thermos. "There's just a drop left there for you."

Cassie suddenly jumped up from her rock and ran across the trail and into the trees. "Something else to show you!" she yelled back.

Lauren drained the thermos and got to her feet as a large tire came swinging by and out over the green pool. She looked up along the length of the rope to see a huge tree branch above. The tire, which appeared to be pick-up size, went across the pool, just inches above the water, and then came back. Cassie ran over and grabbed it as it came by and nearly got pulled off her feet in the process.

"A tire swing!" she exclaimed, her eyes laughing.

"Oh, no," Lauren said. "You're not really suggesting—"

"Come on, Lauren. It's safe. All the kids do it." She peered through the center of the tire, a mischievous look in her eyes.

"We're not kids."

"You'll love it. When's the last time you swung on a tire swing?"

"I've never swung on a tire swing."

"You're kidding! Well, then, you have to do it. Please." Then, very deliberately, she said, "Do everything."

Lauren nodded tentatively, then examined the rope and the sturdy looking branch above. "Okay."

She climbed on the rock she'd been sitting on earlier and tucked herself into the tire, hanging on with both hands to the rope. Cassie held the tire steady until Lauren was ready. Then she pulled it away from the rock. As Lauren's feet left the earth, she felt slightly panicked and held on tighter. Then Cassie let go and Lauren went sailing over the pond, her toes skimming through the surface of the water.

A spontaneous scream of delight came out of her as the tire rose up on the other side and then rapidly came back down. When she passed by again, Cassie pushed and the tire went even higher this time.

My God, Lauren thought, I'm a forty-seven year old woman in a tire swing! Hooray for me!

After a few such exhilarating passes over the pool, she asked Cassie to stop pushing, and the tire gradually reduced its arc and came to a stop. Cassie pulled it over to the rock so she could climb out.

"Did you love it?" Cassie asked.

Lauren nodded. "I did!"

"I knew I could get you to do it if I quoted Faith at you."

"You're a sneaky bitch!"

Cassie laughed gleefully, then climbed into the tire herself and took her turn. Once they had secured the tire back in its tree, they put on their packs and hiked back out. What a magnificent day, Lauren thought. Just like the last few, all of them so fun and carefree, these days with Cassie. She was full of joy and vitality and it spilled over to encompass Lauren, making her feel renewed.

Once they reached the beach, Cassie took hold of her hand and they walked side by side back to the house.

# CHAPTER THIRTY-THREE

They sat next to one another on the front porch on a wide, welcoming, outdoor sofa, drinking expensive single-malt scotch and watching the sun set on the waves. Lauren's mind was emptier than it had been in a long time, which felt thoroughly comfortable. The day had left her tired but peaceful.

For minutes, they had been sitting without speaking, watching the glow of daylight fade from orange to red to purple. The sound of the surf was almost out of reach tonight, just a gentle whisper. A cool breeze came skipping up to the bluff and wafted over them. They were both wearing heavy sweaters, sweatpants and socks. Between the clothes and the scotch, there was plenty of warmth.

"That triple cream brie was over the top," Cassie said. "Completely over the top."

"Good as ice cream, wasn't it?"

"Hell, it was as good as sex."

Lauren smiled. After their long day in the woods, they had ended up snacking for dinner—crackers and brie and some peaches picked up at a fruit stand the day before.

"Your readers," Cassie observed, "those foodies, they're living a luxurious lifestyle."

"Yes, they are. They're privileged people and, for the most part, they know it. Sort of like us."

"True. I feel very lucky." Cassie poured more scotch into her glass. "This scotch isn't half bad either."

"Smooth as triple-cream brie," Lauren said, holding out her glass for a refill.

"This was a housewarming gift. It's been here since I bought the place, waiting for a special occasion." Cassie smiled warmly in the dwindling light.

Lauren felt happy, she realized, then wondered if it was the scotch or the company or the ocean or the cool night air that was responsible. This particular type of happiness, a background feeling like soft music, hadn't come her way in quite a while. But it was familiar from a long time ago and it was the type of happiness she valued most. It was the sort you didn't notice too much, but when you did stop to notice it, it filled you with a deep sense of gratitude.

Cassie folded her hand around Lauren's where it lay on the cushion between them. The glow on the western horizon was darkening. The sky was beginning to pop with stars, just a couple at first, but then they appeared by the dozens. Hundreds.

"How many years till you retire and move here?" Lauren asked.

"Too many. I love it here. I don't want to wait fifteen more years to live here."

"Fifteen? So you want to retire at sixty?"

"That's what I've always planned on. But lately I've been thinking of an alternate plan. I've been wondering if I could practice law here. I wouldn't make the kind of money I can in Albuquerque and I wouldn't be able to specialize, especially not in gay family law. But maybe I could make enough to live on."

"If you really like it here, it'd be worth a try. People need lawyers everywhere. Unfortunately."

The light from inside the house was just enough that Lauren could see Cassie's serene expression. She pulled Lauren's hand to her lips and kissed it, then released it and leaned forward to set her glass on the table. The spot where Cassie's lips had touched her palm tingled. She was feeling hot and fluid inside and slightly light-headed. Enough scotch, she decided.

"I do love it here," Cassie said. "But I didn't really want to come here alone. I figured somewhere between buying this place and retiring, I'd find someone to share it with."

"I'm sure you will." Lauren was worried by the somber expression on Cassie's face.

"I feel like I've already found her," Cassie said quietly. "Found her again."

The way she was looking, so purposefully, Lauren knew what she meant. There was love and longing in her eyes, much more pointed tonight than the minor glimpses of it Lauren had been ignoring up to now. That look transported her ten years back in time to an evening when she'd made a huge, devastating mistake. Cassie leaned closer and reached one hand to Lauren's face, caressing her cheek. Alarmed, Lauren put her hand against Cassie's shoulder to stop her advance.

"What are you doing?" she asked, fear welling up in her.

"I thought—" Cassie's voice was uncertain. "We've been having such a good time these last few days. Being here with you, it's all come back to me. My feelings for you are as strong, stronger even, than they were then. Lauren, I love you."

Lauren sprang up from the sofa. "No! That's not what I want. What I need now and what I needed then is a friend. How could you even think—. You know what a huge disaster that was."

Cassie stood, reached for Lauren and folded her securely in her arms. "Lauren, don't turn away from me now, not after all the years I've spent wondering what we could have had if things had been different. What we could have now. Don't you see? The gods are smiling on us."

Lauren pushed her away. "You mean they killed Faith so you and I could be together?"

"No, that's not what I meant at all. Lauren, please—"

Lauren fled into the house and to her room, shutting the door. Then she lay on the bed and sobbed silently.

Part of her wanted to sink into Cassie's arms and let her take her away, away from her life, away from herself, away from pain, at least temporarily. But another part of her, by no means a small part, wanted none of that, not with Cassie, not with anyone.

To love again seemed impossible and pointless. She'd become accustomed to think that part of her life was over. That part of her was dead. She'd already had her happily ever after.

# CHAPTER THIRTY-FOUR

"Just coffee," Lauren said when Cassie asked if she wanted breakfast.

Cassie spread butter on a toasted bagel. She looked tired and Lauren wondered if she had slept. Lauren sat at the kitchen table and accepted the mug of coffee, taking a tentative sip to test its heat. Cassie brought her bagel to the table and sat across from her.

"We should talk," she said pointedly.

"All right."

"I've had such a good time with you this last week."

"So have I," Lauren said earnestly. "It's been really fun."

"We have so much to offer one another. From the day we met, I felt so close to you. I don't understand why you're saying no...to us."

Lauren met her direct gaze and said, "I just don't want that. You're very special to me, Cassie. I love you dearly and I was so grateful to think I could have you back in my life. As a friend. Sometimes you need a friend more than a lover. I wasn't looking for a lover ten years ago either. We totally screwed that up then and I didn't want it to happen again, not now that we've been given a second chance."

"But everything's different now, Lauren. I know you have feelings for me. You always have. You can't tell me otherwise. I feel like I know you as well as I know myself. And now there's nobody to hurt. You're right. We've been given a second chance."

"At friendship," Lauren insisted.

"No." Cassie shook her head. "That was never a possibility for us. It wasn't then and it isn't now. I can't be just friends with you. You should know that. We tried that once and we failed. This last week, there've been so many times I've felt like taking you in my arms and kissing you. It seems like the most natural thing in the world to me. I thought you were feeling that too. I mean, the only reason I waited this long was out of respect for your sadness. But you've seemed very happy the last couple days. It's been great, hearing you laugh so much." Cassie sighed and shook her head. "The way you look at me sometimes—I just can't believe you're not feeling what I'm feeling."

Lauren lowered her eyes, breaking away from Cassie's intense, challenging stare, and looked at the steam coming off her mug.

"I think you're still feeling guilty," Cassie said. "Feeling that if you allow yourself to love me, you'll somehow be betraying Faith, like before. You've never gotten over that."

"I don't really think that's it." Lauren spoke quietly without looking up.

"Then why won't you give us a chance?"

"I just don't want a relationship. I don't feel that way this time around." Lauren met Cassie's eyes. "I admit I did feel that kind of attraction once. But I got over it. I want you as my friend. I really, really want that, Cassie."

Cassie shook her head. "I'm afraid that just isn't possible.

And, frankly, I think you're deluding yourself."

After a couple minutes of silence, during which Lauren continued staring helplessly at her coffee mug, Cassie said, "I think you haven't given her up yet. You're holding on, trying to preserve your life with her."

Lauren felt tears coming to her eyes.

"She wouldn't approve," Cassie said. "You know what she said. Take both. Do everything. She was all about living life to the fullest."

Choking back sobs, Lauren said, "I'm doing my best to go on with my life."

Cassie got up and came to her, putting an arm around her gently. "I'm sorry I upset you," she said, squeezing Lauren's shoulder. "I'm sure it's been very hard. I didn't mean to push you. I've waited for ten years already. I can wait a little longer. We can take this very slowly, as slowly as you need to."

She kissed the top of Lauren's head like a big sister while she cried. "No third-date U-Hauls for us, hey?" she said, attempting a joke.

"Cassie, I don't want to stop loving Faith."

Cassie wiped a tear off Lauren's cheek. "Nobody expects you to. You don't have to."

Struggling to regain her composure, Lauren pulled away and said, "I think this was a mistake. I shouldn't have come here."

She got up and left the kitchen, heading to the guest room. She pulled her suitcase out of the closet and opened it on the bed, then removed her clothes from the dresser. Cassie brought her a fresh cup of coffee and wordlessly set it on the nightstand, then withdrew, hesitating in the doorway. "We could be so good together," she said softly.

Lauren stiffened, but didn't turn around to look at her. She heard Cassie walk away. She wasn't going to try to persuade her to stay, for which she was grateful. It wouldn't work, anyway. Cassie probably knew that.

# CHAPTER THIRTY-FIVE

Lauren walked out to her driveway in her bathrobe to pick up the Sunday newspaper, which was sheathed in plastic to protect it from the rain. There was a light drizzle misting the plants with a fine, dewy layer. The roses looked especially pretty with beads of moisture on their velvety pink petals.

As she turned back toward her door, she saw Jaspar standing in his driveway, grinning, hunched slightly, the hood of his rain jacket framing his lined face. "Morning," he said heartily.

"Good morning."

"When did you get back?" he asked.

"Two days ago."

"Have a good trip?"

"Yes, it was very productive."

"Productive, was it?" He laughed. "Not romantic? You didn't run off to meet some secret lover?"

"No, nothing like that. It was a research trip."

"Still saving yourself for me, I guess."

She walked past him toward her door. "Yes. You're the only man in my life, Jaspar."

He chuckled. She shut her door and slipped the paper out of the wrapper. No wonder he hadn't noticed she was home. She had been practically hibernating since her return. Leaving Cassie had left her hollow inside. As feeling returned, it came in the form of a familiar background pain that she had been holding at bay for some time. She was both sorry and glad to feel it seeping back into her life. It was what she had left of Faith now, a deep ache. So she had embraced it, spending the last two days doing what some would describe as wallowing in self pity.

Today she'd resolved to do better. She got up early and would spend the day getting back on track. This was the day she had planned to come home all along. Jim would be coming over later to return Cocoa. Emma wanted to come over and look through more of Faith's papers. She was scheduled to arrive at ten.

The last two days Lauren had done nothing at all. She hadn't heard from Cassie. She hoped she wasn't feeling similarly bereft.

She did think occasionally about Cassie's offered explanations for why she wasn't able to accept her as a lover. *She was clinging to her life with Faith. She was still being faithful to her. Loving Cassie still made her feel guilty.* Explanations like that, frequently given in books and movies, were inadequate for real life. The complexity of human emotions can't be summed up so tidily, although we all try, endlessly, to sort, label and file everything, to make sense of our actions.

Putting feelings into words is a way of managing them, but Lauren knew from experience that it didn't work. She had tried to do that before, ten years ago, when she had pigeonholed her feelings for Cassie—*I love her like a sister.* She had momentarily satisfied herself that this was true, allowing herself to continue to love. But the feelings wouldn't conform to the words. They had their own motives which were hidden and impervious to reason. She hadn't been able to control or deter them.

As she thought about why she'd run from Cassie, what the real reason was, she felt too many mixed emotions to explain it. It wouldn't change anything anyway, finding a label that fit. All she really knew was that something in her had led her to reject Cassie's love. The sadness that resulted was as complicated as the feelings that preceded it. Grief, that's what it was. She had become accustomed enough to grief to recognize it. One thing she'd noticed about it is that it never equates to a single loss. It brings with it every loss you've ever had. Every heartbreak and every death comes through your heart like a slow procession of mourners behind a casket, all linked solidly together. There was no way to tell what percentage of this despair was because of Faith or Cassie or her father or her little dog Snicker who got hit by a car when she was nine. The tears she had cried during the last two days were for all of them, perhaps even equally.

Grief, like love, was too convoluted to fathom.

After a cup of coffee and a quick scan of the paper, Lauren cycled through the photos she'd brought back from her trip. Pictures of olive oil, cheese, wine and bread flashed by on her computer monitor. She was impressed with the quality of the photos, better by far than what she normally had to work with. There would be no problem this time finding really good shots to include with the article. On the contrary, the problem would be winnowing her choices down to just a couple. Who knew, she thought, staring at one of the shots, that a hunk of Stilton could be so beautiful?

There were also photos of the ocean, Cassie's house and Lauren, captured at joyful moments. Lots of joyful moments. We did have fun, Lauren thought. She was really a very lovely woman. It had been so easy to fall in love with her once, all those years ago. But Lauren had used all her resources, then, to smother that love. There was no ember left to rekindle.

She approached her work ruthlessly this morning, determined not to dwell on matters of the heart, joyful or sad. After looking through the photos, she began to compose the text of her article. As she got more involved in writing, she began to feel better, began to forget about herself and her debilitating emotions.

By ten, she was able to greet Emma with a smile and a cup of coffee. Emma didn't stop to chat, but went right to work in the den, and Lauren returned to her own work in the family room. An hour later Emma went through to the kitchen to return the empty mug.

"How's it going?" Lauren asked.

"Very well." She stopped near Lauren's chair. "There's a lot of material. And quite a few unpublished articles that seem very polished to me. I wasn't really expecting that."

"Faith was very good at writing everything up. Actually, I helped her with a lot of those articles, but she wasn't good at following through with the business side of things."

Emma nodded thoughtfully. "I remember that about her. I understand your decision to donate all of this to the university, but I've been thinking. There might be another option." Emma leaned against the back of the couch, facing Lauren with her intense blue eyes. "Get someone to edit a collection, maybe even organize these papers and articles into a new book. There may be enough good, original work there. It would be a shame, actually, if all of these insightful opinions were stored away on a shelf in a library where only a few determined graduate students would ever look at them. They should be published."

"Get someone?" Lauren asked.

"I'd like to do it," Emma said hesitantly, then became more assertive. "I think I'm the right person to do it. I was her student. I know how she thought about these subjects. I know what her passions were. And I'm qualified."

It was hard to trust Emma. Lauren still felt deceived. She had to keep reminding herself that Emma too had loved Faith. Emma's desires regarding Faith's work were most likely the same as her own. And she was right about stuffing this material into a corner of some library storage room. It was far from the ideal solution.

"What about your own research?" Lauren asked.

She tossed her head. "Oh, it will continue. Maybe at a slower pace. But this would really be rewarding for me. And so much of the work is already done. All I'd have to do is put it all together in some logical arrangement."

"There would be more to it than that. I'm sure you know that. It would be a big job."

"Yes, well, probably. But I'd be honored to do it. I'd understand if you'd rather it wasn't me, though. I mean, I can see how you might feel some resentment toward me. I'm grateful you're letting me use her work at all."

Lauren shook her head. "No, I—." She stopped herself because she was about to deny any resentment and she knew that wasn't really how she felt. "Actually, I think you're exactly the right person to do it. Let me think about it, though, okay?"

"Yes, no problem." Emma turned to go, then turned back and asked, "What's inside the skull on her desk?"

Puzzled, Lauren said, "Yorick? There's nothing inside it."

"There is."

Lauren got up and went to the den with Emma following. Picking up the skull, she saw a small yellow tube inside. "Strange. I don't remember that."

She upended the skull and shook it gently until the tube fell through an eye socket onto the desk. It was shaped like a test tube, but was plastic. She opened it and extracted a piece of paper, which she unrolled and flattened on the desk. In Faith's flourishing handwriting, the note said, "So long, and thanks for all the lobster!"

"Oh, my God!" Lauren said to herself. And then she started laughing while Emma read the note. Lauren fell into the desk chair, still laughing.

"That's from—" Emma started.

"Yes! *Hitchhiker's Guide to the Galaxy*, paraphrased. It was one of her favorite books."

Emma grinned broadly. "She left that for you."

"Yes. I found one several months ago in a kitchen canister that said, 'Beam me up, Gaia!'"

"She wanted you to laugh."

Lauren nodded, noting the most natural smile she had yet seen on Emma's face.

These sweet gestures of Faith's, planted for discovery after she was gone, were funny and sad at the same time. But definitely welcome. It was like finding her here, just for a moment, winking.

If she had been alone, she would have let her laughter turn to tears, but because of Emma, she controlled herself.

She placed Yorick carefully back on his usual perch, then stood. "Emma, I think I'll say yes to your request to edit and publish Faith's papers. I'm pretty sure she would want that. I'm also sure she would like the idea of you being the one to do it."

By noon, Emma had left with a couple boxes of Faith's papers in her car. They'd decided it would be easier for her to work on these at her own place in Eugene. Lauren was now feeling more inclined to trust her, at least in the business arena. On a more personal level, though, she still clung jealously and guiltily to the letter.

A few minutes after Emma left, the phone rang.

"Lauren," said a vaguely familiar male voice when she answered, "this is Eric Hutchins."

"Eric?"

"I'm at the beach house. There's been an accident. I found your number in my mother's cell phone."

"What's happened?" Lauren asked, feeling terror in her throat.

"Mom's in the hospital in North Bend. That's three miles north of Coos Bay. She fell from the bluff trail. She's got a head injury and a broken arm."

"A head injury," Lauren repeated. "Is it serious?"

"We don't know yet. She's unconscious. The doctor says that's the best thing for her for now."

"When did this happen?"

"Yesterday. I don't know exactly when. A woman walking her dog found her. Then the hospital called me. I drove up last night."

"She'll be okay, won't she?"

"I hope so. Head injuries are tricky. There's some bleeding, some swelling. Puts pressure on the brain. The doctor says it's hard to say at this point. They're still doing tests."

"I'll come down," Lauren said impulsively.

"Oh, no, you don't need to do that. I'll keep you informed if you want. I'll be able to stay here for several days, if necessary. Adele didn't come with me. She couldn't get anyone to take her place at the preschool on such short notice, but she may come up on the weekend. At the moment, everything's under control. Mom's condition is stable. Nothing to do, really. I was wondering if you knew of anyone else I should call. Close friends or— I hate to admit this, but I don't even know if she has...someone."

"She's not seeing anyone," Lauren said. "But I really don't know anything about her friends back in Albuquerque. If you think it's serious enough to call people, I could probably find out from Jennifer."

"No, that's not necessary. It was just if there was someone special. If there was, I thought she should know."

"Right," Lauren said, that phrase, "someone special," vibrating around the edges of her consciousness. "There's her law firm."

"I already called there. I spoke to her assistant."

After thanking Eric for the call, Lauren sat in a hard kitchen chair for several minutes, her mind blank, as if it couldn't comprehend what she'd just been told. Cassie fell off the bluff trail? How could that happen? For a horrible second she had the thought she might have jumped. But that was ridiculous. She wouldn't have done such a thing. Even if she were suicidal, there were much more reliable ways to kill yourself. Why risk becoming a paraplegic? Cassie was much too clear-headed for that. And not suicidal. Not in the least.

Lauren remembered the look of sadness on her face when they parted. But no tears. She isn't a crybaby like me, Lauren thought. Much more solid than me, all around. Obviously, it was an accident.

She was finally able to get up and go back to work, but soon realized no more writing was going to happen today. She began to fear Eric was playing down Cassie's injuries, trying not to upset her. But why would he do that? From his point of view, she was just a friend, and not a very close one. He had never heard of her before a week ago. In fact, it was surprising he had bothered to call at all.

The need to go sit in hospital waiting rooms, inertly, ineffectually, was one of those illogical activities that people felt compelled to put themselves through, she reflected. It gives them a sense that they're doing something, even though they know it isn't something that will make a damned bit of difference.

Although she had always considered herself among the most rational of people, lately she was beginning to change her mind and contemplate the possibility that there was nothing rational about her at all. Because now she was packing a bag and planning to drive back down to Coos Bay to sit in a hospital doing nothing to help an injured woman whose affections she had just rejected.

But a show of support, she reasoned, was never in vain in the midst of overworked doctors and nurses. Being so far from home, Cassie would have no one here except Eric and Lauren.

Just as Lauren was shoving her suitcase into the trunk of her car, her brother's red pick-up pulled into the driveway behind her. This, she thought, is evidence of how distracted I am. She had completely forgotten Jim was coming by to return Cocoa. He stepped out of his truck and waved.

"Perfect timing," he said. "You're just getting home."

She walked over to him as he opened the passenger side door and pulled out the cat carrier. Lauren peeked through the wire frame door at her cat, a dark brown mass of fur punctuated by a pink nose and furious green eyes.

"How's my boy?" she said to Cocoa through the grate.

"He's been a little temperamental, but no trouble."

"I'm not just getting home," Lauren explained. "In fact, I was just getting ready to leave."

"But you said you were coming home today." He looked astonished.

"I know, but my plans changed. I got home two days ago. And now I'm off again. Would you mind keeping him a few more days?"

"No, I don't mind, but are you going to tell me what's going on?"

"Come on in. Let me at least give him a proper hug."

"And me?" Jim pouted.

Lauren reached up and hugged him, then they went inside. He put the carrier on the kitchen floor and opened it. Cocoa walked nonchalantly out of the crate toward his food dish.

224

Lauren picked him up and hugged him tightly, his fur tickling her nose.

"So what's up?" Jim asked, sitting in a kitchen chair. "Where are you off to?"

"Same place. Coos Bay." She filled him in about the accident.

"Are you okay to drive?" he asked.

"Yes, I'm fine." Lauren squeezed Cocoa's head against her cheek. He squirmed until she put him on the floor.

"You know, you never really told me who this woman was. Just some old friend. Some lawyer from Albuquerque. Is that right?"

"Yes."

"Is that all you're going to tell me?"

"There's nothing to tell. Don't go getting ideas."

He frowned. "You don't have to be evasive with me, you know? I mean, I'm the brother you can trust. I'm the enlightened one."

Lauren kissed his cheek. "Yes, you are. And I'm grateful for it. But there really is nothing to tell. If you're sitting around waiting for some juicy, romantic story from me, you'll be waiting a long time. My days of romance are over."

"That's very cynical, Lauren. And sad."

"Not sad to me. I was very happy with Faith for twenty-three years. That's enough. That should be enough for anyone. How many people can say as much?"

He sighed.

"I need to get going, though. It's a four hour drive. I really appreciate you taking Cocoa again."

"No problem. He's good company." Jim stood, then reached down to pick up the cat. "Although I'm not content to spend the rest of my life with only a cat for companionship, even if you are."

# CHAPTER THIRTY-SIX

It was a tiring drive, hampered by rush-hour traffic around Eugene and the unfamiliar layout of North Bend, so it was already six o' clock when Lauren arrived at the hospital. After asking at the information booth for Cassie's room number, she rode the elevator to the third floor. She hadn't been in a hospital for over two years, not since Faith's last pointless surgery. This one, like all of them, felt cold and sterile with its shiny linoleum floor and white walls, devices on wheels parked in hallways, and the occasional patient in a thin shapeless gown to his knees, shuffling along, pushing his rack of drip bags in front of him.

She tried not to think about the last time she'd been in a hospital, a joyless day when Faith was discharged to go home, out of options. In the words of Dr. Hart, "There's nothing more we can do." Faith, though exhausted and perhaps no longer interested in options, had been her straightforward self and said, "So I'm going home to die." Dr. Hart, whose expression was appropriately solemn, had nodded and said, "Without a miracle, I'm afraid so."

Faith had always been an optimist. It was simply her nature, sometimes at odds with the facts. But on that day, at the thought of "a miracle," she had laughed such a bitter laugh that Lauren had shuddered, hearing it. She shook herself to dispel that scene from her mind as the elevator clunked to a stop.

The smell of the place made her nervous, made her breathe less easily. She noticed herself taking deliberate gulps of air. She pushed her anxiety aside and made her way down the hallway until she located Room 324. The door was open to a dimly lit room beyond. She took another deep breath and went in.

With eyes closed and a peaceful, passive expression on her face, Cassie lay under a blanket. A large bandage encircled her head. Her left arm, in a cast, lay on top of the blanket. Her fingers stuck out from the stiff edge of the cast. The wide-necked opening of the hospital gown was tied shut at her shoulder. Lauren moved closer to the bed and reached out to touch Cassie's forehead. It was cool. Then she found her right hand and held it gently, noticing that the skin on her palm was scraped and covered with scabs. She stared at the pale lips, parted slightly, and the darkened eyelids. Her hand was also cool, papery dry, and her face had an uncharacteristically pallid cast—except for the fresh bruise across her jaw.

Asleep, Cassie didn't resemble herself much. Most of Cassie was in the sparkle in her eyes and the liveliness of her face. Still, there was enough of the familiar on this wan and placid countenance to bring to mind the other, the one from a few days ago, exhilaratingly vital, moving through her vast range of expressions.

In her mind, Lauren could see them, the smirks and grins, the arched eyebrows and casual toss of the head, the playful, surreptitious glance, then the unrestrained laugh and all those teeth showing because Cassie didn't care if she looked funny when she laughed. She just laughed. She didn't think about it.

And her eyes. Lauren could envision her eyes best of all,

deep brown, staring unabashedly with an inner light, a joy, an unambiguous love, a look Lauren had first seen ten years ago and then again so frequently in the last week. How could anyone not recognize that look? So deep, sincere and full of unrepentant longing. Lauren had seen it with her eyes, but had kept it secret from her mind because she'd wanted to keep looking at it for as long as she could. That look drew her in, made her want to follow it, made her want to drown in it.

How could she have so frequently and steadily accepted that look without reflecting the same back? She couldn't. And she hadn't. That's why Cassie knew they both wanted the same thing. Because Lauren's eyes must have looked identical—deep, sincere and full of unrepentant longing.

Lauren felt a lump in her throat and tried to swallow it away.

As she stood holding Cassie's hand, her thoughts turned to old memories. The eyes are the window of the soul and the soul is the part of us that falls in love. And the mind is the part where all sorts of interesting things happen…like denial and suppression of feeling. And the heart is just an organ that pumps blood.

The machine monitoring Cassie's heartbeat, with its regular soft beep, was the only noise in the room. As she watched Cassie breathing, looking so vulnerable and so completely absent, something welled up in her from deep inside. It was something huge like a tidal wave, gathering force, building as it headed for the surface. Then, all at once, it slammed into her. She let go of Cassie's hand and turned abruptly, bolting blindly for the door. She made it as far as the hallway before smashing into something—someone. He caught her securely by both arms, then folded her into an expansive embrace, holding her head against his chest as her body fell into an avalanche of wracking sobs.

A half hour later, Lauren sat quietly on a sofa and took another drink from the paper cup Eric had given her. She had gradually calmed enough to comprehend what was happening.

228

He had taken her to a small waiting room on the third floor. While she sat there with her face in her hands, crying, he had managed to get hold of a box of Kleenex and a moistened hand towel. Then he had returned to sit beside her while she blew her nose and wiped her face with the towel and gradually returned to sanity.

The water was cold and welcome. She swallowed, then placed the towel over her eyes, each in turn, before turning to see Eric smiling benignly and a little warily at her.

"Feeling better?" he asked.

She nodded. "Thank you. I'm sorry. I thought I'd come down here to help, but I've ended up just causing you trouble."

"That's okay. Hanging around here is awfully boring. Your nervous breakdown or whatever that was gave me something to do for a while."

Lauren smiled, then blew her nose one more time, wadding up the Kleenex. "You're very good with hysterical women."

"I'm used to it. Job hazard. Not just women. Kids and men too. It's not unusual to be faced with a whole family in some kind of emotional meltdown."

"I'm fine now. I don't know what happened in there."

Eric's face was kind. "You didn't strike me as the type to break down like this, and I wouldn't have expected it anyway given that you and my mother hadn't even seen or spoken to one another for ten years. I mean, not to pry, but you came all this way after I told you it wasn't necessary and now you seem completely devastated. It just makes me wonder."

"I can understand why you're confused." Lauren sighed and stared at the ragged Kleenex in her hand.

"You don't have to explain…if it's private."

She looked up and met his gaze. "If I could explain, I would. Partly it's just seeing someone I care about lying in a hospital bed. It reminds me of…someone I loved. Sorry, I'm being silly. You should ignore me."

"I see," he said. "You were crying over someone else, someone you lost."

"No, no, not exactly." He must think I'm an idiot, Lauren thought. "It was Cassie. Seeing her there reminded me of how

I felt the other time. My partner Faith died two years ago. She had cancer and we spent a lot of time in the hospital over the last year of her life."

"I'm sorry," he said gently.

"But even though this reminded me of that, it wasn't about Faith. I mean, I really do care about Cassie."

Eric sat watching her, his eyes calm. He reminded her so much of Cassie, making her feel like she could trust him and he could understand her.

"I love her," Lauren added.

Before he could respond, they heard a commotion outside the room and saw a nurse running past, following by an orderly. They hurried into the hallway to see them both disappear into Cassie's room. Eric bounded down the hall. Lauren approached more slowly, hearing raised, argumentative voices from inside. Then the orderly shoved Eric out of the room and slammed the door against him.

He turned and looked at Lauren, fear contorting his face. "Seizure," he said breathlessly.

She leaned against a wall for support. She couldn't believe this was happening. Only a half hour after she had realized how much she loved her, Cassie could be dying. She slumped onto a bench while Eric paced outside the room. What she'd told him, or tried to tell him, had been true. Seeing Cassie in a hospital bed, unconscious, had brought up feelings in her that forced her to face the fact that she felt as deep a love for Cassie as she had for Faith. She felt the same connection and the same concern for her well being. She felt like she was lying there with her, broken and struggling to remain alive. And she felt like she would die too if Cassie did. If there was any difference between these feelings and the ones she'd had two years ago with Faith, it was too subtle to register.

If Cassie died, not only would Lauren lose another woman she loved, but she would never have a chance to tell her. Cassie would never know that Lauren had been mistaken about what she wanted, that she'd been driven by fear to deny her feelings. At least there had been time to make sure, with Faith, that she knew how much she was loved.

The door to Cassie's room finally opened. Lauren jumped up to join Eric in greeting the nurse.

"She's calm now," the nurse said. "I'll call her doctor."

"What does it mean?" Eric asked.

"I'm sorry, sir, but you'll have to talk to the doctor about that. I don't know if he'll be in tonight or not."

"When you call him," Eric said authoritatively, "you tell him to call me." He handed the nurse his business card. "I'm her son."

"Yes, sir," said the nurse before walking off.

Lauren stepped toward the door to Cassie's room.

Eric grabbed her arm and held her back. "Are you sure you want to go in there?"

"I'm fine now. Really. I won't fall apart again, I promise."

He looked concerned, but released his hold and followed her into the room. She found Cassie looking the same as before, peacefully absent from their world. There was no evidence of the violence that had struck her a few moments earlier. Eric stood behind her as the two of them watched, wordlessly.

"Do you want to go to the house?" he asked at last. "Maybe get some dinner?"

She nodded. He stepped out of the room. Lauren moved closer to Cassie, looking at her face with a new sense of wonder. She kissed her pale cheek, then stroked it gently. "I love you, Cassie," she said quietly next to her ear.

# CHAPTER THIRTY-SEVEN

Eric and Lauren settled into the beach house together as they maintained their vigil over Cassie. For lunch the next day Eric made a beautiful, garlicky Greek salad with heirloom tomatoes, kalamata olives and feta cheese.

"Considering how small this place is," he said, tossing the salad, "they've got a thriving Farmer's Market. I picked up a huge bunch of basil this morning. I couldn't resist it."

Lauren held out her bowl as he served the salad. "I smelled it when I came in. Lovely stuff."

"I can make pesto," he said. "It won't take but five minutes in the food processor. Then I can freeze it. Leave it there for later, for some rainy winter day when Mom wants the taste of summer."

He had gone to the market after visiting the hospital. There was no change, he reported, when he got back. The doctor had come by, ordered another brain scan. He said that if the swelling didn't go down soon, they might have to operate, cut into Cassie's skull to relieve the pressure. Somehow the basil and the tomatoes had made Eric more lighthearted, even after that news.

"I get the feeling you know my mother very well," he said as they ate, "despite the ten-year break."

"I feel like I do, but I may be wrong. I've always felt that way about her, from the day we met. So I guess it can't be true."

"Actually, it could be true." He took a swallow from his water glass. "Sometimes you can know someone in a different way, like you're on the same wavelength, don't you think?"

"Yes. That's what it is, I suppose."

"I don't feel like I know her much at all." He shook his head, a dark shock of hair falling over his forehead. "I never lived with her for more than two weeks at a time. There wasn't anything routine about that. It was like a holiday. She took me places, like the zoo, and gave me gifts. It was like Christmas whenever I was there. I never really thought of her as my mother. She was more like a family friend or maybe an aunt."

"I know what you mean. My parents were divorced too. I lived with my mother. So my father became this larger than life character. Not a father, not in the everyday sense as someone who punishes you and sets your limits. When I saw him, which was rare, it was like you're saying, not regular life. He was always happy, funny and attentive. I thought he was the most wonderful man. When I was a child, I never thought about how that wasn't how he always was."

"My mother was like that too. Always cheerful, always fun. I don't think I ever even saw her cry. Not once."

Lauren smiled to herself, then said, "But she did cry. She had some bad times. She saw you so seldom, she put on a happy face for you whatever else was going on."

He shrugged and took another forkful of salad.

"Your mother suffered too," Lauren said, impulsively.

He narrowed his eyes at her.

"I don't think you've been fair with her. You should take some time to really get to know her and make up your own mind. I mean, it was understandable that you felt this way as a twelve year old, but you're well into adulthood now. I think you owe her an attempt at least at understanding. You give that much to all these strangers you work with. Why not your own mother?"

Oh, shit, she thought, I've crossed the line for sure now.

Eric regarded her calmly with his mother's brown eyes. "Did you talk about me to her?" he asked.

She nodded, feeling guilty for butting into their family relationships. But she'd started now. "You've only heard one side of the story."

"She could have told me her side at any time," he pointed out.

"I know. I think you're both responsible for this situation. She has a lot of pain and guilt she prefers to keep to herself. Maybe she feels she deserves the anger and hatred you have for her."

"I don't hate her," he said flatly.

"Part of you does. The shy little boy with no friends and no siblings. You obviously blame her for that. You don't allow for the fact that she's just as flawed as anyone else and has made mistakes. Which she acknowledges."

Eric regarded her calmly. "She's never admitted any mistakes to me."

"That's because you've never discussed these things."

He stared momentarily, then stood, collecting the salad bowls. "Maybe you're right. We never really talk about what matters. It's all very superficial. Always has been. It's easier that way, I guess. I think of myself as a pretty good listener. I listen to people talk about their problems a lot, actually. But my mother's never been talkative that way, at least not to me. What did she tell you? I mean, what *is* her side of the story?"

"You should ask *her* that. I don't think I should be the one to tell you."

He nodded thoughtfully. "Yeah, I guess so. I hope she has the chance to tell me herself."

Lauren, hearing the emotion in his voice, said nothing. Then he sat down again and looked at her, his eyes sad.

"The weird thing is," he said, running his hand through his

thick hair, "I didn't expect to feel the way I've been feeling the last couple days. When I got the call from the hospital, I remember feeling nothing at all, except pissed off that I had to be the one to come up here and deal with this. As Adele reminded me, I'm the only family she has. Like I said, though, I don't really feel like we're family. But now that I'm here, I'm having all these feelings, worrying she's going to die, feeling afraid and sad and lonely. I wouldn't have thought it would hit me like this." He laughed lightly. "It seems like you and I are having the same surprise experience."

Lauren regarded him sympathetically, impressed by his ability to open up to her, something he hadn't been able to do with his mother. It was the same for Cassie. She seemed to have no trouble talking to Lauren.

"Maybe it's because of all your unresolved conflict," she suggested. "Sometimes I think the people who have the hardest time when someone dies are those who appear the most removed. It's because they've carried a hurt around deep inside their whole lives. And then it's too late to do anything about it. They're stuck with it. Even people who seem not to care. When it comes right down to it, everybody does care if their mother or father or son loves them, knows them...forgives them."

Eric bit his lower lip in a gesture Lauren recognized as an attempt to control his emotions.

"That happened with Faith's sister Charity," she continued. "She and Faith never got along. The only way they could tolerate one another was to stay far apart. Different states. Though they were sisters, they just never liked each other, you know? But after Faith died, Charity went into a surprising period of mourning. She called me all the time and we talked for hours about their childhood. I've gotten to know her well in the last two years, but in all the years before that, I only even saw her a few times. I went to visit her last month, to take her some trinkets, some family mementos. She spoke so affectionately about Faith. I think she's forgotten that they basically couldn't stand each other."

"That's weird," Eric said.

"Oh, not so weird. Their younger sister died when they were kids. Their parents are both dead. Charity is the only one left now. I think it's natural for her to feel a powerful sense of loss. Because it's not *my* Faith she's missing. It's *her* Faith, her little sister from a long time ago."

Eric nodded. "Did she see Faith before she died?"

"She came out a few months before. Even then, it was all either of them could do to remain civil. Despite how Charity feels right now, there never was much chance they could have any kind of congenial relationship as adults."

Eric nodded thoughtfully as Lauren got up and put the rest of the dishes in the dishwasher.

"What do you want to do this afternoon?" he asked.

"I think I'd like to go to the hospital. I can take my laptop and work on my article."

"Okay. I think I'll fix the gate. The bottom hinge has pulled loose. I can tinker around here. Call me if there's any change."

"I will."

She hoped Eric would have his opportunity to talk to his mother, just as Lauren was hoping to be able to talk to her again herself. It seemed there was a line forming of people with serious messages for Cassie when she woke up.

# CHAPTER THIRTY-EIGHT

Lauren managed to make a comfortable workspace in the hospital room, moving the visitor's chair closer to the window and using the window sill as a shelf for her soda can and notepad. Nurses and nurse's aides came and went through the afternoon, taking Cassie's blood pressure and temperature, replacing the saline solution, emptying the catheter bag. Lauren worked on her article, taking breaks when her eyes or back got tired. A break involved walking around the hospital, going to the restroom, getting a drink of water. Sometimes she took breaks in place and just stared out the window at a cloudy sky. She was not getting much work done. Her mind kept drifting.

Being there still felt familiar to her like the many days she had spent beside Faith's hospital bed, but she was no longer upset by it. Cassie was an entirely different person and this was an entirely different situation. During these private hours, she had plenty of time to think about her own feelings, how she had suppressed them, denied them and run from them. She had time, too, to think about what it meant to acknowledge her feelings for Cassie. But it was hard to think very far ahead under the circumstances. Although she was hopeful Cassie would recover, she knew how untrustworthy hope could be.

At six o' clock, Lauren gathered her things and prepared to leave, stopping beside the bed. Cassie looked so much like she was merely sleeping, as if she would wake up if she were jostled. Or kissed by some handsome prince...or princess.

Lauren kissed her cheek. "I love you, Cassie," she said again, then left.

They repeated this routine the following day. Eric went over in the morning, then came home with his report.

"No more seizures," he said. "Things are looking better. The swelling is down. At the moment, it looks like they won't have to operate."

"That's wonderful news!"

Lauren went over for the afternoon with her laptop and sat as before by the window while Eric stayed at the house painting the fence and gate he'd repaired. At five o' clock, an aide brought in a dinner tray and set it on the bed stand.

"She's not eating. She's unconscious," Lauren said.

"I know, but it's on the orders. The doctor must have thought she might wake up today. So we have to bring it. You can have it if you want."

The aide left. Lauren went to inspect the tray, though she knew she wasn't going to choose hospital food over whatever Eric had planned for dinner. She lifted the pink plastic lid to reveal a plate of meatloaf, mashed potatoes, gravy and waffled carrot coins. She put the lid back. There was a brownie in a tiny plate covered with plastic wrap. She unwrapped it and took a bite. Not bad, she thought. Her diet here reminded her of her college days—soda and dessert.

She nearly choked on her second bite as she heard a gurgle from the bed. Cassie's eyes were open! She was staring right at Lauren in a strangely vacant way, as if she didn't see her, like a

238

blind woman. Oh, God, Lauren thought, don't let her be brain damaged!

Then Cassie blinked and her eyes seemed to gradually focus, but her expression remained blank. It was a haunting look that left Lauren terrified.

"Cassie," Lauren said, drawing near and taking hold of her right hand. "Can you hear me?"

Her eyes moved to meet Lauren's, then her fingers pressed lightly into Lauren's palm. Her mouth moved and she made a guttural sound, a short stutter that sounded nothing like words.

"Oh, Cassie, can't you talk? Do you recognize me?"

She turned her head slowly, looking at the tray of food. She pulled her hand from Lauren's and pointed at the tray, making a noise that sounded like "were."

"Water?"

She nodded weakly.

Lauren poured a cup of water and held it to her lips as she took tiny sips. "Please forgive me," Lauren said, trying to stop her hand from shaking. "This is all my fault. I shouldn't have left you alone. God, what a fool I've been! Now you can't talk and maybe can't walk and who knows what else is wrong with you. Can you move your toes? You don't know who I am, do you? Do you know who you are?"

When she seemed to have finished drinking, Lauren took the cup away. Cassie licked her lips very deliberately.

"What do you want?" Lauren asked. "Are you in pain?"

"Lauren—" she pronounced clearly.

Lauren grabbed her hand again, elated. "Yes! You recognize me."

"I recognize you're a blithering idiot," she said calmly. "My mouth was like cotton. Couldn't move my tongue. Better now. Thanks." Cassie winced. "Oh, shit, my head hurts."


By the following day, Cassie was able to converse normally and appeared to be thinking clearly. Lauren brought her some magazines, slippers, bath robe and loaned her an MP3 player.

"Thank you," Cassie said, thumbing through the music menu. "This will be a good alternative to the TV. It will help block out all the noise too."

Lauren sat back in the visitor's chair, watching Cassie contentedly as she taught herself to work the music player. Lovely, precious face, Lauren thought, even with that scowl of concentration. The scowl gave way shortly to a satisfied smile.

"What are you listening to?" Lauren asked.

"I'm in your oldies folder. Bananarama."

Lauren chuckled. Cassie removed the ear buds and set the device on her bed stand.

"What happened?" Lauren asked. "Why did you fall? Do you remember?"

"It was stupid." Cassie waved her good arm dismissively. "I was walking the bluff trail, as usual. I heard a sea lion barking. Down below. He was making a racket like he was in trouble or angry or something. So I moved closer to the edge to look over."

"And the ground gave way?"

"Right. I knew better. Like I said, it was stupid. The last thing I remember was sliding, trying to grab something, and then that barking. That sea lion was probably just bragging about a fish."

Although Lauren had never seriously considered that Cassie had jumped, she was relieved to have that belief corroborated.

A couple of days passed as Cassie recovered and Lauren alternated with Eric visiting her in the hospital, bringing her books and food treats. Meanwhile, Eric and Lauren were becoming friends, it seemed, sharing meals and a home, united over their mutual concern for Cassie's welfare.

Lauren hadn't spoken to Cassie of love since she'd regained consciousness. Cassie was preoccupied with pain and recovery. A little part of Lauren worried she had knocked the love right out of her head when she fell. Life was like that. Life sought out irony. It would not have surprised her if Cassie had quit loving her at the exact same moment she realized how much she loved Cassie.

They spent their time together watching TV or talking about Cassie's health or stories in the news. For the time being, it was enough. Cassie was herself again. But Lauren had changed. Outwardly, nothing was different. She was happy in Cassie's company, as she always had been. She was content just to talk to her and they seemed never to run out of things to say. But there were new thoughts in Lauren's mind, thoughts she had never before allowed herself. As she sat at Cassie's bedside holding her hand, she wondered what it would be like to wake up beside her every morning and fall asleep in her arms at night. After a lifetime never imagining such things about anyone other than Faith, Lauren wasn't surprised these thoughts took their time coalescing.

For the time being, she kept them to herself, focusing instead on light-hearted topics like the daily routine at the beach house. Cassie found the idea of her son's cohabitation with Lauren vastly more entertaining than it actually was and she wanted to know every detail.

"Which one of you has dominion over the kitchen?" Cassie asked.

"He does breakfast. As you know, I've never been a morning person. But other than that, I'm winning the battle of *chef a la maison*."

"So what does poor Eric do all day if he's booted out of the kitchen?"

"Oh, he's keeping busy. He's very handy around the house."

"I wouldn't think there'd be so many things that need fixing around there."

"No, there aren't. He's moved on to decorative types of things. He's installing some solar lights along the front path, for instance."

"Okay, but no pink flamingoes." Cassie pointed threateningly at Lauren, narrowing her eyes.

Lauren laughed and grabbed her hand, pressing it momentarily between both of hers. She was happy to see Cassie so full of good humor.

One of the regular aides, Eugenia, entered the room with the lunch tray. Lauren released Cassie's hand and cleared a spot on the tray table. Eugenia was an older woman with gray hair pulled into a severe bun. She was friendlier than most, but also garrulous and spoke loudly as if everyone were hard of hearing. That was probably a good thing for a hospital staffer. Lauren found her almost impossible to talk to because she never seemed to expect her conversations to be two-sided, but Cassie just grinned whenever she was in the room. She got a kick out of her, apparently.

"Hello to you," Eugenia said emphatically with a mild Italian accent. "You're looking good today, Miss Cassie."

"Feeling much better," Cassie said.

Eugenia turned to Lauren as she set down the tray. "You'll be taking her home any day now. Good as new. But don't let her do any housework. You do everything. You make her rest. A bump on the head is a nasty thing. Takes a long time to heal. Which one of you cooks? Are you the cook?"

Eugenia turned from Cassie to Lauren. Taken off guard, Lauren sputtered at this question.

"She's the cook," Cassie affirmed, her eyes twinkling with amusement. "She's a phenomenal cook!"

"Oh, that's good." Eugenia stared almost threateningly at Lauren. "So you make sure you give her lots of vegetables. Fresh green and orange like spinach and carrots. And garlic. Lots of garlic. Garlic cures everything. Takes down swelling. My nonna ate raw garlic every single day of her life and she lived to be a hundred. Of course, nobody would go near her, but, eh, that's life. Everything's got the good and the bad." Eugenia shrugged using both hands. "And tomatoes, any way you want 'em. If she doesn't like spinach, you make her lasagna. Put the spinach and a whole head of garlic in there and she'll eat it. Lots of marinara, some pecorino romano or Parmigiano Regiano, whatever you like. You like porcini? Put some in. Nothing fancy."

Lauren stared pointedly at the meal in front of them as Eugenia lifted the lid to reveal some unrecognizable meat under brown gravy, a scoop of instant potatoes and canned corn.

"I know, I know," Eugenia said. "Doesn't matter. At home you can do it right. You want my recipe for *involtini di melanzane*? I come from Abruzzo, so it's a little spicy. Ah, nevermind. You know what you're doing. Good. You know how to take care of this little one. So I'll butt out."

Eugenia was out of the room before she finished her sentence, so there was no opportunity to respond. Cassie laughed with delight.

"Actually," said Lauren, "I wouldn't mind seeing that recipe."

"You understood what she was talking about? You don't speak Italian, do you?"

"Oh, no. I just speak food."

Cassie picked up the spoon and prodded the meat on the tray as if trying to rouse it. "I'll ask her for the recipe next time she comes in. Tell me in English so I know what to ask for."

"Eggplant rolls."

Cassie nodded and took a bite of the potatoes. Lauren reached over and picked up the Jell-O cup, pulling off the foil cover. Then she opened the pint of milk. By now she knew which containers Cassie needed help with.

"Does she think we're a couple?" Lauren asked.

"Sounds like it. Sorry about that. I can tell her we're not if you want."

"No, that's not necessary. It doesn't bother me." Lauren patted Cassie's leg through her blankets. "It doesn't bother me at all."

# CHAPTER THIRTY-NINE

The next day, Lauren talked Eric into going with her to a wild mushroom farm, a trip that would take most of the day. Dressed in T-shirts, shorts and sunglasses, they stopped by the hospital before they left to make a quick check on Cassie, finding her in excellent spirits.

"Now you'll see for yourself," she warned Eric, "what crazy places this woman has been dragging me around to."

"Are you kidding?" Eric said, giving her a hug. "This is going to be awesome!"

Cassie rolled her eyes. "You two were meant for each other."

It was a two-hour drive to the mushroom farm, one of the destinations Lauren and Cassie hadn't made it to when she'd cut her visit short. She was glad to fit it in now. It would complete her research. Eric drove, chatting amiably the entire way. Lauren was enjoying his company. As much as he reminded her of Cassie, it would have been surprising if she hadn't liked him.

At the conclusion of the tour of the mushroom-growing beds, their group was routed through the gift shop. "Do you want anything?" Lauren asked.

"Yeah. I'd like to get one of those blocks with the spores in it to take home. We can grow some shitakes right there in the kitchen window. It'll be cool."

"Okay. I think I'll get a pound of the fresh ones. Maybe we can do an omelet or something."

Eric nodded vigorously. "I'm definitely in the mood for something mushroomy."

After they made their purchases, they drove back. Eric was not as talkative this time, at least not at first. About halfway home, he said, "I've been thinking about what you said, about how I've never given my mother a chance to tell me her side of the story."

Lauren made a noise to indicate she was listening. Eric was looking ahead at the road.

"And, you know, how she suffered too. I think my father was really bitter for a long time. What happened completely shattered his dream of a happy life. It was a simple dream and he thought he'd found it, marrying her and starting a family. I'll bet you've never seen our family photos of their wedding and the first couple years after that, the three of us looking just like a fairy tale happy ending."

"No, I haven't seen them."

"Right. Dad kept them. He said Mom wasn't interested in things like family photos. But, you know, whenever I visited, she took tons of pictures of me." Eric shook his head. "That was always how Dad explained her. He said she wanted to live a life of carefree self-indulgence. Irresponsible and selfish. I guess he really believed that was why she left us, that family didn't mean anything to her."

"Do you believe that?"

"I never questioned it when I was a kid." He knit his thick eyebrows together. "Now, it seems unlikely. Oversimplified

245

anyway. My dad just couldn't find any other way to explain why she would leave. People didn't understand homosexuality back then, that it wasn't a choice. Well, people like my dad didn't, anyway. The most charitable explanation for a lot of people was that it was a mental illness."

"A lot of people still think that."

Eric glanced at her, a concerned look on his face. "I don't."

"No, I know you don't," Lauren assured him. "I could tell that from the day we met. It's pretty obvious your problem with your mother has nothing to do with her sexual orientation. It's your idea that she's indifferent to you that's the problem."

"My whole point of view came from Dad. And she never said a word about any of it. She didn't even talk about Dad or the time when we were a family. I assumed it wasn't something she thought about because it never came up. I thought it wasn't important to her. I do remember wishing she would talk about it, though. At least to say she was sorry."

"Sorry for what?"

Eric glanced at her, looking slightly tragic. "For leaving, for not wanting me."

As they came into Coos Bay, they turned west toward the sea, not yet visible, passing a pasture of grazing cows. That's all anybody ever wants, Lauren thought, to feel wanted. Especially a child. It must have hurt him very deeply to think his mother didn't want him.

"I find it ironic," Lauren said, "that I've always thought of Cassie as so easy to talk to, so open and candid, and to you, her son, she's a virtual stranger."

"You have some special connection with her," Eric observed.

"And you don't? If the two of you really opened up to one another, I think you'd find you're very similar."

Lauren could smell the ocean before it came into view as they headed south on the coast road toward town.

Eric turned to look at her briefly, his dark eyebrows knit together, a searching expression on his face. "You and Mom seem so good together. I'm sort of surprised you don't, you know, *really* get together. You're obviously close. You told me you love her. She's available. You're available. What am I not getting?"

Lauren shook her head. "It's me. I've been a dimwit."

Eric glanced at her, looking confused.

"Or afraid," she said.

"Afraid of what?"

Lauren sighed. "I think I've been afraid of being happy again. Afraid of giving up grieving."

Seeing an electronics store up ahead, Lauren said, "Hey, can you stop at that store? There's something I want to get."

He turned in to the parking lot. "Afraid of being happy? You know, I think I know what you mean. You get so used to feeling a certain lousy way you almost prefer it. I see that with the kids I work with. They're so adaptable. They get used to some crappy stuff. You try to tell them about a new family, what it will be like with home-cooked meals, safety, toys. They don't care. They want what they're used to."

"It happens all the time. The familiar is the most comforting thing of all."

Lauren considered how happy she'd felt last week as she'd gradually let herself live in the moment with Cassie. She remembered too the fear that had come to her at night before sleep, the fear of losing her familiar heartache and the struggle that resulted in her mind. Letting Cassie into her heart couldn't help but displace Faith, at least from the everyday, despite what Cassie had said about the infinite scope of love. Love has no ability to transcend time...or death, not in any tangible way. It was hard to think that Faith would recede and fade into the past and become less real. But there isn't any choice about that when someone dies. Not if you want to find ways to keep living. Maintaining the sharp edge of a lost love requires living in a fantasy, in the past where you both once lived. You can visit that place, but you can't really live there, not indefinitely, not like Lauren had been trying to do.

Eric pulled into a parking spot and cut the engine, then turned to Lauren with soulful eyes. "I guess you've gotten used to living with pain."

"Yes. I've been feeling pretty bad for a long time now. I've been pretending to go on with life, but I've been hanging onto

247

the ache. I think I'm ready to let that go now...if Cassie still wants me."

He put a hand on her shoulder and looked directly into her eyes. "I hope she does."

As they exited the car, he said, "So what are we here for anyway? You need some memory cards or something?"

"You'll see," Lauren said. "A welcome-home present for your mom."

# CHAPTER FORTY

Eric held the front door open for Cassie as Lauren waited inside, tense with excitement.

"Welcome home!" she called as Cassie stepped over the threshold.

She looked wonderful, alert and happy, with color in her cheeks. She held out her good arm to Lauren, who ran over and gave her a careful hug. Then she heaved a big sigh and said, "I'm so glad to be back. And I love the fence and mailbox. They look brand new. And the flowers, they're gorgeous. Everything looks so welcoming."

"Eric's been busy around here," Lauren said. "He's also put up cabinets in the garage. We've got everything very well organized. You can park a car in there now."

It was then that Cassie noticed the music, playing low. "What is that?" she asked and they all stood still to listen until Cassie recognized the song. "'Buttons and Bows'!"

She ran over to the stereo to look at the new turntable as it played a scratchy seventy-eight. Then she turned to look at the others with her face full of joy.

"This is incredible!" she said, turning back to the record. "I haven't heard this song since I was a child. It sounds exactly the same."

"Well, it should," Lauren said with a laugh. "It's the same record."

"I have no idea who Dinah Shore is," Eric said, "but I have to say I've been enjoying these songs. We played a few earlier just to try out the machine. I insisted we hear 'Mairsy Dotes' because it's been intriguing me ever since I read the label. And I still don't get it."

Cassie laughed, her big laugh that showed all her teeth. "This was your idea, Lauren, wasn't it?"

Lauren nodded, completely satisfied with Cassie's reaction. "Eric helped me hook it up."

They arranged Cassie on the living room couch with a small work table, a reading lamp, TV remote and a cup of tea. For the moment, she was content to listen to the old records, so Lauren put on "Red Sails in the Sunset" and watched Cassie's face as it began to play. She sighed deeply and put a hand to her chest.

"The doctor said you should take it easy for a couple of days," Eric said. "Just to make sure not to rattle your brain."

Cassie laughed. "Rattle my brain? I think my brain's been well rattled for years!"

"Are you all set?" Lauren asked her.

"I think so. So when do we eat? I hear you two picked up some gourmet mushrooms that are just begging for a risotto."

"Nope. No risotto. I'm making a mushroom tart. And Eric is making a salad with the rest of the heirloom tomatoes he got at the market."

Cassie grinned. "Lovely!"

"I need to put that tart in the oven," Lauren said, heading for the kitchen.

"So what's the deal with Mairsy Dotes?" she heard Eric ask as she left the room.

"It's mares eat oats!" Cassie exclaimed, then laughed again. "Oh, come on, we'll play it after this one and I'll explain it to you."

Lauren turned on the oven and whisked some eggs into her assortment of chopped mushrooms, then added some Swiss cheese, milk and herbs and poured the filling into a crust. Then she slid it into the oven as "Mairsy Dotes" finished playing in the other room.

Eric came in, shaking his head. "That song is just as weird when you know what it's about."

"Yes, it is. There're some funny songs in that collection."

"She's really happy with the record player. It was a good idea." Eric pulled his salad ingredients out of the refrigerator. "I'm going to be taking off after lunch. You two don't need me here anymore. Besides, I don't want anybody using me as an excuse."

"An excuse for what?" Lauren faced him.

He looked up from his tomatoes and grinned mischievously. "What was it that one song called it? Spooning?"

Lauren, embarrassed, looked away. Eric laughed lightly, then went to work on his salad. When he finished, he wiped his hands on a towel and said, "I think I'll have that talk with her now. I hope it doesn't upset her. Things are going so well. But I guess that was always the reason nobody said anything in the past. To avoid anything negative."

"Good luck," she said as he left the kitchen.

"It smells so good in there!" Lauren heard Cassie say. "Hurry up with that lunch!"

Lauren sat at the kitchen table with a can of soda, trying to imagine what their conversation was like. It didn't matter so much what was said. Just that they were talking, getting it all out into the open at last.

When the tart was done, she took it out to rest for a few minutes and peeked out through the doorway to see Eric and Cassie sitting together on the couch, both of them in tears. Well, that's a good sign, she thought.

She cut the tart and served three slices, then arranged the plates and salad bowls on the table. By the time she put the salad out, she could hear Cassie's laugh, loud and gleeful. I could live with that laugh, she thought. Even in the morning.

Lauren opened the door to the living room. "Lunch is served."

"It's about time!" Cassie complained.

Eric stood and offered her his arm. The two of them walked together into the kitchen, both of them smiling. Eric glanced toward Lauren and winked.

"He's turned into such a good person," Cassie said after Eric left. "I'm vindicated, I think. That's what I told him. Look how good you turned out being raised by your father."

"I hope that's not all you told him."

"No. I told him how hard it was for me to make that decision. I told him about my brief, aborted attempt to take custody. I told him what you wanted me to tell him, Lauren."

"I've been meddling, haven't I?"

"It's okay. Maybe we needed someone meddling."

"Did it help?"

Cassie pressed her lips together thoughtfully, then said, "I'm not sure. I guess we'll find out, won't we? When I move here, we won't be that far away from one another. Who knows? Maybe I'll end up with a tricycle and swing set in the yard."

"I think he wants to have a relationship with you."

"I think you're right. And that makes two of us. I appreciate what you did. He seems to respect your opinion."

By the second day at home, Cassie felt stronger and was no longer content to stay on the couch. After lunch she sat in the front room reading Lauren's article, which was near enough to completion to undergo a critique. Lauren put a stack of old records on the turntable to play low in the background as she cleaned the kitchen. Then she made them both a cup of tea.

"Thanks," Cassie said, looking up from the manuscript to take the cup. "Just finished with this."

Lauren sat in one of the deep-cushioned chairs. "What do you think?"

"I think it's wonderful. You've made it sound much more fun than it actually was." She laughed at herself, then set down the manuscript.

"I hope you're joking," Lauren said.

"Yes. Well, a little. It's very good. I especially liked your description of the Russian bakery and that little old woman running the place. What a character! And your write-up of the mushroom place makes me wish I hadn't missed it. It's a delightful article...and practical."

"Thanks. No changes?"

"I made a couple of notes in the margins. You'll see. Small things."

Lauren nodded, sipping her tea. In the moment that followed, as Sarah Vaughn sang "The Look of Love," they gazed steadily at one another until Cassie set her cup down on the table and turned a serious expression toward Lauren.

"Look," she said, "you've been a terrific help the last few days. It was so generous of you to rush right back here when Eric called you. He shouldn't have done that."

"He didn't ask me to come," Lauren explained. "He was just calling to report what had happened. I came because I wanted to."

"That was really nice of you. I think I'm good to go now, though. I can manage on my own. It's just a broken arm. Besides, I won't be here more than a few more days. I need to get back to work. I've already been here a week longer than planned and my office is starting to get frantic."

Lauren realized with dismay that she was being sent away.

"As much as I enjoy your company," Cassie continued, "we'll soon be back where we were. There's no point going through that again. I was actually really depressed when you left before. It's better if you go now. Your whole thing about wanting us to be friends, it's just—"

She broke off, looking pained. Lauren had almost forgotten that Cassie didn't know everything had changed. She'd been having such a good time inhabiting the house with her like an

253

established old married couple that it had seemed like they'd just moved into a new phase of intimacy without ever discussing it.

She got up from her chair and came to sit beside Cassie, looking purposefully into her eyes.

"Cassie, I love you," she said. "I love you so much. You were right. Being just friends is impossible for us. I had it in my head that a romantic relationship would destroy our friendship. That was stupid. There was never any choice for us but this." Lauren pressed Cassie's hand to her lips.

She looked stunned. "Are you saying you *do* want to be with me?"

Lauren nodded as she noticed the song that was playing. Well, that's timely, she thought.

"'Fascination,'" Cassie said. "It's our song, isn't it?"

Lauren took Cassie's face in both hands and kissed her mouth tenderly. That felt so good, she did it again, then slipped her arms around Cassie's body and kissed her more deeply. Cassie's mouth responded willingly. A wave of warmth spread out from Lauren's center to her limbs. She recognized desire returning. It had never really gone away. It had been lying dormant.

When they broke apart, Cassie said, "I've dreamt of kissing you like that so many times this seems almost unreal to me."

"Let me see if I can make it seem more real," Lauren offered, holding her tighter and closing her mouth over Cassie's. She held on with her one good arm and returned the kisses with an eager insistence that sent Lauren's head spinning.

There was a time, years ago, when she had imagined this kind of intimacy with Cassie and told herself it was wrong to do so, wrong even to think it. But she no longer heard the stern charge of denial. Now all she heard were Cassie's murmurs of pleasure and her own matching inner voice, urging her onward toward love...and life.

# CHAPTER FORTY-ONE

"Faith's article on Sky Mountain is beautiful," Emma told Lauren over the phone. "I really want to include it. I don't see why she didn't put it in her first book. She loved this story and it fit the content perfectly."

Lauren stood in front of Cassie's house, leaning against her car and gazing out at the ocean. "Because she never got there to see it. That was a rule she had for herself. It was okay to mention it as an example, but to highlight it like that, to build a whole chapter around it, she would have had to have the first-hand experience."

"Do you think we could use it anyway?" Emma asked. "Her research was thorough. How much would have been gained by a first-hand observation?"

"It's not the science. It's the details. The atmosphere. She liked to include first-person anecdotes and her own impressions. It was important to her to feel a place. That was her style. I don't think it will sound like her without that."

"You're right. It's one of the things that makes her writing so evocative. I guess I'll have to leave it out. Oh, there's one other thing. I'd like you to write an introduction to this book if you would. I think it will be a moving tribute."

Lauren lowered the phone, feeling suddenly unable to respond.

"Lauren," Emma prompted. "Lauren, are you there?"

She brought the phone back up. "Yes. Thank you. I'd love to do it."

"Great. We'll talk more about that after you read what I've done so far. No hurry, though. You can do it when you get back to Portland."

"Actually, I'm coming home today. Why don't you send me what you've got so far and I'll try to read it in the next couple days."

"Perfect. Lauren, I want to thank you again for giving me this opportunity. I've always wanted to do something to show Faith how much I appreciated everything she did for me. I just didn't know what I could do. This project has been so right for me, to honor her memory. I think she'd approve."

Lauren swallowed, holding back an upswell of emotion. "Approve? Emma, she'd holler and whoop for joy. You know how much she loved attention."

She heard Emma's short laugh and could tell she was also choked up.

Lauren realized, as she acknowledged a tender sympathy for Emma, that she no longer had any anger toward her. She felt a unity with her because of their shared goal, as well as their shared sense of loss.

"Emma," she asked, "are you going to be home later today? Say around one?"

"I could be."

"Eugene is on my way. Would it be okay if I stopped by? I have something to give you."

"Oh, okay, sure." Emma sounded uncertain.

"I'll see you later, then. Bye."

Lauren walked into the house where Cassie was depositing her suitcase just inside the front door. She looked ready to go. Their extraordinary few days had come to an end. This was as long as she could possibly delay, Cassie had decided, without her business collapsing into disarray and her partner going berserk.

"I'll carry that to the car for you," Lauren offered.

"Thanks. And thanks for giving me a ride to the airport. I think everything's buttoned up here."

Lauren reached over and buttoned Cassie's coat. "Including you."

She smiled. "Buttons are a little challenging with one hand."

Lauren put her arms loosely around Cassie and kissed her. Cassie responded with quickening passion in the manner Lauren had come to know well. They stood in a tight embrace inside the doorway, kissing for two or three minutes, during which Lauren's body lurched and flipped and begged for more. They had spent the last two days in bed, learning one another's bodies, learning one another's hearts, and yet Lauren was far from satisfied. Desire is like that. It can go into hiding for years without even peeking out, but once you crack open the door, it's ravenous.

Finally, she disengaged herself and said, "I hate to say goodbye."

"Me too. It always has been so hard to say goodbye to you. Even worse this time. The last couple of days have been magical."

"They have." Lauren remembered that last day in China when they were both trying so hard not to cry. "But it's different now. This time we have so much to look forward to. And it won't be for long. I'll be down there first week of October."

"And Thanksgiving and Christmas?"

Lauren shrugged. "Either place. Or maybe you'll have managed by then to set up your new practice here."

"I'll definitely try, but that's just a few months from now. Maybe we should go somewhere for the holidays. Take a trip."

"Yes, we could do that. Go somewhere south of the equator. I've always liked the idea of traveling to summer."

"Let's keep that in mind." Cassie kissed her softly on the lips one more time. "I guess we should be going."

Lauren nodded, then picked up the suitcase and carried it to the car.

After dropping Cassie off at the airport, she headed inland toward Emma's home in Eugene. She hadn't planned this visit, but it seemed right—the right time, the right thing to do.

She parked in front of a two-story townhouse with a tiny strip of lawn in front, planted with healthy Kentucky bluegrass and edged with beds of azaleas and dahlias, none of them blooming this time of year.

Emma opened the door immediately and asked her inside, saying, "Can I get you something? Iced tea or anything?"

"No, thanks. I'm not going to stay long. Just a few minutes, then I need to be on my way home."

"Well, at least sit down for a minute." Emma pointed her to a comfortable looking chair in the front room.

As she sat, Lauren noticed the tribal artwork in the room—masks, small statues and a few drums—all of them typical Northwest Coast style.

"Sorry for inviting myself over," she said, "but this is something I needed to do in person."

Lauren waited for Emma to sit in the other, similar chair. She felt awkward and Emma seemed nervous, no doubt unable to discern the reason behind this impromptu visit. Lauren decided to just plunge in.

"Before Faith died," she began, "she wrote letters to a lot of people, saying goodbye, saying thank you, that sort of thing. She wrote to people who were important to her. Including you."

Emma looked confused. "Me?"

"Yes. She wrote you a letter." Lauren took the envelope from her pocket and held it between both her hands, still a little reluctant to let it go. "She didn't have a current address for you, so it was returned. But...it belongs to you."

Lauren handed the envelope over. Emma took it in her long fingers and turned it face up to read the address, as if to verify that it was actually intended for her. She undoubtedly noticed the envelope had been opened.

"I see why it wasn't forwarded," she said. "This was my Spring Street address. I sold that place about four years ago."

Lauren met Emma's eye, then said, "The letter came back shortly before she died. Then, later, I read it. Which I shouldn't have done. I won't make excuses for myself. It's just what I did."

"Oh," Emma said, her tone unaccusing. "Well, I might have done the same."

Lauren continued. "When you contacted me last month and came to the house, I should have at least given it to you then. But I didn't. I didn't want to give it to you because I didn't want you to know—"

"To know what?" Emma asked.

"I'm sorry. Why don't you just read it?"

Emma held the envelope for a moment, then looked up at Lauren, who smiled encouragingly at her. Then she opened it and extracted the printed page.

What a strange thing, Lauren thought, to get a letter from a woman who had been dead for two years. What a gift, in many ways, especially for Emma who had wanted so much to please Faith, who had wanted her approval and her love. The letter would give her both. A belated validation, but one Lauren was certain would be welcome.

Emma read slowly with her head bent over the page. When she had finished, she looked at Lauren, her bright blue eyes awash with tears. They both sat there silently looking at one another for a moment. Then Emma stood and came and wrapped her arms around Lauren's neck and they hugged each other and shared a moment of grief and gratitude.

Emma stepped back. "Thank you for giving it to me. I can understand why you didn't want to."

"It seems kind of silly to me now, that I was jealous. I don't blame Faith for being attracted to you. I used to think that took something away from me. But it didn't. It didn't have anything to do with me."

Emma smiled. "I never knew how she felt. She never let on."

"Good!" Lauren stood. "I have a feeling you would have been a lot more persistent if you had known."

"Maybe so." Emma wiped her eyes. "But if I had known you, I think maybe I wouldn't have. I used to think you were so damned lucky to have nabbed Faith. Sort of like you must have caught her in a weak moment, you know? But since I've gotten to know you, I realize she was lucky too. I'm really glad it turned out the way it did. I'm not just saying that. I think the two of you were a very special couple."

Lauren smiled, feeling both sad and thankful.

They walked toward the door. "I'll be anxious to hear what you think of the book," Emma said.

"I'll call you when I've had a look. A few ideas are already brewing in my mind about the introduction. I hope you know how big an assignment that is for me."

Emma nodded. "Oh, I know it will be a challenge. But you're up to it."

Lauren felt light-hearted as she left Eugene and headed home. She thought working with Emma was going to be a lot easier now. Maybe they might even become friends. They had a few things in common, after all.

At three o' clock, she pulled into a MacDonald's and briefly considered having a salad, but then ordered a cheeseburger and fries instead. She took her lunch outside to a round metal table and called Cassie, knowing she would be at LAX waiting for her connecting flight.

"Hi, Baby!" Cassie answered excitedly.

Cassie sounded like she hadn't seen her in ages. Lauren smiled. "Hi, Baby, yourself. How's L.A.?"

"Never rains."

"You sound happy."

"I *am* happy. I'm in love with a beautiful girl. And best of all, she's in love with me. I hope she's happy too."

"Yes, she is. She's insanely happy." Lauren ate a French fry.

"Seems all right, then. Did you see Emma?"

"I did. I gave her the letter."

"Good. I'll bet she was happy to get it."

"Oh, yes. Everyone who got one of those letters was happy to get it. Those were damned good letters! They'd bring anybody to tears. They were so heartfelt."

"Did Emma's bring her to tears?"

"Yes. I think she really loved Faith."

"How does that make you feel?"

Lauren hesitated, dragging a French fry through a puddle of ketchup. "Closer to her."

"Hey, not too close, I hope."

Lauren smiled, recognizing Cassie's counterfeit display of jealousy. "Nothing to worry about. She's not my type. Too much like me."

"So you're okay?"

"Yes. I'm fine. Except that I miss you terribly."

"I know! Me too. Let's start planning a trip together right away."

"We've always done that, you know? Planned our next trip together before the current one is done."

"We need something to look forward to. But, seriously, Lauren, let's go away for the holidays. I don't really like doing holiday things over the holidays. I like your idea about traveling to summer. Can't we do Christmas somewhere summery? What do you say? We can pretend it's July and go scuba diving or something."

"All right. I'm game. But, you know, when you're a grandmother, you might actually have to do Christmas for Christmas."

"Well, I'm not a grandmother yet. This year we can do whatever we damn well please. Deep sea fishing in Baja. Surfing in Hawaii. Drinking rum punch on a Caribbean beach."

Lauren was about to put another fry in her mouth when a thought struck her and her hand froze halfway there. A chill ran up her spine.

"Australia," she said.

"Australia? I've never been there. Great choice. Bottom of the world. It will definitely be summer there in December."

"Cassie, call me tonight. I've just had an idea."

"Okay," she said, sounding intrigued. "Be safe, Sweetie. I'll talk to you tonight."

"Love you," Lauren said, hearing how new that sounded to her ears, despite the fact that she'd said it many times in the last few days. But it was still fresh and made her feel a little giddy. She waited for Cassie's "I love you too," before clicking off the call.

# CHAPTER FORTY-TWO

Lauren dug into the guest room closet to find her largest suitcase, the navy blue one she hadn't used since her trip to England. That had been the last major trip she and Faith had taken, a two-week vacation that revolved around a Viking burial pit excavation in Cumbria. For once, though, they had managed to squeeze in a short vacation that had nothing to do with Faith's research, touring London, Stratford-on-Avon and Cambridge. That had been a good trip, Lauren recalled. During the Cumbria part of their stay, she had escaped one day with the wife of one of the archeologists, two rebellious spouses driving up to see a stretch of Hadrian's Wall while the husband and Faith remained at the dig, poring over skeletons buried in a grave shaped like a longboat.

London had been a dream come true for Lauren. They'd been in Heathrow Airport many times over the years, on their way to or from some far-flung country, but they'd never spent any time in the city itself before that trip. She was glad she'd talked Faith into extending their England trip, that they'd been able to do London together and hadn't put it off for some distant future that would never come, as they had so many other places.

She pulled the suitcase out into the middle of the room, noting the British Airways tag still fastened to the handle.

Lauren wasn't a quick packer. It normally took her weeks to make all her decisions and get ready for a trip like this one. So, now, a month away from the departure date, it was not too early to start. She had just returned from her November visit to see Cassie in Albuquerque, where they had finalized this December plan, their first real adventure together.

The next few weeks would be all about Australia—choosing what to take, planning what to see, talking it all out on the phone from their separate bedrooms each night, as had become their daily routine.

Lauren opened the suitcase just as the phone rang. She bounded into the front room. Checking caller ID, she recognized Emma's number and answered.

"Lauren," said Emma excitedly, "I just read your introduction to the book. I have to say it made me cry. It was so touching. You did a marvelous job conveying a sense of who Faith was and what her work was about with just the right touch of the personal."

Lauren leaned against the back of the couch as Cocoa made a circle around her ankles. "It wasn't easy."

"I don't imagine it was."

"I kept wanting to tell all kinds of things about her that had nothing to do with the subject matter of the book, like what her favorite baseball team was or how much she missed chalkboards in the classroom. I cut out a whole lot more than was left in, in the end."

"You're a good self-editor, then. But you are a writer, aren't you, so no surprise there. I really have no changes to suggest to your introduction. It shows something of Faith as a woman, not just a scientist, and that's what I was hoping to get from you."

"Thanks. It's all coming together so nicely. I know you've put a huge effort into this."

"But I'm having fun," Emma insisted. "I really am. Speaking of fun, have you settled on the dates of your trip?"

"Yes. Leaving a month from now."

"I'm so jealous!"

"I hope we can bring back some usable photos, something for the book cover, at least."

"Me too. I'm so grateful you're doing this, you and Cassie. It's going to make all the difference. I can't thank you enough."

"I'm doing it for me too," Lauren said. "Not just the book."

"Right." Emma's voice was subdued. "I know."

Emma did know, Lauren thought. The two of them had an understanding, mostly unspoken, about their collaboration. Driven by their separate, private need for resolution, their efforts were almost inadvertently combining into a public tribute to Faith.

After hanging up with Emma, Lauren returned to her suitcase, ripped off the old tags, and opened it. She found a white envelope in one of the inside pockets. Pulling it out, she expected it to contain some remnant of a past trip, a pamphlet or ticket from England, most likely. But the envelope was sealed. Her name was written in Faith's handwriting on the front: "Lauren." That's all. Stunned, she stood staring at it for at least a minute, trying to wrap her brain around what she had in her hand. It was Cocoa rubbing against her legs that roused her from her trance.

She sank to the edge of the bed, still staring at the envelope. Maybe it was another of those quips, Lauren thought. But she knew better already. It was more than that. *It was her letter.*

Lauren had sometimes wished she'd gotten one of these letters, but hadn't expected one. Faith could have said whatever she had to say during all those months of her illness. And she did. How could there be anything left to say? Still, holding the sealed envelope in her trembling hand, she was overjoyed to think Faith's last "I love you" was going to be hers after all.

As she sat there, she started to cry just thinking about it, so it was some time before she could actually open the envelope and pull out its contents. Unlike the other letters, this one was handwritten. Lauren wiped her eyes until she could see well enough to read it.

*Dearest Lauren,*

*If you're reading this, I assume you're planning a big trip. Hooray! It makes me happy to think you'll be doing that. I hope you haven't waited until you're eighty, although I do expect you'll still be having plenty of fun at that age. I hope you're still young and have found a new companion to share your life with.*

*I also hope you still have dreams for yourself and you can make them all come true. I regret I couldn't be there to share them with you well into old age, but I don't regret anything else. Our life together was a triumph!*

*You know you were more important to me than anything or anyone. I loved you dearly and never wished for more than I had. You were the fulfillment of my dreams. Never doubt that my life with you was complete and full of joy. I feel like I'm sending you out into the world now to find your own way. I know you are capable.*

*There's just one last request I have of you, my love. If I know you, you've got my ashes sitting on the mantelpiece or some other place of honor. Please take them out somewhere and scatter them. You choose the place. I know you'll choose well. Besides, you know I don't believe anything of me is left in the world, anything that would care one way or another. It's for you that I ask this. It's time for you to say goodbye to me. The only place I wish to reside is in your heart. When all is said and done, that's my final resting place. And, really, Lauren, I doubt your new girlfriend, no matter how sympathetic, will want my remains on her mantelpiece.*

*"Remains" is a funny word, isn't it? I mean, people use it to talk about what's left of the body, like ashes or a skeleton. But I think by now you know much more about what remains when someone dies, and it has nothing to do with something you can touch. I spent my life looking at people's remains. But it was always with an eye to imagining what they were like when they were living. Not what they wore or ate or lived in so much, but what they believed and dreamed about. The human imagination is so interesting and powerful. It takes us well beyond what we can know. It can, and does, create gods and universes. The mind of a single person can create infinity. That's what I believed in, the*

*infinite power of the soaring human imagination. What fascinating things people have dreamt of! The greatest mystery, and the thing most people can't comprehend, myself included, is how that kind of power can't survive something as ordinary as death. What a vast treasury of mythology has come from that mystery! It gave me something to do anyway. I had fun. I was loved. Couldn't ask for more than that.*

*What a lousy poet I would have made, don't you think? No angst! You, on the other hand, have had your share of that. Like me, I know you have trouble believing in magic, but we both believed in love. It's such a gift to offer another person, something to believe in. It's a gift well within your capability. I don't know if I would have believed in it myself if not for you, so thank you for that gift. You're a romantic in the best possible way. You believe in the purity and power of love, in the thing we call "true love." Because of that, I know you'll find it again. Your heart is too generous to keep to itself for long.*

*Just so you don't go looking or have any further expectations, I'm guessing that by now you've found my other notes. I put this letter in a place I thought you wouldn't look for a while, a place you'd come to only when you'd started living again. I'm rejoicing for you in anticipation of your reading it. So this is my last word to you, unless I've been wrong all along and there is something after death after all. Wouldn't that be a huge joke on me?*

*Live happy, my darling girl.*

*Love you so much,*

*Faith*

# CHAPTER FORTY-THREE

It wasn't easy to get to the Sky Island, something Lauren was well aware of. But now that it was actually happening, she was elated. Four days into their Australia vacation, she and Cassie boarded a small plane to take them to Guadalcanal. From there, they hired a boat to tiny Sky Island. The day reminded Lauren of many days with Faith, being whisked off to some remote location by local guides who wondered at these two women from America who came all this way to look at a barren mound of earth or a pile of stacked rocks or a cave containing nothing but some charred wood.

As they waited on the dock for the boat to be readied, Cassie pulled her hat on and said, "Now that this vacation's nearly over, don't you think we should discuss our next trip?"

Lauren smiled knowingly at her goofy grin. "Your turn to

choose." She reached over to tie the straps under Cassie's chin.

"I think I'd like to go to Tuscany," Cassie said decisively, taking Lauren by surprise. "Sample some olive oil. Drink a little Chianti. We could go on one of those foodie tours you mentioned."

Lauren stared into Cassie's eyes, noting how they twinkled with affection and generosity. "I love you," she said.

"I love you too, Lauren. More than I've ever loved anyone. All I want from life for the rest of my life is to be with you and try to make you happy."

Feeling overwhelmed, Lauren squeezed Cassie's hand. She knew she wouldn't get through this day without a few tears. They climbed into the small motorboat to begin their journey.

While Lauren and Cassie sat on deck wearing life jackets, two shirtless young men of Melanesian descent operated the boat, chatting with one another in their strangely familiar but exotic language. Recognizable English words rose and fell with the wind, interspersed among the Creole-sounding Solomon Islands pidgin. Though most of the residents spoke this tongue, the official language was English, so at least the signs and documents were easy to negotiate. The morning arrangements had gone off without a hitch.

As they sped across a calm sea under a brilliant blue sky, Lauren watched the horizon, waiting expectantly for the appearance of the island. Faith was on her mind more than usual today. Not surprisingly, considering her ashes were in her backpack.

"Are you okay?" Cassie asked.

Lauren nodded. "I'm fine. Feeling happy, as a matter of fact."

"Good." Cassie smiled gratefully.

It was true. Her heart was joyful. For a long time, she had been looking backward to find happiness, back to her life with Faith. Now, remarkably, she was looking ahead at a new world of possibility with Cassie, a future full of adventure and fun. She finally understood what Faith had meant when she said every love is different. Lauren's love of Cassie was unique because Cassie was unique and because she herself wasn't the same woman who had fallen in love with Faith at the age of twenty-two. So many things were different now. That was a welcome realization because it meant she could embark on a new life with Cassie while still holding Faith in her heart. There was no need to compromise.

One of the guides pointed to a flat-topped mountain emerging from the waves.

Cassie took hold of Lauren's hand as they both stood to get a better view. The island was a barren volcano jutting steeply out of the ocean. The top of it was ringed in thin gray clouds. Lauren felt herself go cold and shiver. It was like riding into a fairy tale, an improbable story she'd heard many times, seeming always like fiction. It was looking more real, and much bigger, though, as they came speeding toward it.

Mesmerized by the sight, she nearly forgot the task at hand. She roused herself and handed the camera bag to Cassie. "Think book cover," she instructed.

Cassie nodded and stood with her feet planted firmly, aiming her lens at the island as it grew larger. The weather, like everything else today, was cooperating. That layer of marine clouds around the top of the mountain couldn't have been more picturesque, just as Lauren had imagined it.

She sat with her notebook and wrote her impressions as they closed in on the fabled island, aware that she was Faith's recorder in a way she'd never been before.

*A dark brown, nearly barren island juts abruptly out of the waves. Sea stacks loom near its shores, covered with black dots—flocks of cormorants. As your eye climbs from sea level into the clouds, the mountain really does appear to touch the sky. No romantic vision is needed to see it as a stairway to heaven...or the sky spirit world, as these people believed. Looking at it from across the waves, you can't easily dismiss that belief.*

She felt Cassie's steady hand on her shoulder as she jotted down her last thoughts.

*That plateau in the clouds was the final resting place of thousands of Pacific Islanders...and one American scientist whose imagination was captivated by it. She was not a believer, but she was a dreamer.*

Lauren put her notebook away as the boat drifted up to a

shaky wooden pier. One of the guides jumped onto it and the other tossed him a rope. When the boat was securely moored, Cassie and Lauren took their packs and stepped out onto the weathered gray wood of an old dock.

"There's supposed to be a trail," Lauren said.

"Yes, yes," said one of the men. "I'll show you."

He led them away from the dock to a nearby trailhead. It was marked with a worn wooden sign that read, "Sky Mountain Trail."

"You'll wait here?" Lauren asked the man.

He nodded vigorously.

They started up the rocky dirt path, gently climbing, and were soon out of sight of the boat.

"I hope he understood that," Cassie said, "or we'll be stranded here on this deserted island."

"At least we'll be together," Lauren noted.

Cassie narrowed her eyes. "As much as I love you, Lauren, that isn't my heart's desire."

There was only one trail on the island. It led to the top of the mountain over blocky igneous rock. Where the path was faint, there were cairns to point the way. This was one of those trails people hiked for pleasure, for the adventure of mountain climbing. Lauren doubted there were many hikers who knew the incredible story of this place.

She guessed they were following the original trail of the natives, the trail they took while carrying their deceased in dugout canoes. Most ancient trails took the most expedient route unless they were circuitous for superstitious reasons, to confuse evil spirits. This one didn't seem to be. It switchbacked over the most logical places and climbed steadily toward the goal.

"Do you know the title of the book yet?" Cassie asked, sounding out of breath.

"Emma is proposing 'Paradise Regained.' It fits and I like the sound of it."

"That's very clever, playing off her earlier title."

"All the stories are about the afterlife, which, in some cultures, means paradise."

"Like this one."

"Yes, like this one," Lauren confirmed. "This story, the story of Sky Island, is going to be the last chapter."

Cassie stopped walking and looked at Lauren, who also stopped. "The last chapter," she repeated softly.

Her expression conveyed everything—her understanding, her sympathy, her affection. It was often like this between them. So often, words seemed unnecessary. Lauren slipped an arm around her shoulders and turned her to face back the way they'd come.

The boat dock was now visible some distance below. She could see the two men on shore. They were already too far away to tell what they were doing.

Lauren felt a muted euphoria for having made this trek. She'd never done something like this without Faith. She was inclined to tell herself that Faith's spirit was here with her, but then she didn't know what she meant by that. A sense of her. A presence inside. That kind of a spirit, she thought, Faith would believe in.

As they continued walking, Lauren spotted some wood scattered on the rocky hillside. She walked off the trail to get a better look. The gray, splintered wood had evidence of hand carving, gouges made with simple tools.

"I think this is one of the canoes," she said, feeling a rush of adrenaline.

Cassie came and knelt beside her, running a hand over the curved surface of the weathered wood. "Yes, it must be. I didn't know we would actually see anything."

"I wasn't sure. Sometimes these places have been cleaned out by the scientists studying them. Other times not."

They returned to the trail and continued. The higher they went, the more canoes and parts of canoes they saw. Cassie stopped often to take photos. It was eerie to be walking through all these old coffins. Lauren assumed they had been tumbled about over the years by rain, wind and falling rocks. Some were completely shattered. Some were nearly whole. They soon gained some assurance that none of them contained human remains, as they had still seen nothing resembling bones among the debris.

"The bones were probably all collected," Lauren said. "That's commonly done at a site like this. It was an active archaeological dig about forty years ago."

As they climbed higher, the view out to the ocean became obscured by cloud cover. The wispy clouds seemed close enough to touch in places. Their conversation ceased almost entirely for the next half hour as the effort of climbing consumed their energy. Hiking a trail like this was much easier twenty years ago, Lauren thought, as they finally reached a section of the trail that leveled out.

"This is both creepy and beautiful at the same time," Cassie observed, following Lauren on a long loop around the summit.

They were climbing at an easy grade now. They'd lost sight of the peak because of its proximity and the angle of vision from the trail. But all at once they came over a gentle rise and emerged onto a plateau. It was the top of the mountain, a nearly flat, wide expanse of bare rock about five hundred feet in diameter. The convex shape of it testified to an ancient caldera, mostly filled in with sediment. They walked to the center and removed their packs. Where they could see through the clouds, the view was fabulous.

"Why aren't there any canoes here on top?" Cassie opened her water bottle. "Isn't this where they would have left them?"

"Yes. That's what the legend says, anyway. I'm guessing the archaeology team took them, if any were left up here. They were probably the best specimens, most intact. I imagine they still had skeletons in them too."

"What a bizarre thing that must have been to discover." Cassie's voice was hushed, reverential, as they both tried to imagine coming upon that scene.

Lauren unbuckled the strap on her pack and removed the canister containing Faith's ashes. As she held it in both hands, Cassie approached and touched her arm.

"Do you want me to leave you alone?" she asked.

"No. Stay." Lauren's eyes were drawn involuntarily to the sky above. "It seems kind of ironic to be doing this, considering her views on the afterlife."

"I think she would love it," Cassie said. "Such an appropriately symbolic place. I mean, whatever she believed about death, she never lost her enthusiasm for her subject. She admired all the things people did for their dead. It wasn't just cold science to her. You can tell that by reading her book. I think she had a real empathy for them."

"You're right. She would love this. I'm so glad you knew her." Lauren leaned into Cassie, who slipped an arm around her waist.

"Do you have something to say?" Cassie asked.

"Yes. I thought, under the circumstances, the traditional prayer of the people who used this place would be best. This was Faith's own translation, based on the legends she collected from the islanders around here."

Cassie nodded. "Totally appropriate."

Holding the canister in both hands, Lauren began to recite the prayer of the dead, aware that some version of this was said at the top of this mountain thousands of times throughout the ages, but very likely not once in the last two hundred years.

*"From the four corners of existence...*
*From the east comes the sun and the birth of days.*
*From the west comes rest from weary toil.*
*From the south comes the rain and breath of life.*
*From the north comes the wind that blows away pain and trouble.*
*Mother Earth, from you we are born and live and die.*
*Father Sky, to you we fly when our body falls away.*
*Keep our friend safe and hold her gently in your arms.*
*She was a good woman who loved us and whom we loved.*
*We give her back to you with light hearts.*
*May she travel from this place without fear or worry."*

Lauren opened her eyes, feeling the comfort of Cassie's arm around her.

"That was very beautiful," whispered Cassie.

Lauren opened the canister. She stared at it for a moment before shaking out the contents. The ashes blew gently aloft on the wind currents, scattering in a general westward drift, some of them spiraling upward, rising into the clouds. She watched until they all seemed to be gone, landed or blown too far afield to see, until there was nothing but the empty wind.

*Goodbye, Faith*, she thought, emotion clutching her throat.

Cassie took Lauren in both her arms, holding tightly. They stood there embracing on the top of a mountain at the bottom of the world, an image that struck Lauren as profoundly strange, but satisfying. By a silent mutual assent, they released one another and shouldered their packs for the trip back down. Lauren took one more look at the sky and the clouds and the sea beyond.

"Ready to go?" Cassie asked, grasping her hand.

She nodded. "Yes, I'm ready." She squeezed Cassie's fingers reassuringly and they walked to the edge of the plateau hand in hand.

**Publications from Bella Books, Inc.**
*Women. Books. Even better together*
**P.O. Box 10543 Tallahassee, FL 32302 Phone: 800-729-4992**
**www.bellabooks.com**

WITHOUT WARNING: Book one in the Shaken series by KG MacGregor. A story of courageous survival that leads to steadfast love.
ISBN: 978-1-59493-120-8

THE CANDIDATE by Tracey Richardson. Presidential candidate Jane Kincaid always expected to pay the toll the road to the White House would exact, but she didn't expect to have to choose between her heart and her political destiny.
ISBN: 978-1-59493-133-8

ACROSS TIME by Linda Kay Silva. Jessie never dreams that the emptiness of the present might be solved by a call from the past. First in a series.
ISBN: 978-1-883523-91-6

BEACH TOWN by Ann Roberts. Actress Kira Drake nurtures her dreams of stardom from the depths of the closet, which makes any hope of a future with Flynn impossible.
ISBN: 978-1-59493-132-1

CHRISTABEL by Karin Kallmaker. Dina Rowland must accept her magical heritage to save supermodel Christabel from the demon of their past who has found them in the present.
ISBN: 978-1-59493-134-5

TRAINING DAYS by Jane Frances. A passionate tryst on a long-distance train might be the undoing of Morgan's career—and her heart.
ISBN: 978-1-59493-122-2

LIBERTY SQUARE by Katherine V. Forrest. Kate Delafield faces her most difficult situation: a confrontation with her military past. Book 5 in series.
ISBN: 978-1-883523-66-4

THE RAINBOW CEDAR by Gerri Hill. Jaye Burns' relationship is falling apart inspite of her efforts to keep it together. When Drew Montgomery offers the possibility of a new start, Jaye is torn between past and future.
ISBN: 978-1-59493-124-6

WHEN IT'S ALL RELATIVE by Therese Szymanski. Brett Higgins must confront her worst enemies: her family. Book 8 in series. ISBN: 978-1-59493-109-3

BREAKING SPIRIT BRIDGE by Ruth Perkinson. Piper Leigh Cliff returns home to fight for her sanity and life while confront the demons of her childhood. Sequel to Piper's Someday.
ISBN: 978-1-883523-95-4

ROOMMATES by Jackie Calhoun. Two freshmen co-eds from two different worlds discover what it takes to choose love.
ISBN: 978-1-59493-123-9

SECRETS SO DEEP by KG MacGregor. Glynn Wright's son holds a secret that is destroying him, but confronting it could mean the end of their family. Charlotte Blue is determined to save them both.
ISBN: 978-1-59493-125-3

THE KISS THAT COUNTED by Karin Kallmaker. CJ Roshe is used to hiding from her past, but meeting Karita Hanssen leaves her longing to finally tell someone her real name.
ISBN: 978-1-59493-131-4

COMPULSION by Terri Breneman. Toni Barston's lucky break in a case turns into a nightmare when she becomes the target of a compulsive murderess. Book "C" in series.
ISBN: 978-1-59493-126-0

LOSERS WEEPERS by Jessica Thomas. Alex Peres must sort out a possible kidnapping hoax and the death of a friend, and finds that the two cases have a surprising number of mutual suspects. Book 4 in series.
ISBN: 978-1-59493-127-7

HER SISTER'S KEEPER by Diana Rivers. A restless young Hadra is caught up in a daring raid on the Gray Place, but is captured and must stand trail for her crimes against the state. Book 6 in series.
ISBN: 978-1-59493-112-3

BACKSLIDE by Teresa Stores. Virge Young hovers between life and death, reliving the moments that put her in the path of a fundamentalist's bullet.
ISBN: 978-1-883523-96-1

WHITE OFFERINGS by Ann Roberts. Realtor-turned-sleuth Ari Adams helps a friend find a stalker, only to begin receiving white offerings of her own. Book 2 in series.
ISBN: 978-1-59493-121-5

MIDNIGHT MELODIES by Megan Carter. Family disputes and small town tensions come between Erica Boyd and and her best chance at romance in years.
ISBN: 978-1-59493-137-6

WOMEN. PERIOD. By Julia Watts, Parneshia Jones and Jo Ruby. Groundbreaking anthology of essays, short fiction and poetry by women about the one universal trait we all share. Period.
ISBN: 978-1-883523-94-7

BEAUTIFUL JOURNEY by Kenna White. Determined to do her part during the Battle for Britain, aviatrix Kit Anderson has no time for Emily Mills, who certainly has no time for her, either, not when their hearts are n the line of fire.
ISBN: 978-1-59493-128-4

AFTERSHOCK: Book two of the Shaken series by KG MacGregor. Anna and Lily have survived earthquake and dating, but new challenges may prove their undoing.
ISBN: 978-1-59493-135-2

STERLING ROAD BLUES by Ruth Perkinson. Teacher Tenney Showalker is unconventional, as Dean of Education Madeline Wingfield soon discovers. An age of englightenment unfolds as they learn and teach from the inside out and outside in.
ISBN: 978-1-883523-92-3

NIGHT VISION by Karin Kallmaker. Julia Madison is having nightmares. So are all the lesbians she knows. What secret in the desert could be responsible?
ISBN: 978-1-59493-136-9

AS FAR AS FAR ENOUGH by Claire Rooney. Two very different women from two very different worlds meet by accident--literally. Collier and Meri find their love threatened on all sides. There's only one way to survive: together.
ISBN: 978-1-59493-140-6

IF NO ONE'S LOOKING by Jennifer L. Jordan. A three-year old girl is missing and Kristin Ashe must find her, even if she's the last person who's looking.
ISBN: 978-1-883523-93-0

PARTNERS by Gerri Hill. Detective Casey O'Connor has had difficult cases, but what she needs most from fellow detective Tori Hunter is help understanding her new partner, Leslie Tucker.
ISBN: 978-1-59493-130-7

GETTING THERE by Lyn Denison. Kat knows her life needs fixing. She just doesn't want to go to the one place where she can do that: home.
ISBN: 978-1-59493-141-3

BECKA'S SONG by Frankie J. Jones. Mysterious, beautiful women with secrets are to be avoided. Leanne Dresher knows it with her head, but her heart has other plans. Becka James is simply unavoidable.
ISBN: 978-1-59493-138-3

WHACKED by Josie Gordon. Death by family values. Lonnie Squires knows that if they'd warned her about this possibility in seminary, she'd remember.
ISBN: 978-1-59493-139-0

DRESSES AND OTHER CATASTROPHES by Dani O'Connor. Tomorrow. That's Doc's motto. Tomorrow she'll take care of the important things in life. After hoping all her life that tomorrow would never come, it arrives with a vengence. Dresses are only the beginning. Book 3 in series.
ISBN: 978-1-883523-97-8

WORTH EVERY STEP by KG MacGregor. Climbing Africa's highest peak isn't nearly so hard as coming back down to earth. Join two women who risk their futures and hearts on the journey of their lives.
ISBN: 978-1-59493-142-0

SIDE ORDER OF LOVE by Tracey Richardson. Television foodie star Grace Wellwood is not going to be golf phenom Torrie Cannon's side order of romance for the summer tour. No, she's not. Absolutely not.
ISBN: 978-1-59493-143-7

WRONG TURNS by Jackie Calhoun. Callie Callahan's latest wrong turn turns out well. She meets Vicki Brownwell. Sparks would fly if only Meg Klein would leave them alone!
ISBN: 978-1-59493-148-2

SMALL PACKAGES by KG MacGregor. With Lily away from home, Anna Kaklis is alone with her worst nightmare: a toddler. Book Three of the Shaken Series.
ISBN: 978-1-59493-149-9

FAMILY AFFAIR by Saxon Bennett. An oops at the gynecologist has Chase Banter finally trying to grow up. She has nine whole months to pull it off.
ISBN: 978-1-59493-150-5

DELUSIONAL by Terri Breneman. In her search for a killer, Toni Barston discovers that sometimes everything is exactly the way it seems, and then it gets worse.
ISBN: 978-1-59493-151-2

COMFORTABLE DISTANCE by Kenna White. Summer on Puget Sound ought to be relaxing for Dana Robbins, but Dr. Jamie Hughes is far too close for comfort.
ISBN: 978-1-59493-152-9

ROOT OF PASSION by Ann Roberts. Grace Owens knows a fake when she sees it, and the potion her best friend promises will fix her love life is a fake. But what if she wishes it weren't?
ISBN: 978-1-59493-155-0

KEILE'S CHANCE by Dillon Watson. A routine day in the park turns into the chance of a lifetime, if Keile Griffen can find the courage to risk it all for a pair of big brown eyes.
ISBN: 978-1-59493-156-7

SEA LEGS by KG MacGregor. Kelly is happy to help Natalie make Didi jealous, sure, it's all pretend. Maybe. Even the captain doesn't know where this comic cruse will end.
ISBN: 978-1-59493-158-1

TOASTED by Josie Gordon. Mayhem erupts when a culinary road show stops in tiny Middelburg, and for some reason everyone thinks Lonnie Squires ought to fix it. Follow-up to Lammy mystery winner Whacked.
ISBN: 978-1-59493-157-4

NO RULES OF ENGAGEMENT by Tracey Richardson. A war zone attraction is of no use to Major Logan Sharp. She can't wait for Jillian Knight to go back to the other side of the world.
ISBN: 978-1-59493-159-8

A SMALL SACRIFICE by Ellen Hart. A harmless reunion of friends is anything but, and Cordelia Thorn calls friend Jane Lawless with a desperate plea for help. Lammy winner for Best Mystery. #5 in this award-winning series.
ISBN: 978-1-59493-165-9

FAINT PRAISE by Ellen Hart. When a famous TV personality leaps to his death, Jane Lawless agrees to help a friend with inquiries, drawing the attention of a ruthless killer. #6 in this award-winning series.
ISBN: 978-1-59493-164-2

STEPPING STONE by Karin Kallmaker. Selena Ryan's heart was shredded by an actress, and she swears she will never, ever be involved with one again.
ISBN: 978-1-59493-160-4

THE SCORPION by Gerri Hill. Cold cases are what make reporter Marty Edwards tick. When her latest proves to be far from cold, she still doesn't want Detective Kristen Bailey babysitting her, not even when she has to run for her life.
ISBN: 978-1-59493-162-8

YOURS FOR THE ASKING by Kenna White. Lauren Roberts is tired of being the steady, reliable one. When Gaylin Hart blows into her life, she decides to act, only to find once again that her younger sister wants the same woman.
ISBN: 978-159493-163-5

SONGS WITHOUT WORDS by Robbi McCoy. Harper Sheridan's runaway niece turns up in the one place least expected and Harper confronts the woman from the summer that has shaped her entire life since.
ISBN: 978-1-59493-166-6

PHOTOGRAPHS OF CLAUDIA by KG MacGregor. To photographer Leo Wescott models are light and shadow realized on film. Until Claudia.
ISBN: 978-1-59493-168-0

MILES TO GO by Amy Dawson Robertson. Rennie Vogel has finally earned a spot at CT3. All too soon she finds herself abandoned behind enemy lines, miles from safety and forced to do the one thing she never has before: trust another woman.
ISBN: 978-1-59493-174-1

TWO WEEKS IN AUGUST by Nat Burns. Her return to Chincoteague Island is a delight to Nina Christie until she gets her dose of Hazy Duncan's renown ill-humor. She's not going to let it bother her, though...
ISBN: 978-1-59493-173-4

I LEFT MY HEART by Jaye Maiman. The only women she ever loved is dead, and sleuth Robin Miller goes looking for answers. First book in Lammy-winning series.
ISBN: 978-1-59493-188-8

LOVE WAITS by Gerri Hill. The All-American girl and the love she left behind--it's been twenty years since Ashleigh and Gina parted, and now they're back to the place where nothing was simple and love didn't wait.
ISBN: 978-1-59493-186-4

HANNAH FREE: THE BOOK by Claudia Allen. Based on the film festival hit movie starring Sharon Gless. Hannah's story is funny, scathing and witty as she navigates life with aplomb -- but always comes home to Rachel. 32 pages of color photographs plus bonus behind-the-scenes movie information.
ISBN: 978-1-59493-172-7

ABOVE TEMPTATION by Karin Kallmaker. It's supposed to be like any other case, except this time they're chasing one of their own. As fraud investigators Tamara Sterling and Kip Barrett try to catch a thief, they realize they can have anything they want--except each other.
ISBN: 978-1-59493-179-6

BEACON OF LOVE by Ann Roberts. Twenty-five years after their families put an end to a relationship that hadn't even begun, Stephanie returns to Oregon to find many things have changed... except her feelings for Paula.
ISBN: 978-1-59493-180-2